THE STRONGBOW SAGA,
BOOK TWO

DRAGONS FROM THE SEA

DENMARK AND WESTERN FRANKIA
A.D. 845

JUDSON ROBERTS

HARPERCOLLINS*PUBLISHERS*

LIBRARY OF CONGRESS CATALOGING-IN-PUBLICATION DATA
ROBERTS, JUDSON.
    DRAGONS FROM THE SEA : DENMARK AND WESTERN FRANKIA
A.D. 845 / JUDSON ROBERTS. — 1ST ED.
    P.   CM. — (STRONGBOW SAGA ; BK. 2)
    SUMMARY: FIFTEEN-YEAR-OLD HALFDAN'S SKILLS AS AN
ARCHER AND A BLACKSMITH WIN HIM A POSITION ON THE
CREW OF A VIKING SHIP IN 845 A.D., BUT AS WAR BREAKS OUT IN
WESTERN FRANKIA HE BECOMES A SCOUT, SEARCHING FOR THE
FRANKISH ARMY—AND TAKING CAPTIVE A YOUNG WOMAN WHO
IS PREPARING TO BE A NUN.
    ISBN-10: 0-06-081300-8 (TRADE BDG.)
    ISBN-13: 978-0-06-081300-0 (TRADE BDG.)
    ISBN-10: 0-06-081302-4 (LIB. BDG.)
    ISBN-13: 978-0-06-081302-4 (LIB. BDG.)
    [1. VIKINGS—FICTION. 2. WAR—FICTION. 3. REVENGE—
FICTION. 4. FRANCE—HISTORY—TO 987—FICTION.
5. DENMARK—HISTORY—TO 1241—FICTION.] I. TITLE.
PZ7.R54324DRA 2007   2006103263
[FIC]—DC22   CIP
                                                         AC

TYPOGRAPHY BY ALISON DONALTY
1 2 3 4 5 6 7 8 9 10
❖
FIRST EDITION

To Jeanette,
whom my fate finally led me to.

CONTENTS

HEDEBY

Early in the year the Christians number the eight hundred and forty-fifth after the birth of their God the White Christ, my fate led me to the outskirts of Hedeby, the largest town in all the kingdom of the Danes. I arrived there in the late afternoon, tired, hungry, and sore from spending many days atop a horse. At least I had not suffered too badly from the cold on my journey. Though by measure of days it was still the last weeks of winter, the weather had been unseasonably warm ever since the Jul feast, and on the day I reached Hedeby there was a freshness in the air that hinted of the coming of spring.

Hedeby was not just a town. It was a fortress that squatted, fat and solid, against the shore of a shallow inlet along one side of the Sliefjord, a long, narrow gash of the sea cutting deep into the eastern coast of Jutland. A deep ditch ran in a half circle from shore to shore around the entire town. The earth dug from the ditch had been piled behind it to form an earthen wall, which was topped with a wooden palisade.

I paused my horse at the edge of the woods and stared out across the open land that lay between me and the walls of Hedeby. Because of the season, the fields were still bare, with only low, weathered stubble from the remains of last year's crops showing gray against the soil like a grizzled growth of beard against an old man's cheek.

My mare tugged impatiently at the reins, urging me toward the food and shelter to be found in the town. She'd been mine only a matter of days. I had taken her from a dead man. Indeed, much of the gear I carried—my iron helm, my shield, my leather jerkin and small-axe, and even the meager hoard of silver pennies in the leather pouch at my belt—I'd taken from men who were dead. Men I had killed. Only the clothes on my back, the long, heavy bow I carried, and the fine dagger in my belt were truly mine. The dagger had been a gift from Harald, my half-brother and my teacher. He'd given it to me to honor my attaining the age of fifteen, and manhood. It seemed so long ago—had it truly been only a matter of days? The dagger was one of two gifts Harald had given me that night. The other was my life.

Still concealed within the final fringe of trees, I ignored my horse's urgings and sat staring at the town. It was not too late to turn back, and I dearly wished to, for my heart had suddenly filled with fear. Fear of the unknown, in part, for I had never seen a town so huge, nor even imagined so many people together in one place. Even more, though, I was afraid I would not measure up to whatever lay ahead.

I feared the fate that the Norns, the three ancient sisters who set the course of all men's lives, were weaving for me. How could I possibly succeed at the tasks ahead of me? By my years I was now reckoned a man, and admittedly I was tall and strong for my age. But I was alone, all alone, and in my heart, a part of me still felt like a child and longed for someone to turn to for guidance. There was no one, though. All whom I had previously relied upon in times of need—my mother, my brother, even his men—were now dead. The Norns had cut their life-threads and left me to face my fate on my own.

Shame at my own cowardice finally drove me forward. I knew I had to face my fear and overcome it, or I would dishonor myself. I owed a blood-debt. I had deaths I had sworn to avenge.

I kicked my heels against my mare's ribs and we headed down the road that led through pastures and fields toward Hedeby's gate—gaping like a missing tooth in the wall surrounding the town. Ahead, the road crossed a dry moat over a wooden bridge and disappeared through the opening in the wall beyond.

As I drew nearer, I saw an armed warrior was standing guard on the wall beside the gate. He watched my approach, looking out over the sharpened points of the stockade's timbers with a bored expression on his face. The late afternoon sun glinted on his polished helm and mail brynie, and made the sharpened blade of the spear he held flash like fire.

My horse's hooves thumped across the planks of the bridge like a slow drumbeat. As I reached the opening in the wall, three more warriors came into view, squatting on the rampart behind the guard, rolling dice. They were, I knew, warriors from the king's household, royal housecarls who'd been commanded by their lord to protect the town and collect the king's share of the trade that passed through its busy market.

I wondered if they were on the lookout for an outlaw and murderer. That was the lie told about me by the leader of the men who'd killed my brother, Harald. Had the tale made its way this far south? Had it reached Hedeby before me?

I forced a blank, unconcerned expression on my face as I rode through the gate, though my stomach felt twisted into knots and I had to remind myself to breathe. I was prepared to wheel my horse and ride for the forest if the guard challenged me, but he did not. As I passed him, he leaned his spear against the log wall of the palisade and squatted down to join his companions' game. I breathed a silent sigh of relief and entered the town.

Once inside the wall, the dirt track I'd been following became a paved road, surfaced with thick timbers laid side by side in the earth. A short distance off the road, in the band of open ground encircling the town inside the perimeter of the wall, two pigs were rooting in a heap of garbage. They looked up at me briefly as I neared, then plunged their snouts back into the noisome mound. A small boy watching them swiveled his head as I passed, following me with his eyes.

After the many days I'd spent in the open on my journey down Jutland, crossing windswept heaths and dark forests, the smell of the town was overwhelming. Odors of rotting garbage, animal dung, and human waste blended unpleasantly with whiffs of cooking. Smoke from countless fires overlaid all. A barrage of noise assaulted my senses, too.

Dogs barked, pigs squealed, chickens cackled, cattle lowed, and men and women strode up and down the road, babbling back and forth to each other.

Though it had appeared large to me when viewed from the edge of the forest, the town felt even more daunting once I was inside its walls. I felt as though I had wandered into some vast maze. Alleys branched off frequently from either side of the main road. They were lined with houses, row after row of them, all much smaller than the great chieftain's longhouse I'd grown up in.

I did not understand how people could bear to live this way. Why would they wish to?

Finally I reached the town's center. The road opened there into a square of bare, open ground. From the crowd that bustled within, it was obvious this was Hedeby's famed market, where goods from the farthest corners of the world could be bought or sold.

The perimeter of the market square was lined with small, fenced pens, containing sheep, cattle, and squealing pigs. Just beyond them on a low platform, a different kind of beast was being displayed for sale. Three children, two boys perhaps ten years of age, and a considerably younger girl, were squatting in the center of the platform. They looked dirty and hungry, and were wearing only ragged tunics, whose substance appeared to owe as much to the filth caked on them as to the coarse wool they were woven of. They were slaves. It was obvious from the thin ropes looped around each of their necks, tying them together. Even without the bonds, though, I'd have known. I recognized the dull, defeated look in their eyes. I understood why it was there. Where, I wondered, had they been taken? What land had they been snatched away from? What had happened to their homes and their families?

Turning away, I stood up in my stirrups and scanned the market square. Surely almost anything a person might want or need could be found here in Hedeby. What I did not see, though, was what I most hoped to find. I needed to sell my mare and her tack. Her service to me was done, for I had come to Hedeby to join the crew of a ship, a longship hopefully, bound i-viking. But none of the animal pens around the square contained horses, and nowhere I looked did anyone appear to be haggling over mounts. Indeed, there were few horses in the square at all, and those I could see looked to be objects of transportation rather than trade.

I did not know where to turn. It should have been a simple thing. The market was full of people. I had only to ask someone where I might find a buyer for my horse, but I feared appearing a fool. I feared looking like what I was: a green youth from the countryside.

As I took one last discouraged survey of the market square, I caught a glimpse, through a momentary gap in the crowd, of a man intent on a task I'd labored at many times myself. He was short and lean, with a weathered face, seated on a low stool holding a long, narrow stave of wood angled across his lap. He drew a thin, flat piece of steel down the stave in long strokes, shaving fine curls from it, searching for the shape of the bow concealed in the wood. I'd performed the same motions countless times myself in the work shed of Gudrod, the carpenter on my father's estate.

Watching someone labor at so familiar a task somehow made Hedeby seem less strange and threatening. I climbed down from my horse's back and led her closer to where the man was working. As I drew near, I saw three bundles of arrows and a finished bow—the wares he was offering for sale—arrayed on the ground at his feet.

The man glanced up, saw me staring at him, and studied me and my horse.

"My name is Raud," he said, "and if you're looking to buy a bow, or arrows for one, you've come to the right place. Though it appears you have a bow already," he added, nodding at the bow clutched in my hand.

"I do not need a bow," I agreed. "But I saw you working the wood. It was the first thing that has seemed familiar to me in this town since I arrived."

Raud grinned at my confession, but spoke in a kindly voice. "Aye, Hedeby can seem strange to one fresh out of the village. For what purpose have you come here?"

"To join a ship's crew and seek my fortune. But first," I added, "I must sell this horse."

Raud nodded. "Can you use that bow? A wise captain always welcomes skilled archers into his crew."

"I can use it," I answered. There was a great deal I felt uncertain about, especially since arriving at Hedeby, but that much I knew to be true.

He laid the stave he was working on the ground. "May I examine your bow?" he asked. "It looks to be a fine one."

I handed it to him. He rubbed his hands along the long limbs, caressing the wood, and closely examined the sharpened horn nocks, decorated with narrow bands of hammered bronze, which capped each end of the bow, pursing his lips and nodding appreciatively all the while. Finally he stretched his arm out and let the bow balance across his palm.

"May I string it?" he asked. I nodded. He stood, bracing the bow against the arch of his foot, and bent it, sliding the loop of the bowstring up into the top nock as he did. Grasping the leather-wrapped grip, in one smooth motion he pushed the bow forward with his left arm while pulling the string back with his right, coming to full draw. He held the bow there briefly while he studied the curve of its limbs, then eased the string forward. Still not speaking a word, he unstrung my bow and handed it back to me.

"Who made this?" he asked.

"I did," I answered.

"You're young to possess such skill. A longbow such as this is more difficult to make than a flat-bow, and this is as fine a one as I have seen. I could not have done better myself, and that is the high-est praise Raud the Bowmaker will speak of another man's bow."

He looked at the sky. "It will be dusk soon. If you're newly arrived here in Hedeby, I do not sup-pose you have a place to stay the night?"

I shook my head. "I've been on the road for many days, sleeping in the open. I can do it again," I replied.

"That is not necessary," Raud said. "I would not turn another bowmaker out, especially one so skilled. I was thinking of leaving the market soon anyway. Let me offer you the hospitality of my home this night. The fare will be simple, but you can at least sleep under a roof. Your horse will be safe behind my house, and in the morning I'll take you to a man who may wish to buy it. He keeps a stable of horses. It's not unusual," Raud added, "that a traveler will reach Hedeby by ship, but need to continue his journey on land. This man sells mounts to such, and is always looking for sound horses to buy at a fair price."

"Thank you," I said. "I appreciate your kindness." And in truth, the thought of sleeping inside again, with more than just a cloak and a low, open fire to fend off the night's chill, sounded very welcome indeed.

Raud bent down, picked up his bundles of arrows, and handed them to me to carry.

"Here," he said. "I'll make you earn it. But before I allow you to enter my home, you will have to tell me your name."

I blushed, embarrassed that I had forgotten my manners.

"My name is Halfdan," I said.

Raud led me across the market square and through a series of progressively narrower alleys. Finally he stopped in front of a small house and unlatched the gate in the fence around it. The yard contained a pen confining a sow and five piglets, and a garden with chickens hunting for bugs among rows of cabbages.

The door of the little cottage was open. Raud stepped into the yard and called through the open doorway, "Asa, we have a guest for dinner."

Raud's wife, Asa, was a plump woman with brown hair plaited into two braids. Her clothes, Raud's, and their home itself suggested they were poor folk. She had a friendly face and a warm smile, though, and quickly made me feel welcome.

Inside, Raud and Asa's house contained just a single room with a raised hearth in the center and low benches built of wood and packed earth lining three of the walls. A loom stood against the fourth wall, as did two wooden chests, one large and one small.

As Asa put the finishing touches on the evening meal, Raud introduced me to the rest of their family. Hake, their son, was still a toddler. Thora, their daughter, was ten years of age. I wondered about the gap in ages between the two children. As if he'd heard my thoughts, Raud volunteered, "We had another son, Gif. He'd have been seven. He died of a fever two winters ago."

We ate our dinner on a small tabletop that Asa and Thora had taken down from where it hung on one of the walls, and set up across the smaller of the two chests. Thora was determined to be the only person who served me, and sat beside me at table, hanging on every word I spoke. Her attentions caused me much embarrassment, and Raud and Asa much mirth.

Dinner was a hearty stew, with barley, onions, carrots, and chunks of fish, all cooked in an iron pot suspended over the fire. For too many days I'd lived on whatever small game I could kill and roast, unseasoned, over an open flame, or on dried, salted pork, when nothing crossed my path in range of my bow. Though the stew was simple, to me it tasted wonderful.

As we ate, Raud told Asa how he'd met me.

"Halfdan here is a bowmaker, too," he explained. "I met him in the market. He passed near me, and I noticed his bow. It's a fine one, and he made it himself."

Asa looked at me and smiled. "It must be a fine bow, for Raud to praise it," she said, nodding her head. "Everyone in Hedeby knows Raud makes the finest bows to be found south of Ribe."

"Don't believe her," Raud said, "I make the finest bows north of Ribe, too." To Asa he added, "Halfdan hopes to join a longship's crew."

Thora looked at me with big eyes. "Are you a warrior?" she asked, surprise evident in her voice. I felt dismayed by her reaction. If I did not appear a warrior even to a ten-year-old girl, how could I hope to convince a ship's captain I was one?

Asa seemed surprised, too. "What does your

mother think about this?" she asked.

Her question so startled me that I swallowed some soup down the wrong way and choked on it, coughing broth out through my nose. Raud looked embarrassed for me.

"Asa," he scolded, "a grown man does not need his mother's permission to go to sea." He turned to me with an apologetic look on his face.

"Asa's brother sailed with a longship's crew when he was very young—just two years older than Thora. He was only allowed to make the voyage because I vouched for him. I was chief of the archers on the ship. We raided in England, and he was killed there. Asa still grieves for him, though it was more than five years ago."

"Gisli was his name. He was so young," Asa said. "Too young for war. Too young to die. He hadn't had a chance to live. You look young, too," she added.

I did not know what to say. If her loss still pained her so, I did not want to risk stirring her memories up even more. I chose instead to answer her earlier question to me.

"My mother does not know of my plans," I told her. "She cannot know; she is dead. All of my family is dead."

Actually, my half-sister, Sigrid, still lived, but she was as if dead to me. She was now in the power of my enemy, the man who had killed our brother, Harald.

"Many a young man who started with nothing has made his fortune as a Viking," Raud said. "I think your decision is wise."

"And many a young man has died trying." Asa snorted. "I thank the Gods, Raud, that you came to your senses after Gisli was killed. We may not have a fortune, but at least I am not a widow-woman, and our children have a father."

It was my turn to feel embarrassed for Raud. No man likes to be scolded by his wife in front of guests. Raud's face turned red. He set his bowl of stew down on the table, stood up, and walked across the room to where the bow stave he'd been working in the market was now leaning against the wall.

"I'm going outside for a while," he announced. "There is still enough light to follow the wood's grain."

After he left, Asa spoke to me.

"Go on with him, Halfdan. It's not often we have guests, and he misses the company of men. He gave up the raiding life for me. I am grateful. I should not have spoken as I did in front of a stranger."

When I joined him outside, Raud shook his head.

"Pay no mind to Asa," he said. "The Viking life is a good life for a man. I miss it. When her brother died in my care, though, I felt I owed her.

15

She has been a good wife to me.

"I heard in the market that several longships came into Hedeby harbor today," he continued. "It's likely at least one will need more crew. We'll sell that horse of yours in the morning, then you can seek out the ships' captains down by the shore.

"It's a good life," he said again. "Men can die at home, too. I'd rather die quick and clean in battle than sick and weak in bed."

I wondered if Asa's brother would have agreed.

THE JARL

The next morning, after we broke the night's fast with a simple meal of barley porridge, Raud took me to the man whom he'd spoken of who kept a stable of horses. The stable owner's black hair and beard looked greasy, and he smelled like he slept with the animals he kept. After some haggling, though, he paid me in silver for the mare and her saddle. From the grin on the stable owner's face, and Raud's surprised expression when we agreed on a price, I suspected that he'd cheated me. I had no idea how much a horse was worth, or, for that matter, the value of the silver coins he traded for it. Still, I considered I had come out ahead, for the horse had cost me nothing.

It was time to part. Raud held out his hand,

and we clasped wrists.

"Thank you for your help and the hospitality of your home," I told him. "And thank Asa again for me."

"It was our pleasure," he replied. "I wish I could go with you. I miss the sea. I miss seeing other lands. It's a good life for a man, especially when you've no family missing you at home." He clapped me on the shoulder. "You may be young in years, but I'm sure you will do fine. Good luck to you on finding a ship. Good fortune on your voyage, and in your life."

Raud turned and headed back toward his home and family. He did not know me, but even so had been generous with his friendship. I watched him go, part of me wishing I could trade places with him. He longed for the Viking life because he could no longer have it. I longed for a family and a home, because mine were gone. It was my fate, though, to become a warrior. To do so, I had to join a longship's crew. The path I had to follow led to the sea.

I picked my way through Hedeby's alleys until I reached the harbor. This was the first time since I had acquired my shield, jerkin, and helm that I had to carry them and my other gear on my own back. I quickly came to miss the little mare.

After reaching the shore, I stood awhile, watching the busy harbor scene before me. Four longships were moored out against a breakwater, built from trunks of trees driven into the floor of the inlet to provide a protected anchorage. A small-boat was tied against the side of one of the low-slung warships. Closer in, a long wooden dock had been built along part of the shoreline. A number of narrow piers jutted out from it into the water. Several of these had knarrs, shorter and broader than the longships, tied up to them. One of the knarrs must have just recently arrived, for its crew was still unloading it, carrying bales of animal pelts over to an open shed and stacking them under the shelter of its roof. A man stood nearby, cutting a mark on a stick he held each time another bundle was delivered. Two other men stood with him, occasionally reaching out to feel the fur of the pelts when a new load was set down. I approached them and tried to put a confident smile on my face.

"I am looking for the captains of those long-ships," I said. "Do you know where I can find them?"

The three men turned and looked at me. After a moment, the man keeping tally on the stick looked away, his bored expression reflecting his utter lack of interest in my question. His rudeness angered me, and I could feel my face turning hot and red.

The other two men studied my appearance, assessing me from shoes to crown. Their expressions, and the fine clothes they were wearing, made me aware of the condition of my own. They'd been good quality once, but now looked stained and much the worse for wear.

One of the men smiled. It was not an unfriendly smile. I felt encouraged.

"What is your business with the captains?" he asked.

"I hope to join a crew. A longship's crew," I replied.

Now the second man spoke. "Are you a warrior?" He sounded surprised.

"I am," I stated, putting as much conviction in my voice as I could muster.

At my answer, both men looked amused. I was not. Why was it so unlikely? What did it take to make a man a warrior, other than the skill and the will to take the lives of other men? I had killed before.

The man who'd spoken first addressed me again.

"The captains of two of those longships serve Jarl Hastein." He raised his arm and gestured at something behind me. "That's his ship there, on the beach."

I turned and looked where he was pointing. Past the docks, on an open stretch of beach, a longship had been pulled, stern first, halfway up

onto the land. I nodded my thanks to my inform-
ant and strode down the beach toward it.

As I drew near, I saw that cut lengths of logs
had been lined up as rollers from the water's edge
to where the sternpost of the ship now rested, and
the ship's keel had been dragged across them.
Timbers were propped against the hull on either
side to hold it steady. The three top strakes of the
hull on the side I was facing had been staved in,
just back of mid-ship. A piece of sailcloth had been
nailed across the broken timbers to keep the sea
from splashing in. Two carpenters, one standing on
the deck and the other on a short ladder leaning
against the ship's side, were working together at
the break, cutting away the fabric patch and
removing the rivets holding the long, broken
planks in place.

I had never seen such a ship. Her lines were so
graceful, she looked alive. Her hull, broad in the
middle and tapering to a point at bow and stern,
swept up dramatically at either end to the stem-
posts of the keel. The stem-posts themselves, as
well as the top strakes where they joined the stems,
were covered with intricate carving, painted crimson and gold. The carved dragon head mounted
atop the stem-post at the bow also flashed with
gold.

I walked around her, admiring her lines.

My father, Hrorik, had owned a longship, the *Red Eagle*. I had never had the chance to sail on it, although when my father was still alive, and I was still a slave, I'd scrubbed its decks and hull when it was pulled out of the boathouse at winter's end, and had helped paint her with a fresh coat of pitch. The *Red Eagle* had been a fine ship, but it had not possessed the grace of the one I studied now. This ship looked sleek and sinuous, as though it could swim through the sea, rather than sail upon it.

"She's beautiful, is she not?" The voice came from behind me.

"Aye," I answered. "He who built her has brought the wood to life."

I turned to see who had spoken. Two men stood behind me. The closer one was standing with his hands on his hips, gazing admiringly at the ship. He was richly dressed, in a dark red tunic edged around the neck, sleeves, and hem with bands of dark green interwoven with threads of gold. The cloth had a very fine weave and soft drape that rippled with its wearer's slightest movement. I realized it must be silk. My brother, Harald, and my father, Hrorik, had decorated some of their finest tunics with bands of silk at the sleeves and hems. My mother, who'd sewed their garments for them, had let me feel how soft and light the precious fabric was. I'd never before seen a tunic made entirely of the rich cloth, though. It was beautiful. I could not imagine how much it must have cost.

The rest of the man's garb was equally fine. A short, dark blue cape, edged with thick white fur from the winter coat of a fox, hung from his shoulders, fastened by a large, ornate silver brooch. His legs were clad in dark green woolen trousers dyed to match the trim on his tunic, and his feet were shod with boots of a rich, dark brown leather. A sword hung at his belt, its gray steel hilt and pommel inlaid with silver patterns and runes.

The second man, who stood behind him, also possessed a remarkable appearance, though not due to his dress. He was the tallest person I had ever seen. He towered a head and a half higher than his companion, who was himself a tall man. The giant's clothes were also well made, but much simpler than those of his companion. His dark brown hair hung below his shoulders, but was pulled back and secured at his neck with a fat silver ring. Like his richly dressed companion, the giant also had a sword at his belt, though his was unusually long.

"My name is Hastein," the richly dressed man said. Indicating the giant standing behind him, he added, "And this is Torvald, called Starki, the Strong. He is my helmsman. The ship you're admiring is mine. I call her the *Gull*, for the way she skims across the waves."

The man who'd pointed this ship out to me had said it was owned by Jarl Hastein. Despite the wealth reflected by this man's rich dress, I was surprised he was a jarl. He looked to be no more than in his mid- to late twenties, just a few years older than my brother, Harald, had been. With his lean build and carefully groomed golden hair, his appearance even reminded me of Harald. How could one so young have come to rule over an entire district for the king?

"You are right," he said.

I didn't know what he meant. Right about what?

"The man who built this ship did create a living creature," he continued. "He brought the wood she's built of to life. When she needed repair, I brought her back here to Hedeby, to the master shipwright who built her. I would not entrust her to any other."

"What happened to her?" I asked.

"We were chasing a Frankish ship off the coast of Frisia. As we pulled alongside and threw our grappling lines, her captain tried to ram us. I killed him myself for harming the *Gull*.

"It was perceptive of you to see the life in the *Gull*, even when she's beached on the shore," Hastein continued. "The beauty of her lines is not hard to see, but it's when she's in the water that the life that's in her becomes apparent. Do you know ships?"

"No," I admitted. "But I know wood."

At my remark, Hastein shifted his gaze to the bow I was holding in my hand.

"I noticed your bow as I came up behind you," he said. "It is a beautiful weapon. Did you make it yourself?"

"I did," I said, nodding my head.

"You must be quite skilled to be able to craft such a bow." He smiled and nodded, then he and the giant walked past me toward where the workers were removing the broken planks from the side of the ship.

If only I could serve a man such as this, I thought. To be a jarl so young, he must be a great leader. On impulse, I blurted out,

"I can not only craft a bow well, I can shoot one, too."

The jarl stopped and turned back to face me. He had an amused expression on his face.

"And how well can you shoot a bow?" he asked.

For a moment I was at a loss for words. I wanted to impress this man, yet not appear boastful.

"It is difficult to answer your question," I replied. "I could tell you I shoot very well indeed, but how can you know if my standards are the same as yours? What I might view as very skillful shooting, you might think is merely passable. Or on the other hand, I might think a shot I made was disappointing, but, by the standards of another, it might appear a fine shot indeed. There is no way for you to truly know how well I shoot a bow unless you put me to a test."

A spark of interest flickered in Hastein's eyes now, and a smile spread across his lips. "You turn my simple question into a fine distinction. If you're as precise with your arrows as with your words, I will be impressed."

"I wish more than just to impress you, sir," I said, amazed at my own boldness. "I've come to Hedeby hoping to find a berth on a warship, and seek my fortune. I would like to join your crew and serve on your ship. Let me show you my skill with this bow. Pick a target and test me."

The giant, Torvald, erupted with a snort of indignation. "Impudent, beardless lad! This man to whom you speak is jarl over all of the northern district of Jutland. His crew are all handpicked warriors and seasoned men. Children do not serve on the *Gull*."

"I am not a child," I sputtered. "No more than you are a tree that can speak, though in truth you are the size of one. I am a grown man."

26

Torvald opened his mouth, no doubt to insult me again, but Hastein held up his hand to silence him.

"You did not know what you asked," he said to me. "Even were you not so young, I would not bring into my crew any man whom I know nothing about. My men are all well known to me. Their courage, loyalty, and skill at arms have been proved. I know nothing at all about you—not even your name, or who your father was, or where you are from."

Halfdan, son of Hrorik, I started to say, then hesitated. What if the jarl had known my father? He would know of my brother, Harald, if he had, but not of me. How would I explain? I would have to reveal that I had been a slave in my own father's household. What chance then would I have of joining any longship's crew, much less the crew of this jarl?

"My father's name was Eric," I lied. "He was a simple farmer. He's dead now. He died of a fever. We lived near Ribe." If Jarl Hastein ruled over northern Jutland, hopefully he would be unfamiliar with the folk of Ribe in the midlands.

"My name is Halfdan," I added. That much, at least, was true.

The jarl stared at me silently for a moment, the expression on his face unreadable. I met his gaze without blinking or looking away.

"Well, Halfdan," he finally said, "you've made me curious to see how well you shoot your bow." Hastein reached into the pouch at his belt and pulled out a silver coin. "I will not give you a berth on my ship, even if you impress me with your shooting. But if you can make the shot I name, I'll give you this silver denier to reward you for your trouble, and for my amusement."

Hastein turned, scanned the harbor briefly, then pointed out across it toward the end of the timber breakwater.

"Do you see that piling jutting up taller than the others?" he asked.

I did. I nodded, surprised. It was not that long a shot he was proposing.

"There is a knot in it, one hand's length down from the top," he continued. "Do you see it? Are you skilled enough to strike that knot with your arrow?"

The knot was no larger than the palm of my hand. This was more of a test, a shot only a skilled archer could count on hitting. Still, I did not doubt I could make it. I'd learned to shoot a bow hunting squirrels, birds, and other small game. The frequency with which such fare had graced my father's table was a testament to my ability to hit even the smallest of marks.

To shoot the knot would prove me a skilled archer, but I wanted to do more. I wanted to amaze the jarl. Perhaps then he might change his mind. I searched the harbor for a more difficult target. Far down the shore, in some tall grass growing near where the earthen bank of the town wall stopped at the water's edge, I saw movement.

It would be a foolishly difficult shot to attempt. If I could hit this mark, though, it would surely impress any man. On the other hand, if I missed, I would appear a braggart and a fool.

I had come to Hedeby to seek my fortune. Fortunes are more often won by boldness than by caution. I decided to risk it.

"Would you favor fresh duck for your midday meal, Jarl Hastein?" I asked. My voice sounded far calmer than I felt.

"What?" he asked, confused.

Torvald rolled his eyes. "He cannot make the shot you named," he muttered. "He wants to pick another."

"There are marsh ducks nesting in that tall grass," I said, pointing to show him where. "See yonder where one has just wandered out onto the shore? If you would enjoy feasting on duck, I will shoot that one for you."

The distance was well over twice as far as the shot the jarl had proposed.

Hastein stared at me piercingly for a moment. "Some think marsh duck tastes too strongly of fish," he said. "But if you can make that shot, then I will dine on roasted duck, and you will join me."

I strung my bow, then unslung both quivers from my shoulder and selected an arrow I had made and knew shot true. As I laid the arrow across my bow and nocked it on the string, Torvald said, "Ho, boy, have you silver to back your boast? I'll wager two silver pennies you cannot make that shot."

"I'll take your wager, Torvald," Jarl Hastein said, drawing a surprised look from his helmsman. "If he makes it, you will pay me. Now be silent and let him shoot."

The jarl's words startled me, too. Why would he bet on me?

The duck wandered along the water's edge, pecking at the sand, stopping and moving, never still for more than an instant. I watched it, holding my bow ready, but not drawn, and silently berated myself. Why had I been such a fool? Why had I entrusted my future to a duck? If it would not be still, I would have to try and anticipate where it might move between the time I released my shot and when the arrow fell to earth. It was impossible. The foolish creature could go anywhere.

I was starting my draw when a second duck walked out of the reeds, ruffled its wings for a moment, then settled itself down into the warmth of the sand and began preening its feathers with its bill.

"The second duck," I murmured to Hastein, and came to full draw. As I looked beyond the point of my arrow, the shoreline of the town stretched out before me, the houses and work buildings to one side, the sea along the other. My vision narrowed till I saw clearly only the strip of beach leading to where the duck had nestled in the sand. I let all else fade from my sight and from my mind. Finally I saw only the duck itself, then the spot where its neck met its back. At that moment, I released.

Odin guide my arrow, I prayed, as it sped away. And keep the duck from moving.

The arrow arced up and across the stretch of shoreline, then began to drop down, its flight forming a curve as graceful as the shape of a strung bow. Like a thunderbolt thrown by Thor, it fell from the sky and pierced the duck through its side, knocking it sideways and pinning it to the sand. Its mate squawked in terror and took flight.

"Remarkable," Hastein muttered. "That was truly remarkable. I have never seen such a shot." He turned and looked at me. "When you shoot at such a distance, how do you gauge how high you must aim to allow for the drop?"

I shook my head. "When I shoot, I just look at

my target and pick where I want to hit it. When I can see only that point, I release the arrow to find its mark."

"Remarkable," Hastein said again. He turned to Torvald. "You owe me two silver pennies. And as loser of the wager, you should go and retrieve the duck."

"Why did you wager on me?" I asked, while we stood watching Torvald lumber along the shore to where my arrow had pinned the duck to the ground. "You'd never seen me shoot."

"I bet on your confidence," Hastein answered. "You showed no fear that you would fail, and even though you are young, you do not appear to be the sort of fool who would boastfully claim that which he knew he could not do.

"I could have been wrong about you, of course," he continued, "but I consider myself a good judge of men. I would not be alive today, nor hold the position I do, if I was not. And if I had been wrong, it was only two silver pennies. I did not gain the wealth and power I now hold by being afraid to take chances."

I wondered if Jarl Hastein would have chanced his wager on me had he realized how my heart was in my throat when I took the shot.

TELL ME
YOUR TALE

While the *Gull* was beached for repair, Jarl Hastein and his crew were living in tents pitched along the shore. The jarl's tent was striped, made from broad bands of red and white sailcloth sewn together. The tops of the tall cross-timbers supporting the roof-pole were carved into dragons' heads, similar to the one affixed to the stern-post at the bow of Hastein's ship.

A low fire was burning in a ring of stones in front of the jarl's tent. Two iron stakes, forked at the top, had been driven into the ground on either side. A long iron rod, supported by the stakes and spanning the fire, was draped with a string of sausages that dripped fat into the flames.

As we approached, a strange-looking little man emerged from the tent and prodded one of the sausages with a small knife. He was wearing only a long tunic of coarse brown wool, and his head was shaved bald on top, though the fringe of hair remaining on the sides and back was long enough to fashion into a loose plait.

"This is Cullain," Hastein told me, nodding his head at the little man. "He is my thrall. He is skilled at many things, one of which is cooking. Give the duck to him, and he will prepare it."

Cullain. The sound of the name called memories of my mother's voice to mind; of tales she'd told me of her distant home in Ireland. I'd loved the way her tongue had rolled over the names of the Irish kings and heroes in her stories.

"Is Cullain from Ireland?" I asked.

"He is," Hastein replied. "I captured him in a raid on an abbey there. I could have ransomed him back, for the Christians usually pay to recover captured priests, but I've found him too useful. Besides being an excellent cook, he's skilled at brewing ale and mead, and is also a trained leech, who knows how to treat wounds and illness."

My mother had lost her home and the life she'd known in Ireland because of her beauty. This little man had lost his because of his skills. Strange that what should be considered gifts from the Gods could become a curse in a person's life.

"Though your road be long and lonely, may you find peace at its end," I said to Cullain in Latin, as I handed him the carcass of the duck.

He stared at me, startled, then asked, *"How come you to speak the language of civilized men?"*

"My mother was Irish," I replied, *"and learned in the tongue of the ancient Romans."*

Cullain's words caused my mind to drift back to an image of my mother. "You should learn Latin, Halfdan," she would tell me, when I would protest her efforts to teach me. "It is the language of civilization." I'd thought it an unconvincing reason for the slave of a Dane to learn the strange tongue, since, by her own admission, she did not believe my father's people were civilized.

"What are the two of you saying, and how do you know the tongue of the Christian priests?" Hastein demanded.

"I was merely greeting him. I know Latin because my mother taught me. She was Irish," I told Hastein, my mind still on the image of my mother. "She learned to speak and read Latin in a monastery near her home."

"I have spent much time in Ireland," Hastein said. "Only some of the priests and monks there, and a very few of the nobility, can both speak and read Latin. It is very unusual for a woman to have such learning."

"Aye," I answered, without thinking. "Her father was a king, and the monastery was near his lands. That is why the priests taught her."

Hastein stared at me silently for a moment.

"How strange," he finally said. "Your mother was the daughter of a king in Ireland, but your father was merely a farmer in Ribe?"

For a moment his comment confused me. Too late I recalled the lie I had told him about my father. Before I could try to invent a story, Hastein spoke again.

"I suspected earlier that you were lying," he said. "No man needs to think before answering when asked his father's name or where he calls home, but you hesitated when I asked you those questions. The truth is like a well-known path our footsteps can follow without thinking. Lies are not so familiar, though. Your voice betrayed you then, as your face does now. Its expression is more honest than your tongue was earlier."

My face, which seemed to have a mind of its own, had indeed confirmed Hastein's accusation by flushing a brilliant red.

Cullain, who had laid the duck beside the fire ring and entered the tent, now staggered back out almost hidden beneath a huge bundle of thick brown fur—the pelt of a large bear—which he spread on the ground. When he was done, Hastein seated himself on the skin, his legs crossed. Torvald sat down beside him, to his right. Hastein pointed to the empty spot at his left.

"Sit," he told me. I would rather have crawled away in shame, but his voice had a tone of command in it I dared not disobey. I had already shown the jarl disrespect by lying to him. If I turned my back on him now and fled, I feared he might set the giant on me.

"It will take some time for Cullain to prepare the duck. While we wait, we will talk. Let me warn you not to try to deceive me again, for I am deemed more cunning than most men. I wish to know who you are, and why you felt a need to conceal from me the truth about yourself. Now tell me your tale."

I dared tell him naught but the truth. But my life had led a twisted path, and I did not know where to begin. Sensing my hesitation, Hastein prompted me.

"Who is your father? Who are your people?"

Who were my people? I remembered the day when my brother, Harald, had taken me to see the burial mounds of our ancestors.

"My father's name was Hrorik," I began. "He was the son of Offa, who was son of Gorm, who was son of Haldar Greycloak. My father was called

Strong-Axe, and he was a chieftain."

"I know of him," Hastein said. "I have met him and have raided with him. I heard a rumor that he died."

"It is true. He was gravely wounded in battle during a raid on England. My brother, Harald, brought him home. Hrorik died the night after they returned."

"I know of Harald, too," Hastein said, nodding his head. "I remember a lawsuit was brought against him at the Thing up on the Limfjord, charging him with killing a man. I helped judge it. The killing was ruled to be lawful. It occurred in a duel, as I recall."

Hastein looked me in the eyes. "I do not recall hearing that Hrorik had another son, though. Who are you?"

Though it was difficult, I held his gaze, and did not look away.

"My name is Halfdan, as I told you," I said. "Hrorik was my father. My mother was the daughter of a king in Ireland, as I said, but Hrorik took her in a raid and kept her as his concubine. She was his slave."

"And are you a slave, too?" Hastein asked. "Perhaps a runaway? Though it is growing out, your hair still shows traces of having been cut shorter than a free man would wear it."

I shook my head.

"No," I answered. "It is true I once was a slave. But on the night he returned home from England, before he died, Hrorik freed me."

"And your mother? Does she still live?" Hastein asked.

Now I did look away. I did not want the jarl to see the tears that came to my eyes.

"No," I said. "She, too, is dead. Her body was burned with Hrorik's on his funeral pyre. She agreed to accompany my father on his death voyage to the next world, if he would free me and acknowledge me as his son."

I missed my mother, but that was not what brought the tears to my eyes. I still felt pain that she had died for me; that she had bought my freedom with her death. I should not have let her.

"Why did you try to hide this from me?" Hastein asked. "And why are you here in Hedeby, looking to join a ship's crew? If Hrorik acknowledged you as his son, could you not stay in the household? Does Harald not wish to share the inheritance with you?"

"No, that is not true, not at all," I stammered. I did not want anyone to think ill of Harald. "Harald was the finest man I have ever known. I loved him. He embraced me as a brother. He trained me in the skills of a warrior and the manners of a free man."

"You speak of him in the past, as if he is dead," Hastein interjected.

"He is," I replied. The thought of Harald's death almost brought tears to my eyes again. "He was murdered. That is why I feared to tell you who I am. The man who killed Harald hunts me, too. And he has spread lies about me, to conceal his own misdeeds. He claims I was among the men who killed Harald and his followers."

"Harald Hroriksson is dead?" Hastein asked. "Murdered? I had not heard that. I have been away, scouting the coast of Frankia. It is grave news. How did it happen?"

"Harald and I had traveled, with a few of his men, to Hrorik's smaller estate up north on the Limfjord," I explained. "It happened there. The farm was attacked during the night. We tried to fight them off, but there were too many. In the end, everyone on the farm—even the women, children, and thralls—was slain. Everyone but me."

"How did you escape?" Hastein asked.

"In the last assault, Harald gave his life, cutting a path through the enemy so I could flee. I did not want to leave him, but he ordered me to go. He said someone had to escape. Someone had to live, to avenge the dead."

"And you say these men who killed Harald are

also hunting you?" Hastein asked. "Who are they?"

"Their leader is called Toke," I told him. "He is Hrorik's foster son."

I could see the surprise in Hastein's face.

"I know Toke," he said. "He is a chieftain. I met him once in Dublin. I have never raided with him, but he is said to be a fierce warrior, fearless in battle. He is not a man I would suspect of such treachery. And why would he kill his own foster brother?"

"He is a berserk," I said. "When he lived in our home, he was much given to evil moods and fits of violence. No one, save Hrorik and Harald, was safe when his black moods came upon him, and eventually he dared to challenge even Hrorik's authority. Finally Hrorik banished him. But after Hrorik died, Toke returned, seeking a share of the inheritance. He was greatly angered to learn Hrorik had left him nothing."

"But with Harald dead, and if there is no other male heir, then Toke might still hope to inherit," Hastein suggested.

I nodded. "I believe that is his plan. He and Harald quarreled fiercely, and Harald ordered Toke to leave and never return. I thought blood would be spilled that night, but Toke and his crew left peacefully. I know now he was but biding his time."

"And you say Toke killed Harald and all of his men?"

I nodded again. "All who were with us. I do not know how Toke discovered that we had gone to the small estate on the Limfjord with only a few men. But Toke and his crew landed in the night and surrounded the longhouse. Harald knew we were badly outnumbered. He negotiated for the women and children to leave safely, but once they were outside the longhouse Toke and his crew killed them all. They wanted no witnesses to their treachery. Then they set fire to the longhouse. We tried to break out and fight our way to the forest, but there were too many of them."

Hastein shook his head. "Murder of women and children?" he asked. "After their safety had been promised? And murder of a foster brother? It is a grave accusation you are making. It is very hard to believe this of a chieftain like Toke."

I felt I knew what Hastein had left unspoken. Toke was a chieftain, a respected warrior and leader, while I was but a former slave. Why should my word be trusted? I could feel my face turning red with anger.

"Does noble birth guarantee honorable deeds?" I exclaimed. "You see Toke as a chieftain, but you know him only by reputation. I know what he is truly capable of, because I have seen it. He is a

Nithing, a man without honor. I have sworn to kill him and all of his warriors who helped slay Harald, and I will do so, or die trying."

Torvald, who had been silent up until now, snorted derisively. "I think the latter is more likely," he said. "Toke has killed many men. I myself saw him kill a man once in a duel in Dublin. You would not stand a chance against him."

"Do you not recall men once said the same about me?" Hastein asked Torvald, in a quiet voice, "when I was vying with Grim Ormsson for the right to rule as jarl in the north of Jutland?"

Hastein turned back to me, and continued. "My father had been jarl before me," he explained, "but when he died, I was just a young man. Grim, a seasoned chieftain and warrior, thought he was more fit to rule than a beardless youth. Perhaps the king suspected the same, for he did not intervene when Grim and his men marched against me. My father's housecarls supported me out of loyalty to his memory, but few others stood with me. I was counseled to cede the right to be jarl to Grim, and swear allegiance to him. I was told I would not stand a chance against Grim. Yet today I am jarl, and Grim's bones are moldering in his burial mound. I am jarl because I dared to face the fate the Norns wove for me, despite the fact that few but me believed I could succeed."

Hastein was silent for a while. "I rule over the lands around the Limfjord for the king," he finally said. "I am responsible for maintaining the peace there. If all of the inhabitants of an estate have been murdered, it is my concern. I must think on this."

Hastein leaned back on one elbow, stretched his legs out in front of him, then called out, "Cullain!"

The little thrall, who had been squatting beside the tent, gutting and plucking the duck, looked up.

"Bring us wine," Hastein ordered. "And something to eat while we wait for you to cook that duck. I am ravenous."

I was hungry, too. Cullain brought us a wooden platter laden with a large slab of cheese, a loaf of bread that smelled freshly baked, three silver goblets, and a pottery pitcher. Setting the tray on the ground in front of Hastein, he pulled a knife from the block of cheese and used it to cut three sausages from the string roasting over the fire.

After adding the sausages to the supply of food on the platter, Cullain lifted the pitcher and poured liquid from it into the three goblets.

Hastein took one of the goblets and passed it to me, saying, "You are my guest at this meal. Good health."

Cullain passed a second goblet to Hastein, who this time kept it and took a long drink of its contents, then sighed contentedly. While Hastein drank, Torvald reached forward and took the third goblet. He, too, took a long drink, then belched appreciatively afterward.

I looked suspiciously at the liquid in the goblet I was holding, then took a cautious sip. The liquid was a deep, rich red, almost the color of blood, though thinner. Hastein grinned at me.

"Have you never drunk wine before?"

I shook my head. I'd drunk ale, and on a few occasions mead, but never wine.

"This was part of the cargo from the ship I took off Frankia. The one that damaged the *Gull*. The priests of the White Christ drink wine like this in their rituals. They believe it turns into the blood of their God and protects them from death. From what I've seen, it holds no power in that regard, but it's a fine drink nonetheless."

Hastein leaned forward, cut a piece of bread and topped it with slices of sausage and cheese, then reclined on his elbow again. "Help yourself," he said to me, nodding at the tray of food. Torvald took a knife from his belt and stuck it in one of the sausages. He raised it to his mouth and ripped a large chunk off of one end. I waited to be sure he was finished at the tray before cutting myself some bread, cheese, and meat. I thought it might be unwise to come between a giant and his food.

"You said the men who killed your brother, Harald, are also hunting you," Hastein said. "What did you mean?"

"During the final fight, I escaped into the forest. When morning came, Toke sent warriors, aided by trackers and dogs from a nearby village, to hunt me down."

"Why did the villagers help him?" Hastein asked.

"Toke told their headman that bandits had attacked the longhouse and slaughtered its occupants. He said he'd been camped nearby and was drawn by the flames, but arrived too late for anything but vengeance. Toke claimed he and his men had killed all of the bandits, save one who had escaped. He was referring, of course, to me."

"And the villagers' headman believed this tale?" Hastein asked.

"He, like you, knew Toke," I replied. "I suppose he, too, found it hard to believe such a noted chieftain would murder all of the occupants of a farm, including his own foster brother."

"Toke cannot let you live," Hastein said with a grim smile. "You can give the lie to his tale. You could reveal his treachery.

"It is a long way from the Limfjord to Hedeby," he continued. "How did you escape the hunters? Or do they pursue you still?"

46

"I am at home in the forest," I said. "More so than most men. Their advantage was not as great as they believed, and it made them careless. I did not kill the two villagers, for I had no fight with them. But none of Toke's men from that first hunting party still live. I am sure, though, that Toke will send others."

"Your tale is difficult to believe," Hastein said. "Few men could survive being hunted as you describe, much less prevail. And you are not much more than a boy, with no experience in battle, and were only recently a slave, to boot." He took a long drink of wine, then just stared at me, saying nothing.

It had felt good to tell my tale to Hastein. It was like a lightening of the burden I carried for someone else to know of Toke's treachery. But as Hastein's silence dragged on, my spirits sank. He did not believe me.

Finally he spoke.

"Your tale is difficult to believe," he said again. "Yet I find there are some signs you speak the truth. Your appearance is consistent with your words. The cut of your hair, and the amount of time it looks to have been growing out, matches the facts you have told me. And your clothes, though somewhat stained and ragged now, obviously were at one time of fine quality, and appear to have been made to fit your size, rather than stolen. Words may lie, but such things do not. Are there any other facts you can tell me that support your story?"

I let my mind retrace the events I had lived through in recent days.

"I know the name of the headman of the village, who spoke with Toke. He is Hrodgar."

Hastein nodded. "I know him," he said. "He is a good man."

"And the trackers Hrodgar sent to aid Toke's men are named Einar and Kar," I continued. "In the end, Einar joined forces with me, and helped me overcome the last of Toke's men. He knows the truth. He heard Toke's man confess before he died. And I have these."

I reached into one of my quivers, and pulled out two sticks, carved with runes. Hastein took them from me.

"What are they?" he asked.

"They are the names of Toke's men who attacked the farm. Einar carved them on these sticks for me. We made Toke's man tell us before we killed him." I did not mention to Hastein that I could not read runes, so did not know what the sticks said. That was a problem I would deal with when the time came.

"If this Einar heard one of Toke's men confess,

as you have said, he is an important witness," Hastein said. "I would like to speak with him."

Hastein was silent again for a while, then let out a long sigh. "I have never been able to ignore murder and treachery, and the work of Nithings," he said. "It is a weakness of mine. But I have no time now to attend to this. Far greater matters are about to be set in motion, and I am a part of them.

"Yet I wonder," he added, "if it is the Norns who have caused your path and mine to cross. When weaving the fates of men, rarely do the three sisters cross the threads of separate lives without a reason. I have learned to watch the path my life follows for the telltale footprints of fate. I wonder if the shot I saw you make today was not a sign for me—a sign that your fate has been touched by the Gods. And if that is so, I do not believe it is an accident that we have met."

He sighed again.

"There is no way around it," he said. "I must keep you with me for now, until I have time to investigate your accusation against Toke, and decide what must be done. Despite your youth and lack of experience, you will join the crew of the *Gull*."

4

THE GULL

I was surprised at Hastein's words. Torvald was more than surprised. He was indignant.

"My Jarl," he exclaimed. "This is but a beardless youth. He cannot join the crew of the *Gull*! We are all chosen men."

"You have heard his tale," Hastein replied. "He has more experience fighting than you would expect from his age. And you have seen him shoot his bow. No archer on the *Gull* could make the shot he made today, not even Tore."

Hastein turned to me. "But Torvald is right. The men will not like it. They have all seen many campaigns, and have proved their worth. Do not expect their acceptance to come easily. You will have to earn it."

"This will cause bad feelings," Torvald said,

shaking his head. "It is a mistake."

"It is my decision who serves on my ship," Hastein retorted. "The crew will abide by my decision, as will you. And you are my second in command. I expect you to ensure there is no trouble over it."

Torvald sprawled back on the bearskin, leaning on one elbow and frowning fiercely. He reached for his goblet and took a long drink from it, but said nothing more.

"As a member of the *Gull*'s crew," Hastein told me, "you will be entitled to one share in the felag, the fellowship of all the crews of my three ships. That means you will have one share of any common plunder we win. Any individual plunder you take will be your own.

"I've seen that you are a master archer. You tell me you are also skilled in the forest, and I've heard you speak the Latin tongue, which is likely to prove useful on this voyage. Have you any other talents I do not know of?"

"I can craft bows and arrows," I answered. "And since I was ten years of age, I worked as a blacksmith's helper on my father's estate."

A slow smile spread across Hastein's face. "This is another sign for me," he said. "The blacksmith on my estate on the Limfjord slipped on ice this winter and broke his leg. It has not healed well, and he is not fit to go to sea. The *Gull* has been without a ship's smith on this voyage. . . . Until now."

He turned to his helmsman. "You see, Torvald. It is meant to be. And this will help the men accept him."

Torvald only grunted. He looked doubtful.

Hastein waited, looking at me expectantly, but I said nothing. I was certainly not going to protest working as the ship's smith. I was glad to be on the crew at all.

"As a blacksmith, you possess a valued skill beyond that of an ordinary crewman," he finally said. "An experienced warrior would bargain for additional shares in the felag. I will not take advantage of your inexperience. You'll be entitled to one and one-half shares rather than one."

Hastein glanced at the gear I had lugged with me to his camp. In addition to my bow and two quivers, and the small-axe and dagger stuck in my belt, I had a shield, a helm, a rolled bundle containing two cloaks and a metal-studded leather jerkin, and my food pouch and waterskin. It was all I owned in the world.

"Obviously you do not have smithing tools," Hastein observed. He reached into a small leather pouch hanging from his belt and pulled out several silver coins. Handing them to me, he said, "Use these to buy the tools you'll need. At the end of the voyage, you can repay me if you wish to keep them. Use any silver that remains after you've bought your tools to buy pigs of iron."

I took the coins but sat staring at them in my hand, saying nothing. I could feel my face turning red.

"Is there a problem?" Hastein asked. "Do you think you'll need more silver?"

"I know the tools I'll need," I answered, looking at the ground instead of into his eyes, "but I have been a thrall most of my life. I do not know the fair value of the things I need to purchase, or the worth of this silver. I do not know how to buy what I need."

"You are a strange lad indeed," Hastein said, "though what you say is consistent with your tale. Torvald, accompany Halfdan and be sure he is not cheated." Torvald rolled his eyes but said nothing. I felt I was sinking ever lower in his esteem.

"And as for you," he said, looking back at me. "You were wise to tell me the complete truth. I will not hold it against you that you were born a thrall. But you should know that many men will judge you by what you were, rather than what you are. It is a thing best kept secret."

After the meal, Torvald and I set off into the town. I suggested that we find a blacksmith, and see if he had any extra tools he would be willing to sell, but Torvald insisted we go first to the market square.

"If you truly know nothing about the value of silver, or how to bargain, you need to learn," he insisted. "If you do not, you will soon embarrass yourself in front of the crew. It will be hard enough as it is to get them to accept you. Tore in particular will not like it."

"Who is Tore?" I asked.

"He is the leader of the archers in the *Gull's* crew. In battle, you will usually fight under his command. If he accepts you, the rest of the crew will at least tolerate your presence. But Tore will not be pleased to have one as young and inexperienced as you fighting under him."

Torvald sighed. "It is just like the jarl," he said, "to make a decision like this, then leave it to me to make it work. I must think of a plan." He sighed again. "The jarl is fortunate to have me to depend on."

When we reached the market square, we wandered through the wares that had been set out for trade or sale. Torvald often stopped and bargained vigorously for some item. Though he never bought, his negotiations with the merchants helped me begin to understand the value that lay in the silver coins I carried. To my surprise, it was not the type of coin—whether an English penny, a Frankish denier, or even a coin stamped in Hedeby itself—that set its value. It was the weight of the silver that mattered. The one time Torvald actually did make a purchase—a skin filled with Frankish wine, which we passed back and forth between us as we wandered—he did not even use a coin to pay. Instead he pulled a thin, twisted silver bar, that looked like it might once have been part of an arm torque, from the pouch at his belt and chopped a small piece from it with his knife.

Despite his initial grumbling to Jarl Hastein about bringing me into the *Gull*'s crew, I found Torvald to be a pleasant and entertaining companion. He smiled often, laughed easily, and seemed to enjoy having a listener eager to hear his tales about Hastein and the crew of the *Gull*. Torvald was, I learned, not only the helmsman of Hastein's ship, but also the warrior who carried the jarl's standard in battle and fought at his side. Hastein and Torvald had been friends since childhood, and—to hear Torvald tell it, at least—most of the jarl's successes would not have occurred but for Torvald's assistance. I wondered if Hastein held the same view.

I was tilting my head back to take another swig from the wineskin when Torvald nudged me with his elbow. A nudge from Torvald was like a shove from a lesser man, and I staggered sideways, squirting wine across my face instead of in my mouth.

"Look there," he said. "That man is selling sea

chests. I knew someone would be selling them in a port town like Hedeby. Now it is your turn. Bargain for one and buy it."

I looked in the direction Torvald was pointing. A short distance ahead of us, an old man with a grizzled gray beard was sitting on a long, low wooden chest. Another was nearby, its lid propped open. The man, who was wearing a simple tunic and trousers of rough gray wool, was whittling on a fat stick with a thin-bladed knife.

It had not occurred to me that I would need a sea chest until Torvald mentioned it, but as soon as he did, I recalled watching my father and his crew prepare for their voyages on the *Red Eagle*. Each member of his crew had had such a chest, to store his gear in and to use as a seat when he was rowing.

"How much should I pay for it?" I asked Torvald.

He shrugged his shoulders. "Find out how much he's asking for one," he suggested. "Then offer him less."

The graybeard looked up from his whittling when I approached.

"Did you make these chests?" I asked him. He nodded. I looked at the chest he wasn't seated on. It was beautiful craftsmanship. Its planks were made of a dark, tight-grained wood I didn't recognize. They felt as smooth as steel, and gleamed as though they'd been rubbed with oil. The hinges were of brightly polished bronze, and two bands of the same metal wrapped the chest near either end to strengthen it. An ornate bronze plate cast in the design of a writhing serpent was set into the wood on the front of the chest, with a slot for a key cut in its center.

"How much do you want for this one?" I asked. I did not need so fine a chest, but its beauty awakened in me a longing to possess it.

"That one?" the old man asked, and paused a moment, while he let his eyes slowly take my appearance in, from head to foot. "That one's my finest work. I'll sell it for three silver pennies— Hedeby penny-weight," he added.

The price, and the old man's look, brought me back to my senses. The chest was beautiful, but it was not for such as me. I looked at the one the man was seated on. Though of a similar size to the fine chest, it was far plainer. Its planks were of pine, and its hinges and catch were rough iron forgings.

"May I look at this one?" I asked. The old man stood up, straightening his back slowly as if it hurt him to do so. I opened the lid of the pine chest. It moved smoothly on its hinges, and mated well with the main body when closed. The planks were joined tightly together at their edges.

"How much do you want for it?"

"One silver penny," the old man replied.

Torvald snorted, and began making a show of scanning the market square, as though looking for another seller of chests. I appreciated the hint.

"I'll give you a half," I said.

"Hedeby weight?" the old man asked.

His readiness to accept my offer seemed a sign that even at half a penny, I was paying too much, but I nodded, and fished from my belt pouch one of the English pennies I'd taken from Toke's men when I'd killed them. The old man took a small set of scales from a pouch at his belt, weighed the coin, then set it atop a nearby block of wood and laid the blade of his knife across it.

"Do you agree this cut is fair?" he asked.

I nodded again. He hammered on the back of the blade with the stick he'd been whittling and it was done.

As I'd suspected, we ended up having to locate a blacksmith to find the tools I needed. It turned out there were two smiths in Hedeby. The first had no tools to sell, but the second, an old man, had an extra set he'd once carried on sea voyages: a mid-weight hammer, its head flat-faced on one side and wedge-shaped on the other; a set of short iron tongs; a block of hardened steel, about the size of one of Torvald's fists, to use as an anvil; and a small bellows made of leather and wood. I paid him what he asked without haggling, and felt myself lucky.

I loaded my newly acquired tools into my sea chest and hoisted it onto my shoulder. We used the rest of Hastein's silver to buy five bars of rough cast iron, which Torvald threw up onto his shoulder like they were sticks of firewood, and carried with far less apparent effort than my sea chest was costing me.

When we returned to the campsite, Hastein was gone. Cullain was busy preparing the evening meal for Hastein and the captains of his other two ships, who would be joining him. Torvald immediately invited me to eat with him that evening.

"You may share my tent tonight, too," he said, gesturing grandly at a large cloak draped over crossed sticks to form a simple lean-to shelter, standing beside Hastein's tent. "We have a large tent pitched on the shore for the rest of the crew to sleep in, but since they do not know yet that Jarl Hastein has invited you to join us, you would not be welcome there. Cullain," he called, before the little Irishman could escape. "When you cook the evening meal for the jarl and his guests, be sure to cook enough for Halfdan and me, too."

Cullain, the top of whose head barely reached the middle of Torvald's chest, glared at him but said nothing.

"When will the crew be told about me?" I asked Torvald.

"I think it best that they not learn until we're ready to sail," he replied. "I have a plan."

While I arranged my helm, cloaks, quivers, and other gear inside my sea chest, Torvald disappeared. He returned bearing a section of oak plank roughly as long as a man's forearm, and as broad as the span of a hand. I wondered if it had been cut from one of the broken strakes removed from the *Gull*'s hull, for it was weathered, stained from being coated with pitch, and was pierced on one edge by a hole for a rivet. Two fresh holes had been bored in one end of the board, and a length of rope, knotted at one end, was draped through one of these holes.

"What is that for?" I asked him.

"You will see," he replied, smiling. "In time."

During the last hour of daylight, and later by the light of a small fire we built in front of his shelter, Torvald sat working on the board, digging a shallow hole in it with the point of his knife. When I asked him what he was doing, he answered only, "In time."

I watched with interest when Hastein returned, accompanied by the captains of his other two ships. Both men looked to be as much as ten years older than Hastein, if not more. Their tunics were well made, of fine, brightly colored linen—expensive, though not as fine as the silk Hastein wore—and fine swords hung at their belts. Torvald told me their names: Svein captained the *Sea Wolf* and Stig the *Serpent*. Both appeared to be what Harald would have called "men of consequence," yet they were content to follow Hastein, a much younger man. I longed to learn more about this jarl whom I, too, was now committed to follow.

We ate and drank well that night, dining on the same food and drink Cullain prepared for Hastein and his captains—a privilege, I gathered, granted to Torvald as the jarl's helmsman and personal guard. I found myself becoming quite fond of wine, despite my initial mistrust of its appearance. Torvald entertained me during our meal with more tales of his adventures with Hastein.

After we finished, Torvald returned to his project with the board. He continued picking at the center of the plank with the point of his knife—a large seax poorly suited for such work—until he'd dug out a round hole in the wood almost as deep as the thickness of my finger. Finally he pulled a silver coin out of his pouch, laid it over the hole, nodded with satisfaction, and hammered it with the pommel of his seax until he'd seated it firmly in the wood. Torvald looked quite pleased when he'd finished, and held it up for me to see.

"What do you think?" he asked.

"If it is supposed to be a silver coin hammered into a board, it is very fine indeed. Otherwise, I'm not sure."

Torvald laughed.

"What is it for?" I asked.

"In time," he answered.

The repairs on the *Gull* were completed by mid-morning of the following day. Hastein and Torvald summoned the crew, and with much straining they pushed the ship back down the log rollers into the water. Once she was afloat, an anchor was set to keep the ship lying parallel and close in to the shore.

All around me, members of the crew stripped their clothes off, stowed them in their sea chests, and began wading out through the waist-deep water to load their gear on board the ship. Provisions—barrels of salted pork, live chickens in cages, kegs of ale, sacks of barley, and barrels of fresh water—were brought to the shoreline and ferried out in the *Gull*'s small-boat.

Torvald bustled from one end of the ship to the other, supervising the crew as they loaded the provisions and their gear. As helmsman, it was his responsibility to see that the weight aboard ship was evenly distributed.

Hastein, who'd been watching the refloating of

his ship from the shore, walked over to where I was standing, watching the loading.

"Why haven't you loaded your gear on board yet?" he asked.

"Torvald told me not to," I replied. "He said to wait until he summoned me."

Hastein frowned at my answer. "Why?" he demanded.

"I do not know," I answered. I'd been wondering the same myself.

"We need to finish loading the ship and get underway. Get yourself and your gear aboard. And find a position near the stern," he added. "If we fight at sea I will likely be there, and I like my best archers near me, so I can direct their fire."

I'd brought my sea chest and the pigs of iron to my vantage place on the shore, so I could bring all aboard ship when Torvald signaled that it was time. I bent over, picked up two of the rough iron ingots, and laid them across my shoulder.

Hastein looked amused. "What are you doing?" he asked.

"I am taking these pigs of iron out to the ship," I answered. As you directed, I thought. I was surprised it was not obvious.

"Are you going to wear your clothes in the water?"

Actually, I had intended to. I was already nervous about the crew's initial reaction to me. It could not help if I was naked when they first met me. The contrast between my youthful body and their heavily muscled and scarred ones would only highlight my lack of age and experience. But I did not want Hastein to think me a fool.

Reluctantly I stripped, stowed my clothes in my sea chest, and began carrying the pigs of iron out to the ship. The water was extremely cold, and the rough metal ingots heavy and uncomfortable against my bare skin. It took two trips to carry all of them. Each time I arrived at the ship's side, Torvald reached over and took the heavy bars from me like they weighed nothing.

On my final trip, I carried my sea chest on one shoulder and held my shield and bow, which were too large to fit in the chest, high with my other hand. When I reached the ship's side, Torvald was away, up in the front of the vessel. I stood, my teeth chattering, wondering how I was going to get on board. Finally, a pair of hands reached out and took my bow and shield. I waited, but they did not come back for my chest.

"Some help," I called, and a man leaned over the side.

"Are you lost, little one?" he asked. He took my sea chest from my shoulder and set it on deck, then extended an arm and helped me climb aboard.

"Thank you," I told him, once I was on deck.

"It was nothing. I enjoy fishing," he replied, "and you're the biggest fish I've caught in a long time. Though still a little small for this ship."

The men around us laughed. Their faces were all bearded and weathered from lives spent outdoors, and even the youngest of them looked years older than I did.

As I stood there naked, cold, and shivering, I felt painfully aware that to these men I must have looked no more than a boy. The effect of the cold water had accentuated that appearance. I found my sea chest, dressed as quickly as I could, then turned to look for my bow and shield.

A man seated on a chest nearby was holding my bow across his lap. He had strung it. When he saw me looking at him, he spoke. "What's your name, boy?" he asked.

He was not tall. In fact, he was shorter than I was, but below his thick black beard his torso was massive, thicker twice over than mine, and his arms, bulging under the short-sleeved tunic he was wearing, were heavily muscled.

"Halfdan," I answered, and hoped there was nothing more he wished from me. He had a thick, heavy brow above his eyes, jutting out now in a scowl.

"I am Tore," he said. "I was looking at your bow."

When I said nothing, he continued. "It is well

made, and has a heavy draw. Few men choose to shoot a bow this strong. I am the only man among the crew of the *Gull* who does."

No longer, I thought.

"This is a very fine bow for a boy like you to possess," he continued. It had angered me that he'd presumed to string my bow. The tone of his voice and the sneer on his face were angering me even more.

"I agree," I said. "It is a very fine bow, for anyone to possess. But it is mine. And I am not a boy." I held out my hand for it, but he did not give it to me.

"How did a *boy* like you come to own such a fine bow, and what are you doing on this ship with it?"

"I made it," I answered through gritted teeth. "My bow and I are aboard this ship because I am an archer, and a member of this crew."

Tore's face turned red at this news. "I am the chief archer on this ship," he said. "I was not aware we were getting another archer in our crew."

Torvald's voice came from behind me. "And I was not aware, Tore, that Jarl Hastein was required to ask you before he added a new archer to the crew. I do not think he's aware of that, either, but he's up at the bow right now. Come, let us go ask him, if you'd like."

"The jarl chooses whom he pleases," Tore said

sullenly. "But we are all experienced warriors here. A boy like this does not belong in this crew."

Torvald tugged at his beard and looked puzzled.

"I confess, it seemed strange to me, also, that the jarl should invite him to join us. He *is* a blacksmith, though, and we have none. Perhaps that is why the jarl offered him a position. And I understand he does have some skill with his bow."

"Some skill!" Tore roared. The loudness of his voice caused men the length of the ship to turn and stare at him. "Many men have some skill, yet few have the right to serve on the *Gull*."

Torvald shrugged his shoulders. "Perhaps he has more than just some skill," he suggested.

I wondered what Torvald's plan was, and when I would see it. So far, things did not seem to be going well.

Hastein made his way to the rear of the ship. "Is there a problem back here?" he asked. "Torvald, you are supposed to be getting my ship under way."

"It is this boy, my jarl," Tore said. "It dishonors us all to have one so young and inexperienced serve with us. We are all chosen men who have proved our worth."

A number of the crew had gathered around us by this time, and they murmured their agreement with Tore. I saw no friendly expressions on the faces staring back at me.

"You speak the truth, Tore," Torvald said. "We have all proved our worth, but this boy has not. It is not only an insult to have him in our company. It could be dangerous, too. We do not know if he can be depended on in a fight."

"Aye, aye." The men around us murmured louder now, and their glares at me were even more hostile. I stared at Torvald, stunned by his words. Hastein also looked surprised—and displeased. The muscles in his jaw clenched, and his face began to turn red, the color creeping up his neck above his tunic like a rising tide.

"Perhaps, Tore," Torvald suggested, "we should test him now. We could set a mark, and you could shoot at it against him. A boy this young should not hope to serve with us unless he can beat our best. Only if he outshoots you can he stay. If you win, you can throw him back overboard."

Jarl Hastein and I both glared at Torvald, but he smiled broadly back at us. "I like this plan," he said. "I think it is a good one."

Tore seemed to like the plan, too.

"Do you want to leave on your own now, boy?" He sneered at me. "Or do you want to be thrown off the ship?"

Torvald had walked over to his sea chest and opened it.

"This would make a fine mark to shoot at," he said, and pulled out the board with the coin embedded in it.

Torvald walked the length of the ship to the bow and, using the rope attached to the board, tied his target to the front stem-post of the ship, below the gilded dragon head. Then he sauntered back to where we stood, whistling a tune as he walked. By now, everyone in the crew had taken an interest in what was unfolding.

"That coin is a small mark," Tore said. "Where do you propose we shoot from?"

"From the stern deck, of course," Torvald said. "You're a master archer. Too easy a shot would insult you. One arrow each. The closest to the coin wins the contest."

I held out my hand to Tore.

"What do you want, boy?" he snapped.

"I cannot shoot without my bow," I answered. He turned his head and spat.

"You think you have a chance of besting me?" he demanded. I said nothing, but met his gaze without flinching, and hoped I looked more confident than I felt. Finally Tore slapped my bow into my outstretched hand, then reached behind him and lifted his own from where it lay, wrapped in a deerskin case, behind his sea chest. He stripped the case off the bow, stood, and strung it.

I opened my sea chest and carefully selected an arrow from one of the quivers inside. I checked and smoothed the feather fletching, then sighted along it, to be sure it had not taken a bend since the last time I'd shot it.

Tore, apparently not one to brood or ponder before taking action, stepped up onto the small, raised deck beside the steering oar at the stern of the ship, and laid an arrow across his bow.

"I will shoot first," he announced.

"Tore," Torvald said, "I will bet you three silver pennies to one that this boy outshoots you."

Tore lowered his bow and glared at him. "Damn you, Torvald," he said. "Do you think to throw me off that easily? That is a wager I'll take and win."

Up and down the ship, other men began to call out. "Will you give me that wager also, Torvald?"

"Three pennies to one for me on Tore, Torvald."

"I'll take your silver, too."

A look of concern flitted across Torvald's face, as though he was regretting the words he'd spoken. Then he shrugged his shoulders and said, "Very well. Who wants the wager?"

In all, thirteen men came forward—fourteen, counting Tore. Torvald stood to win fourteen silver pennies if I outshot Tore. But if I lost, it would cost him forty-two. I wondered if Torvald was still pleased with his plan.

Tore raised his bow again and pulled it back to full draw. Men scurried away from the center of the deck and the arrow's path. The ship was rocking gently from the waves lapping against her hull. I watched Tore's knees flex with the motion, compensating, while his upper body remained still as stone. He held his arrow at full draw for a long time, aiming the shot.

When Tore finally released, all heads turned, following the arrow's flight. It streaked the length of the deck and thudded solidly into the oak board, two finger-widths below and only slightly to the left of the coin. Had it not been low, his arrow would have nicked the coin's edge.

I was impressed. Tore, judging from the broad grin on his face, was also. He stepped down from the stern deck and swaggered past Torvald. As he did, he reached out a hand and jiggled the pouch at Torvald's belt. "This will soon be lighter," he said with a smirk.

I stepped up onto the stern deck and turned to study the shot I had to make. My arrow would have to pass beside the mast and over the oar rack. I stared at the target in the bow, trying to gauge how to compensate for the rocking of the ship. I was used to solid ground underfoot. I cursed

Torvald under my breath. He obviously was no archer, and had no idea how difficult a shot he'd set as a test.

Hastein was seated on the top strake of the side, a short distance away, watching me. The anger was gone from his face now, replaced by an expression of curiosity. Perhaps he viewed this as another chance to weigh whether it was fate, woven by the Norns, that I should join his crew. But it was not the Norns who would have to shoot my bow. This shot was mine alone to make or miss.

Torvald looked back and forth from Tore's arrow, embedded in the target, to me, with a worried expression. Tore was gloating at the helmsman's obvious concern. The sight of it did nothing to boost my confidence.

Torvald walked back until he stood directly in front of me, took a deep breath, then let it out in a long, loud sigh, as if already lamenting the pending loss of so much silver. Then, while his back was turned to the rest of the crew, he winked.

"Fourteen silver pennies," he whispered. "It was a lucky day when I met you."

"I am glad you are so pleased with your plan," I muttered at him, pretending to be examining the limbs of my bow. "I am not. If Tore bests me, I will be cast overboard. But if I prevail, you will win much silver from my labors, while all I will gain is the ill will of my shipmates who will lose their wagers to you."

"Do not worry yourself about that," Torvald assured me. "This is a good-natured crew, for the most part. They'll think it a fine jest."

A fine jest? And what if Torvald had miscalculated, and I could not best Tore's shot? I was seething. It would not help me concentrate on my shot.

From down the deck, Tore jeered. "Do you plan to shoot, or will you just jump overboard and save me the trouble of throwing you?"

"Oh, yes, I can tell this crew is good-natured," I whispered. "Perhaps Tore is right. Perhaps it would be better for me to concede, and not even shoot at all. Thanks to your plan, no matter what the outcome of this contest, now I can only lose."

An alarmed look crossed Torvald's face. He stepped closer to me. "You cannot do this," he said. "I will lose forty-two silver pieces. And I will be a laughingstock. Tore will never let me forget this."

Torvald's look of concern raised my spirits considerably. At least now I was not the only one worried about the outcome of his ill-conceived plan.

"What are you doing, Torvald?" Tore barked. "Move aside and let him shoot."

"Half," I muttered. Torvald frowned, looking confused. I explained. "Half of the silver you win

73

will be mine. My skill is worth that much."

A scowl flashed across Torvald's face, then vanished just as quickly, like smoke in the wind. He laughed loudly, then whispered to me, "Done, Halfdan. Very well done, in fact. You have learned to bargain well."

Torvald stepped aside. I raised my eyes and let them find the silver coin, glinting in the sun at the far end of the ship. I let my anger and my fear wash away. The sounds of the waves lapping against the hull, and the catcalls of Tore and the crew faded, as the image of the coin grew in my mind until it filled it. In one swift movement, I raised my bow, drew, and released.

The arrow's flight seemed endless, as though the Gods had slowed time itself. It skimmed over the top of the oar rack, and whispered past the mast. Then, as it neared the ship's bow, time returned. The arrow slammed into the center of the silver coin with such force the oak board split from the impact. The two halves of the shattered board parted and the arrow, its iron head jutting through the pierced coin, dropped onto the deck with a clatter.

For a moment, there was only silence. Then every member of the crew, even those who had lost wagers, roared in amazement.

When the noise died down, Jarl Hastein

stepped forward and placed his hand on my shoulder.

"This is Halfdan," he announced in a loud voice. "I have invited him to join our crew. As you have noticed, he is a trifle young compared to the rest of you. He is a blacksmith, though, and we will need one on this voyage. And I believe he may possess some other skills that could prove useful."

The crew laughed. Hastein continued speaking.

"Do you accept Halfdan, then, into our felag?"

The men grunted and nodded their heads. They still did not look happy at the prospect, but at least their expressions were no longer hostile.

"Tore," Hastein said, turning to face the scowling loser. "Halfdan is an archer. You are the leader of my archers. He will fight under your command. Do you accept him now?"

Tore's expression looked like he had just taken a large mouthful of something that tasted very bad, but he, too, nodded. He had agreed to the test, and now was bound by it.

"Aye," he said.

"Then let us get the *Gull* underway," Hastein cried. "We have wasted enough time on Torvald's games. The king has summoned me to council."

THE KING'S COUNCIL

On leaving Hedeby, we sailed for the island of Sjaelland, where King Horik had a large estate. According to Torvald, the king usually chose to winter there. The journey marked my first time at sea in a long-ship.

My shooting exhibition, arranged by Torvald, had provided me a foothold of acceptance in the *Gull*'s crew, but nothing more. It did not take me long to realize that to these men, who'd sailed and fought together many times, I was still an outsider. In battle or other danger, they knew they could depend on one another. They did not know whether they could trust me with their lives.

Tore, whom I'd bested with my bow, seemed

determined to find out as much as he could about me, as quickly as possible. Even before we got under way, he began.

"Put your sea chest here," he gruffly ordered me, pointing to the oar hole second from the rear on the steer-board side. "I row at the last oar on this side. If you are going to fight under my command, I want to keep an eye on you."

I wondered if he hoped to catch me making mistakes, thinking he might still see me ejected from the *Gull*'s crew. If so, my initial performance must have encouraged him. When we were ordered to take our oars down from the racks where they were stowed and prepare to cast off, I selected the wrong oar—one of the shorter ones, because I thought it would be easier to handle. Tore corrected me.

"Not that one," he said, taking the oar from my hands and returning it to the rack. "At the bow and stern, where the hull is narrower, we use the longer oars, so our reach will match the rowers in the center. These shorter oars are for the men who row at the midships positions. Have you never served on a longship before?"

Red-faced, I shook my head. "No," I said. He rolled his eyes.

A short time later, when we slid our oars out through the holes in the ship's sides and began pulling in time to Torvald's chant, I demonstrated my inexperience again. Rowing with such a long and heavy oar was not a simple matter. A low swell caught the blade of my oar after I'd raised it up out of the water and was pushing it forward for the next stroke. The resistance when I wasn't expecting any almost knocked the oar from my hands, and broke my rhythm. It took two full strokes before I was pulling smoothly again in time with the rest of the crew.

Tore, who was seated immediately in front of me, had been rowing with his head turned to the side, watching my oar as he pulled on his own. He shook his head, and I felt my face flush again.

I studied Tore as he rowed. He made it look easy. He rocked back and forth on his sea chest, his legs braced in front of him and his broad back and shoulders pushing and pulling the big oar in long, smooth movements. I began timing my own strokes to the movements of his back, and by the time we reached the mouth of the fjord, was beginning to feel more comfortable with the rhythm. Still, I was grateful when Torvald barked out the order to ship oars and raise the sail.

Beyond the mouth of the Schliefjord, the wind was blowing steadily, and in a favorable direction. The *Gull*'s big red-and-white striped sail filled and the ship surged forward across the swells. I could feel her hull flexing and shifting under my feet like a living creature.

The wind held steady all that day. I found myself with time on my hands, and little with which to fill it. I was used to having work to do. A slave seldom has time for leisure, and even after I'd been freed, my days had been occupied with Harald's lessons. I found myself brooding. No matter where I tried to send my thoughts, they kept returning to Harald's death, and my mother's. Their faces haunted my mind and pulled at my heart.

I needed work for my hands. Perhaps a task that kept them busy would occupy my mind, too. Opening my sea chest, I pulled out the metal-studded leather jerkin I'd stowed inside. There was a small hole in the front, over the belly. I would use this time to stitch it closed.

Tore and several of the crew lounging nearby were discussing the best way to breach a wooden stockade. Tore argued it was best to pile brush against its timbers and try to burn an opening through. Odd, another archer, who rowed at the oar across from me, scoffed at this idea.

"And if the fire spreads?" he asked. "You'll burn everything of value inside. Climbing the wall is best—at night, while most inside are asleep."

Listening to them, I felt a pang of loneliness. I

wished I could join in their banter. It was a foolish desire. It was safer to be ignored, as I learned when Tore suddenly turned to me and asked, "And you, Halfdan? Tell us, how would you breach a stockade?"

How could I answer such a question? My brother, Harald, had taught me as much of the ways of a warrior as he could before he'd died. But I had never been to war, or gone raiding.

"I have never assaulted a stockade," I admitted.

Tore feigned a look of surprise, and glanced at Odd and the others to see their reaction. They were staring at me curiously now. I felt certain they were wondering again why Hastein had invited me to join their crew.

"You have never assaulted a stockade?" Tore continued. "I suppose that is not so strange after all, in one as young as you. Surely you have been in battle, though. Or are you too young for that, also?"

"Yes," I answered. "I have fought in battle. I have killed men and I have seen comrades killed."

Tore and the others stared at me expectantly, as if waiting for me to continue, but I did not. My past was not their business. I tried to change the subject.

"Do you have a needle?" I asked. "I need to repair a cut in my jerkin."

"Let me see it," Tore said and held out his

hand. Reluctantly, I passed the jerkin to him. He examined it closely, paying special attention to the two dark stains, one below the neck opening and the other on the belly around the cut I wanted to stitch.

"This looks like blood," he said.

"It is," I admitted.

"Yours?"

I shook my head.

Tore stuck his finger through the hole in the leather, and wiggled it.

"This is small," he said. "About the size an arrowhead would make."

It was true, but I said nothing. Tore would not let it be. "Did you shoot the arrow?" he asked.

I did not want this conversation. But Tore had asked me a direct question. It would be rude to ignore him, and I did not wish to give insult.

"Aye," I responded.

Again Tore and the others stared at me silently, as if expecting me to continue and tell them more. Again I did not.

"So you took your jerkin from a dead man?" Tore asked. "A man you killed?"

I remembered stripping it from the body on the hilltop, the body of one of the men who'd hunted me. I nodded slowly.

"I did," I said.

"I myself took my mail brynie from a Frank I killed," Tore said, raising his eyebrows and pursing his lips. It was the first time he'd shown any approval of anything about me. "How did it come to pass?" he asked. "How did you come to kill the man who wore this jerkin?"

I'd had enough. I reached out my hand for my jerkin. "It was a private matter," I told Tore. "Between the dead man and me. Between other dead men and me. I do not wish to share this tale with you."

I rolled the jerkin back up, replaced it in my sea chest, then turned and started to walk away, propelled by my need to escape Tore's questions. Behind me, I heard an indignant snort.

I should not have turned my back on Tore and the others. It was offensive, as though they were not worth my attention. They will never accept you, I told myself, if you insult them. I stopped, loosened the string tying the waist of my trews, and stepped to the ship's side. I did not really need to empty my bladder, but it gave me a reason to have walked away. I glanced back at the stern. Tore was watching me.

"He is a shy one, our new shipmate," he said. I did not think he was referring to my walking away to relieve myself.

* * *

King Horik's estate on the island of Sjaelland overlooked a bay edged with a sandy beach. In the
afternoon of the third day after leaving Hedeby, we
lowered the *Gull*'s sail at the mouth of the bay and
prepared to row in across the last stretch of water.
Hastein's other two ships, the *Sea Wolf* and the
Serpent, hove to on either side of us and also
unshipped their oars. When all three crews were
positioned and ready, Torvald roared out his
rowing cadence, and the oars of all three ships rose
and fell in time, beating the water and propelling
us toward the shore.

"Pull, pull, pull, pull . . ." Torvald shouted. His
chant was echoed by the grunting breaths of the
rowers, as we heaved on our oars.

The three longships sped side by side toward
the shore, their oars all moving in perfect cadence,
the three crews working together as one. Even I
managed to keep the rhythm.

Torvald stood on the small, raised deck in the
stern, steering the ship and gauging our approach
to land. Suddenly he lifted his fist high above his
head.

"Raise!" he shouted. We kept pulling on our
oars, maintaining the rhythm he'd established with
his chant, but now all eyes were on Torvald. His
fist dropped and his voice boomed out again.

"Oars!"

The *Gull*'s thirty oars rose out of the sea in unison. To either side of us, the crews of the *Sea Wolf* and the *Serpent* also raised their oars, and held them extended straight out from the sides of the ships as we coasted the final stretch to land.

Torvald released the handle of the tiller, reached behind him, and heaved with both hands on the line attached to the trailing edge of the steering oar, pivoting it up and clear of the bottom.

I could feel the *Gull*'s keel beginning to grate on the sandy bottom, and moments later we ground to a stop, our bow jutting up onto the beach.

Torvald pumped his fist once over his head. Around me, the men of the three ships' crews roared out a single cry.

"Hastein!"

The jarl had arrived for the king's council.

While Hastein and his captains, Svein and Stig, left to call on the king, the rest of us set up our camp for the night. Dark clouds hovered low on the horizon, threatening rain, and the afternoon wind blowing in off the water carried a chill, so we lowered the mast and, using the yard as a center pole, stretched the sail over the deck to form a simple tent to shelter us during the night.

Other longships, eight in all, were also moored along the shore, their prows pulled up onto the sand and their sails tented. Torvald pointed to the one closest to our three ships. She had sixteen pairs of oars, one more than the *Gull*, and her hull was painted black.

"There lies the *Raven*," he said. "She is the ship of Ragnar Logbrod."

I knew I had heard the name in tales told round the hearth on long winter evenings in my father's longhouse. Now, though, I could remember nothing of what I had heard, save the strange nickname: Hairy-Breeches.

"Who is he?" I asked.

"He is a war-king," Torvald answered. "Perhaps the greatest who has ever lived, a true wolf-feeder. He does not rule over districts in the name of the king, like Jarl Hastein, though he is related by blood to the king's line. Ragnar owns but a modest estate up on the Vik above Jutland. Yet at war or raiding, if Ragnar is present, men will choose him to lead."

A steep hill overlooked the bay. I could see, silhouetted against the sky on its crest, the great longhouse of the king surrounded by smaller buildings. A procession was winding its way down from the summit toward the shore.

Thralls from the king's household drove ox-carts, some laden with firewood and others with barrels of ale, down to the beach and unloaded them in front of the ships. Following behind the carts, other thralls drove a small herd of cattle. Two of the cattle were allotted to our three ships. The king was providing a feast—albeit a simple one of only beef and ale—for the crews of the chieftains he'd called to council.

We slaughtered the cattle on the beach and built fires, then spent the rest of the afternoon watching the carcasses roast on great spits above the flames. Hastein's slave Cullain supervised the cooking, periodically testing the carcasses with a sharpened stick or directing crewmen standing near the fire to turn the spits. No one seemed to mind taking orders from the little thrall, for we were all hungry and looked to him to remedy that for us.

While we waited, one of the kegs of ale was tapped, and every man fetched a cup from his sea chest and gathered round. I had no cup—it was a piece of gear I would need to add to my kit—but Torvald had a spare, and loaned it to me. While we waited for the beef to cook, we drank.

Not long after darkness had fallen, Cullain declared the meal ready.

I sliced a chunk of beef as big as my fist from one of the carcasses and impaled it on the point of my dagger, since I had no plate nor even slab of bread to set it on. Torvald, who was standing beside me, did not concern himself with such niceties. After attacking the carcass with his seax and carving off a piece almost the size of a small cat, he sheathed the big knife and carried the slab of meat in his fist, occasionally ripping pieces from it with his teeth as we made our way back to where we'd left our cloaks spread on the ground, our cups beside them.

I swallowed the first few bites without even chewing them, but once the fiercest pangs of hunger were quelled, I leaned back on one elbow and chewed each bite slowly, with my eyes closed, savoring the flavors of the meat. Being able to eat my fill of beef still felt strange to me. I could not forget my years as a thrall, when I could only watch others gorge themselves on the rare occasions when a cow or bull was slaughtered, while I hoped at best for scraps.

Torvald, sitting cross-legged beside me, was obviously enjoying the meal, too. He grunted whenever he ripped a new bite from the great slab he clutched, chewed with loud smacking of his lips, and sighed in pleasure each time he washed down a mouthful with a long swallow of ale. His beard was stained with grease from the meat, as was his sleeve, which he periodically wiped across his chin to keep the meat juices from running down his neck.

Tore and Odd, who had earlier spread their

cloaks on the ground near us, approached carrying pieces of beef and freshly filled cups of ale. I'd learned during our journey from Hedeby that Tore and Odd were close comrades, who could usually be found in each other's company. In appearance, they were a strangely matched pair. Tore, the younger of the two, was short and bowlegged, with a chest as round and large as a barrel, and massive, heavily muscled arms. His looks made me wonder if there was a dwarf somewhere in his lineage. Odd, the oldest member of the *Gull*'s crew, was tall and gangly. Where Tore had thick black hair, Odd's was thin and stringy, light brown streaked with gray, and so sparse on top he usually wore a fur-rimmed cap to cover his head. Tore had a black beard so long and dense it hid what little neck he had—his head was very closely attached to his shoulders. Odd wore a long, drooping mustache, but every few days he painstakingly scraped his chin clean of beard with a small knife.

To my relief, Tore had not pestered me with questions during the afternoon while we'd tarried on the shore, waiting for our dinner to cook. Perhaps the abundant supply of ale had temporarily mellowed his mood.

"Did you see, Torvald?" Odd asked, as he settled himself on his cloak. "One of the other ships here is the *Raven*. Ragnar's ship."

Torvald nodded. Tore did, too.

"Aye," Tore said. "If Ragnar is here, for certain it is war the council is discussing. It takes the scent of blood to lure Ragnar to a council."

"Hastein confides in you, Torvald," Odd said. "Does the king want to lead the Danes to war against the Franks? Was that why Hastein took us scouting down the coast of Frankia?"

Torvald did not answer right away. He tilted his head back, as though examining the stars that glittered above us through scattered rents in the cloud cover, then jutted his chin out while stretching his neck. Only after his efforts were rewarded with a loud belch did he respond to Odd's question.

"Sometimes Jarl Hastein confides in me, and sometimes he chooses to keep his own counsel. He is my jarl, though, and I trust him and have pledged to follow him. As have you, Odd, and all the rest of his housecarls. He will tell us what we need to know, when we need to know it."

"Men say Ragnar killed a dragon once," Tore said, changing the subject. "A great serpent that spit fire and boiling poison from its mouth."

Now I remembered what I had heard long ago about Ragnar. It was a tale old Ubbe, the foreman on my father's estate, would tell sometimes, when my father and his men would gather round the warmth of the main hearth, drinking and sharing stories to pass the long winter nights.

"Aye," Odd said. "I have heard the dragon's breath charred Ragnar's shield when he closed in to attack."

"Yes," Tore added. "And Ragnar wore special breeches he'd made of bearskin with the fur still on, that he'd boiled in pitch then rolled in sand to protect his legs from the fire and poison. That is why he is called Logbrod."

Torvald snorted and rolled his eyes. He glanced at me, as if expecting me to agree with his opinion. I was surprised. What Tore had said matched the tale I'd heard.

"You scoff?" Tore asked. "It was a clever plan, and a bold deed, worthy of a great hero. I do not believe *you* could defeat a dragon."

"It would be hard to do," Torvald agreed. "First I would have to find one. I have never seen a dragon, though I have traveled much of the world. I do not believe they exist."

"Dragons are rare creatures," Odd suggested. "Few men have had the fortune—or misfortune—to see one. That does not mean they do not exist. There are too many tales. There must be some truth behind them."

"You have never seen the Gods, either, have you?" Tore challenged. "Does that mean they do not exist?"

"I have felt the power of the Gods," Torvald

answered. "I do not need to see them. And besides, I know the truth of how Ragnar got his name. There was no dragon, though there were breeches made of bearskin."

Now it was Tore's turn to look dubious.

"So you, Torvald Starki, know the 'true' tale of Ragnar Logbrod, and how he got his name? Did the great man himself confide this tale to you?"

"No," Torvald said. "I heard his son, Bjorn Ironsides, tell the tale to Hastein. According to Bjorn, it is also how he won his own name, and how his brother Ivar came to be called the Boneless."

Odd grinned. "I have long wondered how Ivar won that name. Tell us the tale."

Torvald shook his head. "I cannot tell it," he said.

"Why not?" Tore demanded. I wondered if Torvald had been sworn to secrecy.

Torvald looked at his cup and sighed. "Because the tale is long, my throat is dry, and my cup is empty. I could never finish the telling. My voice would surely give out . . . unless you fetch me more to drink."

Odd started to rise. "I'll refill your cup for you," he offered.

Tore pushed him back down, scowling. "You will not," he said. "It is beneath your dignity to wait on Torvald. You are his equal. I am his equal.

Yet he always tries to get me, or you, or some other member of our crew to do his work for him. We will not play his game. We are not his servants. He can fetch his own ale."

"But I want to hear his tale," Odd complained.

Torvald lay back on his cloak, with one arm behind his head to pillow it, and began rooting in his mouth with the forefinger of his other hand, searching among his teeth for trapped shreds of beef. He seemed content, in the face of Tore's outburst, to endure his thirst.

I too wanted to hear Torvald's tale about Ragnar. It would not offend my dignity to wait on Torvald in exchange for his story. I had been a thrall, and was used to serving others. I drained the dregs in my cup and stood up.

"My cup is empty," I said. "I am going to refill it. Can I fill your cup while I am up, Torvald?"

When I returned, Torvald began his tale.

"Ragnar has fathered many sons, by two wives and several concubines. Four of those sons still live and are famed warriors in their own right: Ubbe the Frisian, born of Ragnar's first wife, Thora; Ivar the Boneless and Bjorn Ironsides, born of his second wife, Kraka; and Sigurd Snake-Eye, born of a woman Ragnar captured in a raid on the Wends.

"When his sons were young, Ivar was always a favorite because of his quick mind. Like his father, he was born to lead men in battle. It is said that by the time Ivar was only eight years of age, there was no one in Ragnar's household, save Ragnar himself, who could best the boy at the game of hnefatafl, and as a grown man, he, like Ragnar, can plot the moves of ships and companies of warriors more easily than most men move game pieces on a board.

"In the winter when Ivar was ten years of age, he and Bjorn, who was but eight at the time, accompanied Ragnar into the forest to check a deadfall trap he had set, hoping to catch a wolf that had been hunting dangerously close to their homestead.

"When they reached the trap, they found it had done its work well. The great wolf lay dead inside, its back broken by the falling log.

"While Ragnar skinned the carcass, the two boys roamed through the surrounding forest. On the side of a low, rocky hill, they found a hole leading into the ground. Bjorn told Hastein that he and Ivar thought it might be a troll's lair. Emboldened by the knowledge that their father was near, they decided to explore the cave, hoping to find the troll's treasure. Since he was the oldest, Ivar crept into the cave, while Bjorn waited outside, guarding against the troll's return."

Torvald paused and looked at his cup. "It is

empty again," he said, and looked at Tore, smiling expectantly.

"Mine is still full," I said, and passed it to him before Tore could renew their argument.

"Was it a troll's cave?" Odd asked. I was wondering, too.

"No," Torvald replied. "It was the cave a great she-bear had chosen for her winter's rest, while a cub grew in her womb.

"The bear was asleep, partially covered by a drift of leaves at the back of the cave. In the dim light, Ivar could see only a great mound. Not realizing what it was, he foolishly tried to find out by prodding it with his spear.

"No doubt you have heard that it is unwise to awaken a sleeping bear. Ivar quickly learned the truth of that saying. Enraged by Ivar's rude behavior, the she-bear awoke with a roar. Ivar fled out of the cave with her close on his heels. When he reached open ground, the deep snow slowed him and the bear brought him down with a swipe of her paw.

"Ragnar ran toward the sound of the growls and young Ivar's screams. Just as he reached them and saw the she-bear standing over Ivar, mauling him with her massive paws, Bjorn ran up to the beast and thrust his small spear into her side, trying to draw her away from his brother. The great bear turned and swatted Bjorn aside with one blow, sending him flying through the air.

"Bjorn told Hastein that the blow temporarily knocked the life from him. By the time he returned to the world of the living, his father was kneeling over him. Beyond, the bear lay dead in the snow beside the bloody, broken body of Ivar.

"Ragnar carried both boys back to the safety of their longhouse. Although Bjorn was badly bruised and in great pain, the bear's attack had broken no bones. Ragnar said his ribs must be made of iron to have withstood such a blow, and the name stuck— he has been known as Bjorn Ironsides ever since.

"Ivar, however, was badly injured. His scalp, face, and back were torn by the bear's claws, and the force of her blows had shattered both of his arms, a leg, and many other bones besides. He soon caught a fever, and was not expected to live. But the boy's will was strong, and he refused to give up his life.

"The fever burned Ivar's body for ten days. When it finally broke, the household rejoiced, believing the worst had passed. However, try though they might, Ragnar and Kraka could not wake Ivar. Bjorn said it was as though his brother's body still lived, but his spirit had gone.

"A witch-woman lived in the forest, a day's ride from Ragnar's estate. She was believed by the folk of the district to be a shape-shifter, and was widely feared. But when the fourth day dawned after the breaking of Ivar's fever and he still had not awakened, Ragnar sent for her."

A shape-shifter! I marveled that Ragnar would dare to deal with such a one, even to save his son.

Torvald continued. "Bjorn said that Ivar's flesh had no more color to it than ice, and his body had grown so thin, the outlines of every bone, including those that had been broken, could be seen through the skin. The witch stood over him, chanting in a strange tongue, and carved a spell in runes on Ivar's chest with a knife made of bone. She licked the blood that flowed from the cuts, and put her mouth over Ivar's to breathe his breath. Then she told Ragnar what she had learned.

"The witch said the she-bear had been a shaman among its kind, and it was angered over the death of its unborn cub. Its ghost had stolen Ivar's spirit, and was claiming his life in payment. She told Ragnar the only hope for Ivar was to persuade the spirit of the bear to accept another life in exchange for his son's.

"From among the animal skins covering his bed, Ragnar took the pelt of a bear, and fashioned from it rough trousers, a cloak with slits cut for his arms, and a hood to cover his face. Wearing these shaggy clothes, he went into the forest, accompanied only by the witch-woman and a slave, a boy close in age to Ivar.

"Later that night, when Ragnar and the witch returned, they bore with them the bloody skull of the she-bear, a token of the covenant Ragnar had made. The rough fur breeches he wore were stained red with blood. The slave boy was never seen again."

What, I wondered, had Ragnar done? What sort of evil pact had he entered into? Had he, too, become a shape-shifter, part man and part beast?

"Ivar awoke the very next morning. It took many months, though, for his shattered bones to grow whole again. It was long before he could even feed himself. Summer came before he regained enough strength to leave his bed and walk. The two servant girls who cared for Ivar during that time called him the boneless boy. Now he is a man and fully recovered, but for a slight limp, but he is still known as Ivar the Boneless— though few today know the true reason why."

"If this story is true, why is the story about Ragnar and the dragon told?" Odd asked.

"It is the way of skalds," Torvald replied. "They gain their fame and win rewards from kings and other great men by composing fine tales about bold deeds. Slaying a dragon that breathes fire and spits poison is the kind of story men like to hear.

Entering into a dark pact with a shape-changing witch does not make so fine a tale."

I was disturbed by Torvald's story. What sort of man was Ragnar? And what of the poor slave boy who had died? What of his family? It was not something that would concern men like Torvald, Tore, or Odd. But I had been a slave. And I had seen my own mother die as a sacrifice, offered because she was merely a slave. I did not think Ragnar was a leader I would wish to follow.

My thoughts were interrupted by the sight of Hastein striding into the ring of light around the fire, followed by Svein and Stig. The jarl turned his head this way and that, searching the faces of the men sitting in the firelight and the shadows beyond. Stig touched his arm and pointed in our direction.

Hastein walked over to us and spoke to Torvald.

"We leave tomorrow morning at first light. Be sure the crew and ship are ready."

Torvald, whose mouth was full once more with a large portion of beef, merely nodded his head and raised his cup in acknowledgment. Hastein stared at him for a moment, then shook his head.

"I am glad to see you did not go hungry this night, while I was in council atop the hill in the king's longhouse," he said. "In his feast-hall, we dined well also, though when in the presence of the king, it's considered unseemly to wear your food upon your face and clothing."

Hastein turned and walked to where the *Gull*'s prow rested on the sand at the water's edge. He climbed the gangplank to the bow, then stepped up onto the edge of the top strake and balanced there, one hand on the neck of the gilded dragon's head.

"Warriors!" he cried in a loud voice. "My brothers of the sword. I have just returned from the king's longhouse. I have come to tell you what was decided in the council of the King of the Danes." The men seated around the fires ceased talking and turned their attention to Hastein.

"As is known to you all, the lands to the south of our kingdom are ruled by the Franks. Their holdings are vast and rich, yet these men are greedy, and are constantly seeking more.

"Once, the lands that border the south of Jutland were the home of Saxon tribes, a folk who worshiped the same Gods as we. But in the time of our fathers' fathers, the Frankish King Charles, he whom the Franks call 'the Great,' developed a lust for the lands of the Saxons. For many years he warred against them. The Saxons resisted bravely, but the might of the Franks was too great. The Frankish king burned the Saxons' villages and slaughtered their people by the thousands. After the final battle, when the strength of the Saxons was finally broken, ten thousand of their folk were sold into slavery, and the slave markets from Hedeby to the Araby kingdoms were glutted with their women and children. Those few not killed or sold were driven from their lands and scattered in the wild regions far to the east. It is important that those deeds not be forgotten, for they show the nature of our enemy.

"Then the Frankish King Charles turned his eyes upon our lands. But we Danes are free men, and will always remain so. Godfred, who ruled in those days as king, was not cowed by the might of the Franks. At his call, the people responded and built up the Danevirke. When King Charles marched north against us with a great army, King Godfred sailed south in a mighty fleet and fell upon Frisia, carrying death and destruction behind the flank of the Frankish force."

At Hastein's words, I remembered hearing tales of King Godfred and how he had summoned the Danish folk to fight off the invading Franks and build the Danevirke, the great earthen wall running across the base of the Jutland peninsula. Godfred had been a real hero. No false stories needed to be made up about him. The truth of his deeds made fine tales.

"King Charles of the Franks and King Godfred signed a treaty, bringing peace between our peoples,"

Hastein continued. "But the Franks did not long honor the agreement. During the reign of Louis, the son of Charles, the Franks again attacked across the Danevirke. Again, though, they found the courage and might of the Danes too great, and they were driven from our lands.

"For many years since that time, peace existed between the Danes and the Franks. But as wolves can smell blood from a great distance, so we Danes can sense weakness in a foe. King Louis was not the man his father was. Now Louis is dead, and his three sons are weaker still, and fight among themselves. The Frankish Empire has broken into three kingdoms, each at war with the others.

"While the Franks are divided, they are weak. Already, in recent years, we Danes have tested their defenses and have fattened our purses at their expense. We have sacked their towns of Dorestad, and Ruda, and Quentovic, and Nantes. We have tasted the wealth of the Franks, and have found it ripe for the taking.

"This spring," Hastein continued, "we will strike the Franks with more than just raids. We shall carry the fire and steel of war deep into their heartland. The Franks shall long remember this as the Year of the Danes."

My head was spinning, as much from excitement as from the ale I'd drunk. I could not believe my good fortune. We were going to war. What an adventure it would be!

"King Horik himself will lead one attack against the Franks and their fortress of Hamburg," Hastein continued. "A second fleet will attack the western kingdom of the Franks. Ragnar Logbrod will lead this second army, and we shall sail with him. We will attack Ruda near the mouth of the Seine River, then sail on up the river, sacking every town, village, and monastery we encounter, until we force the Frankish king to call out his army against us. When he does, we will crush them."

Hastein drew his sword and brandished it over his head.

"Wealth, honor, and glory await us!" he cried.

All around me, men burst into cheers. Some drew their swords and waved them overhead. I raised my cup and joined in the cheering, too. I was a warrior now. I was a member of Jarl Hastein's crew. I would follow him to fight our enemy and keep our homeland safe. The dreams of my childhood had come true. I was a Viking.

6

GHOSTS AND
OTHER SPIRITS

The next morning, we sailed from Sjaelland, as did the other ships that had been beached along the shore below the king's longhouse. Once beyond the mouth of the bay, they scattered. Even our sister ships, the *Sea Wolf* and the *Serpent*, set courses that caused them to slowly veer away from us.

"Where are they all going?" I asked Torvald. We had a fine, brisk wind blowing steadily from the east, so once we'd raised and set the sail my time was my own. I chose to spend it in the stern, where I could talk to Torvald as he steered. Hastein, who was standing nearby, heard my question.

"Armies do not raise themselves," he said. "The king gave war arrows to every ship's captain who attended the council. We each have chieftains to deliver King Horik's summons to. The king is claiming his scot. He is calling on the Danes to bring their men and ships to war."

Because he ruled over the lands surrounding the Limfjord in the north of Jutland, it was Hastein's lot to carry the king's summons to the chieftains who lived there. We pressed hard after leaving Sjaelland, and covered the first leg of our voyage, to the mouth of the Limfjord, in just over two days. Once upon the fjord, however, our pace slowed greatly. We stopped at every village and every chieftain's longhouse we passed, and Hastein went ashore carrying the symbol of war, a single arrow painted red from feathers to tip.

A king's summons, it seemed, could not be delivered quickly. There were formalities to be observed. At each stop, we would lower the *Gull*'s sail and, after hanging a shield below the dragon's head on the prow as a sign we came in peace, row in to the shore. Hastein, dressed in polished helm and mail brynie, and accompanied by Torvald, Tore, and a handful of other warriors from the crew, all wearing full armor, save for their shields, would march down the gangplank, to be met ashore by the local dignitary we were calling on. Speeches would be exchanged. I, who like most of the *Gull*'s crew was left on board the ship, could not hear them. They were usually long, though. It must have been thirsty work, for invariably at their end the chieftain or village headman would call for ale. Several times they even insisted on holding a feast. Such hospitality, once offered, could not graciously be declined. It made for a slow journey.

It was an uncomfortable time for me. I had passed this way only weeks earlier with my brother, Harald, and a handful of his men. That journey had led to Harald's death. Each day I saw landmarks along the shore that I recognized. Invariably they stirred up painful memories. Someday, perhaps, I would welcome seeing Harald's face again with my mind's eye, and would remember our good times together with pleasure. Not now, though. My loss was too recent, and the pain still too fresh.

One afternoon, the wind died and we had to row the ship. I was glad for the diversion. I let my mind wrap itself around the simple task of moving the big oar back and forth, and lost my thoughts in feeling the muscles of my back and shoulders straining to pull it through the weight of the sea.

I realized suddenly that Hastein, who had relieved Torvald at the steering oar, was staring at me. When my eyes met his, he turned and looked toward the shore. I turned my head, and looked where Hastein was gazing.

The jarl had steered the *Gull* close to the

southern shore of the fjord. We were passing a small cove. A massive slab of stone, jutting from the water like a great gate post, formed one side of the entrance to the sheltered inlet. Beyond, the shore was lined with a sandy beach, bisected by a narrow stream that emptied into the cove. I knew this place. A small longhouse had once overlooked the water here. A long, low earthen mound, still too fresh for any growth to have taken root, now marked the spot where it had stood.

"Mind what you are doing!"

Tore's voice, tense with anger, roused me. I had stopped rowing, and was holding my oar straight out over the water. Tears were flowing down my cheeks. I had no way to wipe them. The oar demanded my hands and my attention. I ducked my head, hoping no one would see, and resumed rowing.

My hope was in vain. Once I regained my rhythm and my composure, I glanced up. Hastein was watching me closely. Torvald, standing beside him, was also staring at me. Even Odd, rowing opposite me, was looking at me, surprise evident on his face. At least Tore's back was to me, so he could not have seen, but I had no doubt that Odd would tell him I had been weeping as we rowed.

The sun had not moved much farther across the sky by the time we came to our next stop. While

Hastein and his guard donned their armor, a crowd of villagers gathered on the shore. They parted to let an old man pass through to the front. He had a long, thick gray beard and was carrying a pitchfork, as though he'd come straight from the byre or the fields. He stopped when he saw the ship, and a smile creased his face.

"Jarl Hastein," he cried. "Welcome. It has been too long since you have graced our village with your company."

I had seen the old man once before, though only from a distance. It was Hrodgar, the headman of the village, who had sent men to help Toke hunt me.

Hastein and Hrodgar seemed to know each other well. They embraced when Hastein stepped from the gangplank onto the shore, and Hastein dispensed with the formal speech he'd given at our earlier stops. Instead, he and Hrodgar walked back to the village side by side, talking and laughing, trailed by the townsfolk and Hastein's small guard of warriors.

"The jarl and old Hrodgar have long been friends." Odd had walked over to where I sat on my sea chest, watching the retreating crowd.

"Hrodgar was one of the first to swear allegiance to Hastein after his father died," Odd continued. "He and the men of this village fought for

Hastein in the troubles that followed. Though an old man, he is no bench decoration, afraid to go to war. He is a brave warrior and a loyal friend. Do you know him?"

I shook my head.

"Are you from these parts? Do you have people in this district?"

What you really want to ask, I thought, is why was I weeping earlier.

"Some of my folk once lived not far from here," I answered. "But no more."

My answer was true, but it left much unsaid. The grave-mounds of my father's brother and father, and of his father's father lay not far from here. And beneath the new mound we had passed were the ashes of my brother, Harald, and his men.

I pulled a cloak from my sea chest, wrapped it around myself, and lay down on the deck.

"No doubt the jarl will be here long, if he visits with an old friend," I said. "I think I will use this time to sleep." I pulled the cloak over my head, and willed Odd to go away and leave me in peace. He was kind enough to do so.

I awakened with a start. Someone's foot was nudging my back.

"Wake up!"

I pulled the cloak from my head. The bright sunlight blinded my eyes and made them water.

Tore was standing above me. Beyond him, I could make out the indistinct form of another man.

"The jarl sent me to fetch you," Tore said.

The man behind him stepped forward and kneeled down, grasping my shoulders with his hands. "By the Gods," he exclaimed, "it is you!"

"Do you know this boy?" Tore demanded.

"I know this warrior," the man replied. "Do not be deceived by his years. He is a true wolf-feeder. I would be proud to fight by his side any day."

"Einar?" I asked, my mind still fogged from sleep.

"Aye, lad," he replied, "it is me, and surprised I am to see you so soon again, and in such fine company. You have done well. You serve the jarl himself now. Well met! Well met indeed!"

It was a shock to see Einar, but a pleasant one. Though I hardly knew him, Einar had fought for me. He was probably the closest thing to a true comrade—someone I knew would stand beside me, no matter what—I had. I held out my arm to clasp wrists with him, but he pulled me into his arms and embraced me. "Well met," he said again.

I stowed my cloak in my sea chest, then turned to Tore. "Do I need to wear my armor?" I asked. Hastein, Tore, and the rest of the men had armed themselves before going ashore. It was just for show, I knew, but I did not want to spoil the effect Hastein desired to create.

Tore shook his head. "No," he said. "Just come with me."

Einar walked with us. He was, as ever, talkative.

"I told Hrodgar about you, of course, when I returned to the village," he said. "I knew there was a strong chance your fate might never lead you back this way again, but I felt it important that he know the truth of what had happened. Of *all* that happened," he added, then winked at me several times, and nudged me with his elbow. Tore stared at us curiously, but said nothing.

I appreciated Einar not actually mentioning Toke's treachery, and the murder of Harald and the others, in front of Tore. I would have appreciated it more, though, had he not made it so obvious there was a secret he was keeping—one that involved me.

There were nine longhouses in the village. We went to the largest. Inside, Hrodgar was seated at a table positioned close to the fire burning in the central hearth. Hastein sat with him, in the place of honor to Hrodgar's right. Torvald and the rest of Hastein's men lounged on the benches along the side walls, drinking ale and talking with men from the village.

We stopped in front of the table. "Here is Halfdan, my Jarl," Tore announced, unnecessarily.

"So this is the one who killed my hounds," Hrodgar said. It did not seem a promising greeting.

I could tell it aroused Tore's interest, though, from the look on his face.

Hastein nodded to Tore. "Thank you," he said. "You can leave us now." Tore's disappointment was visible, but he turned and walked away.

"Jarl Hastein has been asking me about the attack on Hrorik's farm," Hrodgar continued. "I have told him what I observed, and what Toke said had happened. He also asked to see Einar here and speak with him. The jarl has told us how he met you, and of your tale."

Hrodgar stared at me silently for some time, his wrinkled face expressionless, masking his thoughts. Then he shook his head and sighed.

"I confess I do not see much of Hrorik's looks in you," he said. "But your face, your eyes in particular, do remind me of your mother. I remember when Hrorik brought her back here from Ireland. She was a beautiful woman. It did not surprise me that he was much taken with her. Nor did it surprise me that she came to be with child."

Hrodgar sighed again. "At least Hrorik's line is not ended," he said. "It was Niddingsvaark that was done that night. Fell deeds and foul. And none would ever have known, had you not escaped. Toke was clever. The face of a kinsman gave him good cover to hide his lies and treachery. He has a heavy blood-debt to pay."

When Hrodgar spoke those last words, I felt a

surge of relief. Not until then could I tell whether
he still believed Toke's lies.

"I have sworn to see him pay it," I replied.

"Perhaps someday you will. Einar tells me you
are a warrior to be reckoned with, and Hastein says
you are the finest shot with a bow he has ever seen.
That is high praise. I would like to see you shoot
someday. I suspect I shall have the opportunity.
The men of our village own a small ship. We use it
mostly for trade, but we will send it filled with warriors to answer the king's summons. I have decided
that I will lead them myself."

A woman, neither young nor old, had stepped
to the table with a pitcher of ale, and was refilling
Hrodgar's and Hastein's cups.

"Father," she exclaimed. "You are too old to
go to war."

"You are right, daughter, about one thing. I
am old—and I am in danger of becoming too old.
Only fools shun risk in the hope of a long life, for
there are worse things than death on the spears.
Old age shows men no mercy. I have outlived two
wives and a son, and my bones ache now every
morning when I rise like they once did only after a
hard day's work in the fields. I do not desire to die
in my bed, too weak to care for myself. I am a man,
and if I die like one, I will not regret it. Now bring
this warrior a cup, too, for no doubt he is thirsty,"

he said, waving his hand at me. "Come, Halfdan," he added. "Sit with me and quench your thirst. I would talk with the son of my old friend Hrorik Strong-Axe."

Hrodgar did me great honor by asking me to join him and Hastein at his table. At one point, I glanced across the hall and saw Tore standing beyond the hearth, staring intently at me. It is a good thing a man cannot burst from curiosity. Were it possible, Tore would surely have been at risk.

Within a week after we reached Hastein's estate on the Limfjord, other ships began arriving. Soon the shoreline of the fjord was lined with longships, and the land beyond teemed with warriors. I had never seen so many folk together in one place before, not even at Hedeby.

The captains and their men quickly became impatient to set off for Frankia. The king had forbidden strandhogg on Danish lands, so the army was forced to buy its provisions while it waited, rather than stealing cattle and other fare from the surrounding villages and farms. Though at first Hastein was pleased at the opportunity for profit while the army mustered at his estate, before long he became alarmed at how rapidly his herds were being depleted.

"An army is like a dragon," he complained. "It

is big and dangerous, and eats all the time."

Every day men were sent into the forests, hunting game to help feed the warriors. And each day, I was among those sent. Because of his skill with a bow, Tore was also among those chosen to hunt. However, Tore's skills apparently did not include those of a woodsman. It gave me secret pleasure to see how often he returned from the forest empty-handed. I made sure he noticed that I always brought in a kill.

By the time a month had passed since the king's council, more than eighty ships had arrived at Hastein's estate. The black-painted longship of Ragnar Logbrod, the *Raven*, was among them, and Torvald told me that Ragnar's sons Ivar the Boneless and Bjorn Ironsides had also joined the fleet. The ship from the village, captained by Hrodgar, arrived, too, and I was pleased to learn that Einar was among her crew.

"There is news you should know," Einar told me. "Four days after Jarl Hastein visited our village, three warriors rode in from the south. They were sent by Toke to learn what had happened to the men he'd ordered to find and kill you. Hrodgar told them Toke's warriors had been killed in an ambush by the outlaw they had hunted. He did not reveal that he had learned of Toke's treachery, but the three did not seem satisfied by his account. It was clear they found it suspicious that both Kar and

I survived, and only Toke's men had died."

"So Toke knows I am alive," I said.

"Aye. I think it is a good thing we will leave for Frankia soon. Toke has too much to lose if his treachery becomes known. He has no choice but to hunt you down and kill you."

Einar's words made me realize that during recent weeks, in my excitement at my new life and the prospect of war, I had pushed thoughts of avenging Harald's death to the back of my mind. I felt ashamed. I felt disloyal to Harald and the others who had died with him. More than any-thing, though, I felt afraid. In my heart I could not deny that I was no match for Toke. And now he knew I still lived, and would be hunting me again. How long would it take him to pick up my trail? I wondered if any of the villagers had told Toke's men of the youth who sailed with Hastein's crew, and who had been greeted so warmly by Hrodgar.

That night I dreamed of Toke. We were in the forest and he was chasing me. No matter how fast I ran, he kept drawing nearer. Then suddenly he was upon me, raising his sword—Harald's sword, Biter—to strike. I turned and tried to shoot him, but as I drew my arrow back he swung the sword and cut my bow through, the wood parting with a loud crack at the blow.

I awoke with a start and sat up. I was not in the forest. I was in Hastein's great longhouse. All around me, on the side benches and on the floor, men snored peacefully, wrapped in their cloaks. A thrall was standing at the main hearth, breaking branches and throwing them on the fire, which had burned low.

The rest of the night, every time I closed my eyes I saw Toke's leering visage in my mind. I knew I was not yet ready to face him. There was no way *I* could best him.

That night I foolishly let my fear rule me. But my long night of sleepless brooding made me no safer from Toke; it merely made me tired. And when daylight came, I learned that, for a while at least, I need not fear Toke finding me.

While the members of Hastein's household and the crews of his three ships broke the night's fast with a simple morning meal in the great hall of the longhouse, Hastein climbed up onto one of the tables and addressed us.

"Ready the ships, and ready your gear and stow it on board. Ragnar and I have agreed. Tomorrow we sail for Frankia. Bjorn Ironsides will remain here to lead any latecomers to join our fleet. The rest of us need wait no longer. It is time to carry war to the Franks."

The hall erupted with cheers.

"Hunters, do your best today," Hastein continued, when the noise died down. "We will all feast tonight!"

The afternoon shadows were stretching long across the ground by the time I returned to Hastein's estate. I led my heavily laden horse, draped with the carcasses of a wild sow and her two piglets, to the meat shed near the longhouse. Hastein was standing nearby, surveying the results of the day's hunting. Three men were with him, one old and two younger, all chieftains by the quality of their dress.

The old man stared at me intently as I unloaded my horse and gave the carcasses to the blood-soaked thralls in charge of butchering the night's meat. He was tall and very thin, almost gaunt, with cheeks that looked hollow under his high cheekbones. His skin was weathered and creased with wrinkles. On top his head was bald, but his hair—mostly white with a few scattered strands of black—hung down to his shoulders from the sides and back of his head and blew loose in the evening breeze. His posture was slightly stooped, and he stood with one hand resting on the head of a long-handled great-axe, as if he was using it as a walking staff. Strangely, a large raven was perched on his shoulder.

"Who is this boy?" the old man asked, turning to Hastein. "He looks to be a skilled hunter."

"His name is Halfdan," Hastein replied. "He is the newest member of the *Gull*'s crew."

"He seems very young to serve on the *Gull*. Is he kin of yours?"

"No, Ragnar," Hastein said. "Despite his age, he is the finest shot with a bow I have ever seen. That is why he serves on my ship. That . . . and other reasons."

I looked at the old man curiously. So this was Ragnar Logbrod. I had not expected so famed a war leader to be so old.

Ragnar turned back to me and met my gaze. His eyes, peering out from under thick brows, were so dark they looked as black as the feathers of his raven. "I was watching when you came out of the woods," he told me. "For a moment I thought I saw someone following you. Someone, or something."

I turned and looked back over my shoulder, in the direction I had come from. Could it have been one of Toke's men, already on my trail?

"I was watching, too," Hastein said. "I saw nothing."

One of the other men laughed. "Do not be surprised," he said. "Father often sees things that other men do not." The face of the man who spoke was marked by four parallel lines, the white tracks of old scars, running across his brow and down one cheek to his neck.

"Do not mock the second sight, Ivar," the old man said. "Though you do not possess it, it has served me well more than once. The Gods give us all different gifts. To you they gave a second chance at life, when by rights you should have died. To me, Father Odin gave the second sight, and glimpses into the world of the spirits that it offers."

I wondered if Ragnar's connection to the spirit world was truly a gift from Odin, or a result of his unholy pact with the witch-woman and the spirit of the slain bear. Regardless, his words alarmed me and startled me into speech.

"The world of the spirits?" I asked. "Do you mean you saw a ghost following me?" I wondered if Harald had come back to chide me because his death was not yet avenged.

Ragnar smiled. "I did not see a ghost," he said. "I am not certain I saw anything at all. If I did, though, it was most likely a fylgja."

"What is a fylgja?" I asked.

"It is a follower. A spirit guardian. Sometimes they take animal form and can be seen by all, like my raven friend here. I call him Munin, after one of All-Father Odin's two ravens. Munin came to me fifteen years ago, and has remained near my side ever since. Other spirit followers are invisible, and can only be seen in dreams—or by one strong in the second sight."

I looked behind myself again, and shivered

involuntarily at the thought of an invisible spirit creeping in my wake. Ragnar smiled again. He meant, I think, to be reassuring, but the sight reminded me of a wolf baring its teeth.

"Do not be concerned," he said. "A fylgja will not harm you. It is a protector who whispers in your ear to warn you of a hidden threat, or by the slightest breath turns aside an enemy's speeding arrow shaft. Such things, which men consider fate, are often the work of a fylgja. They can give you the gift of special luck, also. Ivar is said to have good weather luck, and Bjorn here finds wealth in most of his ventures. Men say that death for my foes follows me."

"And you, Hastein?" Ivar asked. "What follows you?"

"Hopefully women," Hastein replied, grinning. "Many of them, all beautiful and willing." Bjorn and Ivar threw back their heads and roared with laughter, but I noticed that only a thin, humorless smile crossed Ragnar's face. He seemed a grim man, such as would seldom enjoy mirth.

"Come," he said to Hastein. "It will be time soon to offer the sacrifice. Let us make ready."

Toward one end of the cleared lands surrounding Hastein's estate, the ground rose and formed a low bluff that overlooked the waters of the fjord. A solitary oak, the massive spread of its branches attesting to its age, crowned its peak.

Hastein, as chief godi of his district, had selected a great bull—almost pure white in color—as an offering to the Gods to seek their protection for our voyage. It would be sacrificed on top of the bluff overlooking the fleet.

Before joining the crowd that had gathered to watch the ritual, I cleaned up from the hunt and donned new clothes Hastein had given me. They were trousers of green wool and a tunic of bright blue linen made by a female thrall in his household who was skilled at sewing.

"I am your chieftain now," he had told me when I offered to pay for them. "It is the way of things that from time to time I give gifts to the men who serve me. And I have a reputation to maintain, which includes the appearance of my men," he added. "Though your clothing was clearly well made, it has seen hard use. It will do for when you are on board ship or in the forest or battle, but when we are at feast or council, I do not wish you to look like a field hand."

By the time I joined the crowd of warriors standing around the base of the bluff, the bull had already been wrestled into position beneath the branches of the great oak. Each of its front legs had been secured with short lengths of rope to sturdy stakes that had been hammered into the ground. Longer ropes had been attached to each of its rear legs, and thrown over a massive branch of the oak. The ends of these ropes were held by a group of men who, by the look of them, had been selected for their size and strength. Torvald and Tore were among them.

Hastein stepped up to the bull and wrapped his arms around its horns. It rolled its eyes, bellowed mournfully, and tried to shake its head and throw him off, but he braced his legs in a wide stance and held on. Torvald and the others heaved on the ropes, pulling again and again until it was hanging, head down, its front hooves barely touching the ground.

Ragnar, who like Hastein was the chief godi over his own lands and people, approached the bull from the other side. Both he and Hastein, I noticed, were wearing thick gold rings on their sword arms. My father had had such a ring, the oath-ring of a priest. I wondered what had happened to it.

From a scabbard at his belt, Ragnar drew a knife with a long, slender, sharply pointed blade. Looking up at the sky, he cried out in a loud voice: "All-Father Odin, Lord of War and Death! Mighty Thor, Master of Storms! Hear us! We, your people, ask your aid and blessing this night. We are setting forth to make war upon the Franks. They are followers of the White Christ, and are your enemies as well as ours. Protect our ships from storms as they sail upon the sea and give us a fair wind that our journey may be swift. Accept this blood sacrifice, and with it the honor that we offer you. Give us a safe voyage, and victory!"

When Ragnar shouted the last words, Hastein wrenched the bull's horns with all his strength, twisting its neck, and held its head steady. Ragnar drew back his arm and plunged the long knife deep into the bull's neck. As the creature gave a great bellow of pain and anger, Ragnar twisted the knife in a circular motion, then pulled it free and stepped back to avoid the crimson stream that gushed from the beast's neck.

"Behold," he cried. "The earth drinks the sacred blood!"

Ivar and Bjorn stepped forward, bearing broad, shallow copper basins that Ragnar filled with the blood draining from the dying bull. In the chill of the night air, wisps of steam rose above the filled bowls.

Once both basins were filled, the jarl released the bull's head. The dying beast tried to hook him with its horns as he stepped away from it.

"It dies well, with courage," Hastein said. "The Gods will be pleased. Let it suffer no more."

Ragnar stepped in again with his long knife and

sliced through the bull's throat. Within moments, its struggles ceased. Hastein gave a signal, and thralls from his household scurried forward to begin butchering the carcass. Hastein turned and addressed the crowd in a loud voice. "Let every pot this night contain meat from this bull. Let every warrior taste of this sacrifice. Tomorrow we join together in a great undertaking, to carry war to the land of the Franks. Tonight we feast together and celebrate the beginning of our voyage. Let us go now to the shore, and bless our fleet."

Hastein and Ragnar, each carrying a branch cut from a spruce tree, led the way down from the bluff, followed by Ivar and Bjorn. As they passed through the crowd, many kneeled and bowed their heads. When they did, Ragnar and Hastein dipped the branches they carried in the basins, and sprinkled the warriors with blood.

"It brings good luck," a voice said from behind me, "getting anointed with the blood of the sacrifice."

I turned to see who spoke. It was Tore. He, Torvald, and the others who had assisted with the sacrifice had made their way down from the bluff and joined the crowd that now trailed behind Ragnar and Hastein, watching as they anointed the prow of each ship. As they painted the stem-posts with blood, Ragnar and Hastein chanted, "Let breakers spare thee, and waves not harm thee. Turn aside from rocks that lurk beneath the surface, and fly before the wind like a bird."

"If you think the blood brings good luck, why are you not out there getting your face painted red?" Torvald asked.

Tore scowled. "I intend to," he said. "Do you mock the power of the Gods, Torvald? What will protect us, if they do not?"

"I will depend on my own strong right arm," Torvald answered. "I have more faith in it than the blood of a dead bull. I wager there are many men who have been painted with the blood this night who will not make the return voyage from Frankia. They cannot avoid their deaths if it is their fate to perish in the land of the Franks. You or I cannot, either, and I do not intend to stain my good feast clothes with bull's blood trying to."

"You tempt the anger of the Gods with your lack of faith," Tore said. He turned and hurried off in the direction the procession had gone.

Torvald turned and grinned at me. "Well," he said. "Aren't you going, too?"

I looked down at my new feast clothes. This was the first time I had worn them, and I thought they looked very fine.

"No," I said, but I hoped I was not making a mistake.

7

SEA WOLVES

It is a long journey from the Limfjord to the western kingdom of the Franks, and being out on the open sea in winter—even the relatively mild, late winter of that year—made for a cold, uncomfortable voyage. Our journey carried us so far south, though, that after a time we could feel the sun's rays growing stronger every day, and the wind's bite seemed less harsh as it blew across the water.

All of the lands we passed, once beyond the base of Jutland, were ruled by the Franks. I began to worry. Surely any people strong enough to conquer and hold so vast an empire were capable of fielding armies far larger than the force of warriors I sailed with. We numbered just over ninety ships, although Bjorn would likely bring more when he followed. When Hastein had first told us of the plan, it had seemed a bold stroke to send a fleet of longships to strike deep within the heartland of the Franks. I now hoped our boldness would not prove to be dangerous folly.

Hastein and Ragnar agreed it would be wise to conceal from the Franks, for as long as possible, the fact that an invasion fleet was sailing down their coast. They hoped to strike our first blows against the western Frankish kingdom before their king had time to muster an army.

By day, our fleet sailed out of sight of land, its ships so numerous they seemed to cover the sea. Only at dusk would we row in to shore and anchor for the night in protected coves or along sandy beaches, our dragonships thick upon the water like a nest of serpents. Each morning, we arose early and, before the sun burned away the mists shrouding the coast, our crews would strike their tents, row clear of the shore, raise sail, and be gone.

Each day, Hastein and Ragnar told a handful of captains to take their ships in to land, so their crews could forage. Every night the beasts and crops these crews scoured from the farms and villages they visited were divided among the fleet. Our warriors needed food, and there was not room enough on our ships to carry sufficient provisions for so long a voyage. Because small raids along the coast by passing pirates were common, Hastein and Ragnar reasoned they would not cause too much alarm, and probably not even draw notice deeper in the Frankish heartland.

Finally a morning came when the *Gull* did not follow the fleet as it sailed out of sight beyond the horizon. Our sister ships, the *Sea Wolf* and the *Serpent*, also remained behind. At Hastein's command, we donned our armor, lashed our shields in place in the racks along the ship's sides, and kept our helms and weapons close at hand.

Mail shirts are rare and expensive, but among the hand-picked warriors of the *Gull*'s crew, I was the only one who did not have one to wear. Tore, who for once seemed in a cheerful mood, clapped his hand on my shoulder after I pulled on my thick leather jerkin.

"Soon enough you'll have better than this," he said. "Most of the warriors in the Franks' armies have mail shirts. Many a member of this crew acquired his brynie with steel rather than silver."

"Is it our turn today to search for food?" I asked.

Torvald, who was standing nearby unwrapping his mail brynie from the sealskin bag he stored it in, answered. "No," he said. "We are scouting. By Hastein's reckoning, we are nearing the mouth of the Seine, the river that flows from the heart of the west kingdom of the Franks. We do not want to overshoot it. The fleet will travel at a slower pace from this point on. They will wait out beyond the sight of land for our signal, while we search for the river's mouth."

"If we are just scouting for the river, why do we arm ourselves?" I asked.

Tore snorted. "This is the land of the enemy," he said. "We do not know what we will encounter. Only a fool follows an unknown path without taking care for what or who may lie beyond the next bend."

The *Gull* hugged the coastline. Shortly before noon the land began curving away to the east. Hastein signaled to the *Sea Wolf* to pull alongside. When the ship was within hailing distance, he called to its captain, Svein.

"Sail out to the fleet," he said. "Tell Ragnar we have arrived at the bay, and that he should look for us among the islands on the north side of the estuary. I will find a place there for us to camp and hold a council. Tomorrow it begins."

As we sailed on, the long beaches and rocky cliffs that had lined the shore in recent days gave way to low, marshy islands, interspersed with numerous sandbars. Even the sea itself changed, its color taking on a muddy hue.

Hastein ordered us to lower and secure the sail, and signaled the *Serpent* to do the same. We unshipped our oars and moved forward again more slowly, with a man in the bow throwing out a weighted line, checking the depth of the water to be sure we did not run aground. Hastein stood beside him, and occasionally signaled a change of course to Torvald, who was manning the steering oar in the stern.

Suddenly Torvald raised his hand to shade his eyes, and stared off into the distance. As I rowed, I glanced over my shoulder in the direction he was looking, but could see nothing.

"Hastein!" Torvald called. "A sail! Ahead, and off the steer-board side."

"Raise oars," Hastein commanded, and as the ship coasted slowly to a stop he ran back to the stern and stepped up on the raised deck beside Torvald. He stood there for a few moments, searching the sea, then shook his head.

"I do not see it," he said. "You have eyes like a hawk."

Torvald raised an arm and pointed. "There," he said. "It is just a speck of white that flashes above the horizon now and again."

Hastein searched in the direction Torvald was pointing. For a long time he watched the sea in silence, while we in the crew watched him.

Finally he nodded.

"I spy it now," he said. "It is still far away, but drawing closer. With our sail lowered, its crew will not be able to see us."

The *Serpent* glided alongside our ship. Stig, her captain, called to Hastein. "What do you see?"

"It is a sail," Hastein replied, pointing. "Headed out to sea from the river's mouth."

Stig turned and looked. "Aye, I see it now. It looks to be a fair-sized sail, but is moving slowly. A trader, I'll wager, fat through the beam. A merchant ship that size has probably come downriver from Ruda."

"Do we take her or let her pass?" Torvald asked. Hastein was silent for a few moments as he stared in the direction of the approaching merchant ship.

"We take her," he finally replied. The men of both crews gave a muted cheer.

"We will hunt her like wolves hunt a deer," Hastein continued, talking to Stig. "I'll take the *Gull* farther down the bay, toward the river's mouth. We'll stay close to the shore. If the Frankish captain holds his present course, he will not see us when we pass. You lie here in wait. Once the Frank draws near, head out to intercept her. If she runs for the sea, it will be up to you to catch her, but I do not think she will. It should not take her captain long to realize you are faster than his ship. If he has any wits at all, he'll turn and make for the river's mouth. When he does, we'll catch him between us."

Hastein raised his voice. "And all of you, on both ships, heed this: If the trader's crew resists, they do so at the risk of their lives. But let no man kill the Frank's captain. He will know the river, and we will need a pilot to guide us on it in the days to come."

We took up our oars again and got underway. Torvald steered us close to the low islands that lined the shore, always keeping a watchful eye on the crewman checking the water's depth from the bow. With her sail lowered, the *Gull* lay so flat against the water as we cut across the broad swells that only the bare stick of her mast and her golden dragon's head on the bow rose up above the height of the waves on either side. From a distance, she must truly have looked like a dragon that had swum in from the open sea, searching along the shore for prey.

"How far in toward the river's mouth shall we take the *Gull?*" Torvald asked.

"A ways yet," Hastein replied. "The closer we get to the river's mouth before we spring our trap, the narrower the bay will be, and the Frank will have less room to maneuver."

We rowed on a while in silence. I was bursting with curiosity to know what was happening. Apparently Tore was, too, for finally he asked, "Jarl Hastein, where is the Frank? Can you see the *Serpent*?"

"The trader still sails on," Hastein told him. "I do not see the *Serpent*. No, wait. There she is." Hastein watched silently for a while, then spoke again. "The Frank has seen her. He's trimming his sail and coming about. Raise oars," he cried, then, "Rest a bit, my brothers, while the Frank turns and heads back this way. We have come far enough. The trap is set."

Including himself and Torvald, Hastein had crewed the *Gull* for this voyage with thirty-nine men, nine warriors more than were needed for the ship's fifteen pairs of oars. Now he ordered two of the extra crew members to relieve Tore and me. They had already strapped on their helms and swords, and did not look pleased.

"Tore, Halfdan, bring your bows and come with me to the bow," Hastein told us.

The remaining extra warriors were already there, pulling coils of thick rope from the small storage area under the raised bow deck and tying grappling irons to them. Two of them took one of the ropes back and secured it to the base of the mast. The other three remained in the bow with Hastein.

"When we hook the Frank," Hastein instructed them, "you will board his ship with me, while Tore and Halfdan cover us with their bows. Remember, all of you, I want the captain alive."

Hastein stepped up on the bow deck, checked the position of the merchant ship, then waved to Torvald.

"Torvald, turn the ship," he cried. "Move us out into the bay. It is time to show ourselves to the Frank, and let him see his doom."

"On my command," Torvald cried. "Steerboard side back oars, port side pull. Ready! Stroke, stroke, stroke. . ."

Slowly the *Gull* rotated in place until her bow was pointed out toward the mouth of the bay. "Ready!" Torvald called, and the men raised their oars up out of the water. "Ready!" he cried again, to prepare them, then, "Pull!"

All working as one, the rowers dipped their oars into the sea, then rocked back on their sea chests, pulling the long, wooden blades through the water. The *Gull* moved forward in uneven surges at first, thrusting ahead on each stroke and gliding more slowly in between, picking up speed until she was slicing through the waves toward the approaching merchant ship.

Watching from the bow, I could see the *Serpent* following behind the trader, her oars flashing in the sun as they dipped in and out of the water. The squat trader bobbed and bucked across the waves, looking slow and ungainly compared to the two sleek hunters charging through the sea toward her.

Tore, standing beside me in the bow, pointed at the merchant ship. "Look at her sail," he said. "They are resetting it. What is the Frank doing?"

The answer came a moment later when the trader, whose course we'd been approaching at an angle from the front, veered and headed straight for us.

"Thor's hammer!" Hastein exclaimed. "She has a doughty captain. He intends to ram us unless we give way."

In turning toward us, though, the merchant ship had also turned closer to the wind. She started losing speed and losing ground to the *Serpent*, which was closing rapidly on her now. Arrows flashed in a high arc from the *Serpent*'s bow toward the merchant ship. I saw some splash into the sea, but others dropped down onto the fleeing Frank. The range was still too far for accurate fire, particularly from a rocking deck, but the arrows must have driven the trader's crew into cover, for one corner of her sail began flapping, but no one moved to bring it under control.

The merchant ship was still bearing down on us

and closing fast, but by now it was clear the *Serpent* would reach her first. The Frank's captain was alone on her raised stern deck, crouched low against her side rail for cover, one hand on the tiller of the steering oar, the other clutching a shield close against his side.

The *Serpent* eased up along the merchant ship's steer-board side. As she reached the trader's stern, two warriors in her bow twirled grapples around their heads and let fly. The iron hooks clattered up onto the Frank's rear deck in front of her captain, and the warriors who'd thrown them braced themselves against the *Serpent*'s side and hauled on the ropes, setting the hooks against the trader's rail and swinging the *Serpent*'s bow toward her.

The Frank's captain lunged forward and swung a small-axe, severing one of the grappling lines. Two arrows streaked from the *Serpent* and thudded into the merchant ship's rail near the second grapple, driving him back to the cover of the stern.

A warrior climbed up onto the top strake in the *Serpent*'s bow and balanced there waiting to leap, holding himself steady with one hand on the ship's dragon head, while others behind him hauled on the remaining grappling line, pulling the two ships closer and closer together. The rowers on the *Serpent* had already pulled in their oars to prevent them from being broken between the ships, and her weight was beginning to drag on the merchant ship, slowing her even more.

We were very close now. "Raise oars!" Hastein shouted. "And pull them in!" Torvald heaved on the tiller, swinging us so the *Gull* slid past the merchant ship on her port side. She towered above the low-slung deck of the *Gull*. As we passed the Frankish ship, three grapples, two thrown from our bow and one from amidships, arced out and hooked her.

The Frank was caught from both sides now. Aboard the *Gull*, men let their oars clatter to the deck and seized the grappling lines, pulling our ship up tight against the side of the trader. Hastein swung his shield across his back by its long strap and stepped up onto the *Gull*'s top strake, grabbed the rail of the trader, and pulled himself up her side. The two other warriors in our bow did the same, while Tore and I scanned the rail of the Frankish ship, arrows nocked and ready on our bows.

Suddenly a Frankish sailor rose up above the rail. He swung a wooden mallet and smashed it into the face of the warrior climbing to Hastein's left, crumpling him, unconscious, back onto the deck of the *Gull*. I pulled my bow to full draw, but before I could shoot, Tore put an arrow through the sailor's mouth and he fell backward out of sight.

Hastein reached the top of the trader's rail and straddled it with his legs. He pulled his shield around to his front, drew his sword, and dropped from view, down onto the main deck of the Frankish ship. The other warrior who'd boarded with him did the same. I could no longer see them, but I heard screams of terror and pain. After a few moments, the screams ceased.

By now three warriors from the *Serpent*, one of them her captain, Stig, had clambered onto the raised stern deck of the merchant ship. They cornered the Frank's captain in her stern where he had no room to move, and began edging toward him, step by step, their shields in front of them. The Frank cowered behind his own shield, his eyes peering over its top edge, his right arm holding his small-axe cocked and ready behind him.

Suddenly Stig and his warriors lunged forward, smashing their shields against the Frank. As he staggered back, he swung an off-balance blow with his axe, but Stig caught it easily on his shield. The warrior beside him turned his own axe in his hand and swung it in a short, hard chop, striking the Frank on his wrist with the back of the axe head. The Frank howled in pain and released his weapon. Stig raised his sword and hammered its pommel against the Frank's head, dropping him to the deck.

More warriors clambered up the side of the trader from the *Gull*, but aboard the Frankish ship all was quiet now. The fight to take her was over.

Hastein came into view again, leaning over the rail of the merchant ship. "Halfdan!" he called, panting as he spoke. "Come up here. I am going to question the Frank's captain. I need you to translate."

"Here," Tore said, holding out his hand. "Give me your bow and quiver. You will not need them now."

"Thank you," I said, and handed them to him. As I turned and began climbing the trader's side, Tore added, "Fetch my arrow for me, while you are on board the Frank's ship."

As I swung my legs over the rail of the Frankish trader, I looked down. The man Tore had shot was lying below me on the main deck of the ship. The bodies of seven more sailors lay scattered beyond him. The deck was stained with blood that was draining from their many gaping wounds. I lowered myself gingerly to the deck, and stepped carefully between the red rivulets that were spreading farther and farther with every rock of the ship.

The man Tore had killed was sprawled on his back, the shaft and feathers of Tore's arrow jutting out of his mouth. The arrow had entered at an angle from below and pierced his skull. I grasped it just below the feathers and gave a tentative tug. It did not budge.

I wished Tore had come to retrieve his own arrow. I should have told him to. It was too late now, though. He was expecting me to get it. I did not want him to think I was afraid of blood and death.

The dead man's eyes were open. I felt like he was watching everything I did. For a moment I considered breaking the arrow and telling Tore it was not worth retrieving, but I did not want to sully my own honor with a lie. I braced one foot on the dead man's forehead, covering his eyes, and, looking away, pulled hard. With a sucking sound, the arrow ripped free.

I climbed up onto the elevated stern deck—much higher and larger than the small, raised deck on the *Gull*—where Hastein was waiting for me. Someone had thrown a bucket of water on the trader's captain to revive him. He was propped against the side of the ship now, both legs splayed out in front of him, holding his head in his hands and groaning. A thin, watery trickle of blood ran down one side of his face, and his hair was matted with more blood where Stig had hit him.

"Tell him," Hastein instructed me, "my name,

and that I am a jarl among the Danes."

Speaking in halting Latin, I told the Frank, *"This man speaking to you is named Hastein. He is a jarl, a great leader among the Danes. You are his prisoner now."*

The Frank lifted his head when I spoke. He stared at the arrow in my hand, a horrified expression on his face. Blood dripping from the arrow was forming a small puddle on the deck.

"Where are my crew?" he demanded, speaking directly to Hastein in our tongue. "Have you killed them all?"

"They chose to fight rather than surrender," Hastein answered. "It was an unwise choice. It cost them their lives."

At Hastein's words, I thought of the bloody deck I had just climbed up from. The dead men were all simple sailors. None had armor or even shields. I'd seen no true weapons down there, just the wooden mallet, a long-handled gaff hook, and a few knives. Those men had stood no chance against experienced warriors with shields, armor, and swords. I wondered how much opportunity Hastein had really given them to surrender. If he'd spoken to them at all, I doubted they'd understood.

Hastein's next question seemed to confirm my suspicion. "How is it you speak the language of the

North?" he asked the trader's captain. "Few Franks know our tongue, yet you speak it well."

"I make my living by trade," the Frank responded. "In years past, I have often sailed with cargoes to your land. I am not an enemy of the Danes. You had no cause to attack my ship and kill my crew. Jarl or no, you are nothing but a common pirate."

By the end of his speech the Frank's voice was quivering, and tears began to run down his cheeks. "Some of my crew had sailed with me for more than ten years," he added.

"What is your name?" Hastein demanded.

"Wulf," the Frank replied.

Hastein squatted on the deck beside the Frank. "I am sorry the loss of your men grieves you," Hastein told him. "I, too, have felt the pain of such losses. There is no shame in your tears. But you say you are not my enemy. You are wrong. You are a Frank, and I am a Dane. Your kings have warred on my people in the past. It was they who made us enemies. It is your misfortune that they did so. Do not blame the Danes because we do not forget past wrongs."

"It was not by my choosing that the Franks made war upon the Danes in times past," Wulf retorted.

"No," Hastein agreed. "It was not your choice.

And now the Danes return war to the Franks, and that is not your choice, either. It is your fate, though, and the fate of all Franks who cross our path. You cannot escape it."

Hastein stood up again. "Did you sail from Ruda?" he asked.

"Aye," Wulf answered, nodding his head. "It is my home. Though now I fear I shall never see it again."

Hastein smiled. It was a cold, hard smile.

"I think you will see Ruda again," he said. "I think you will see it soon, in fact."

We camped that night on a long, low island near the river's mouth. The merchant ship's cargo included casks of wine, which Hastein distributed among the fleet. While the warriors of our army drank to celebrate the end of our long journey south, the army's leaders—Ragnar, Hastein, and Ivar—met in council around a fire Cullain had built in front of Hastein's tent. Members of the *Gull*'s crew milled on the shore around them, drinking, laughing, and enjoying the feel of solid ground underfoot again. I lingered close to Hastein's tent, listening to what they said in council. This was my first experience at war. I wanted to know what was planned.

"It has been a long journey to reach this

point," Ragnar said. "But the Gods smiled on us. The weather held clear, and we lost no ships. I hope Bjorn has as fair a voyage when he follows us with the rest of the ships for our fleet."

"Aye," Ivar agreed. He was leaning on one elbow, with his legs stretched out straight beside him, drinking wine from a silver cup. "If we move very far upriver, away from the safety of the sea, we will need every warrior who was promised—and wish for even more."

Ivar drained his cup and held it out in Cullain's direction. "More wine," he said.

"Ivar is right," Hastein said. "It will take the Franks some time to gather their forces. But once they do, we must be wary, for their armies can move swiftly, and they are hard fighters. I have fought them before. And we are certain to be outnumbered."

"We must move swiftly, too," Ivar said. "Before the Franks have time to react to our presence. On the morrow our men must spread out over the countryside on either bank of the river, and scour it for horses. Once mounted, our raiding parties can strike fast and deep across the Franks' lands. With luck, we can hit them hard and be gone before their army has time to react."

Ragnar shook his head. "We have not come so far, with so great a force, just to pillage some villages and monasteries, then retreat back to our own land. The men do expect plunder, and we will let them take it. They would be difficult to control if we did not. But we have come for more—we have come to bring war to the Franks. Their power weakens, while ours grows. We must use this opportunity while our enemies are in disarray to strike them a severe blow. We would dishonor ourselves if we failed because we feared what the Franks might do."

I felt Ragnar was right. We were here not only for plunder, but also to protect our homeland. Surely Hastein agreed—it was he who told us so, that night after the king's council.

"We are deep in the land of the Franks," Ivar argued. "When they move against us, do you expect to be able to stand and fight against a far superior force? And if we sail too far upriver, they may try to block it behind us, and cut off our line of retreat. I think it is a risk not worth taking."

"Perhaps there is a way to lessen the risk," Hastein suggested. "We need a secure base for our army. A base strong enough to cause the Franks to hesitate to attack, if it is defended by an army the size of ours. With such a base we can protect our ships and wait for the Franks to make a mistake. From its safety, we can make the Franks play our game, but without it, we will be forced to only react to the moves of their army. It is like playing hnefatafl. He who only reacts to the moves of his opponent usually loses."

"This is not hnefatafl. We are not playing a game with pieces on a board," Ivar said. "We are moving ships and men in a distant and strange land. We are in Frankia. Where would we find so strong a base?"

"Ruda," Hastein replied.

8

RUDA

"You must be mad!" Wulf exclaimed. "I would never betray my own people!"

"Do not think of it as betraying your people," Hastein told him. "You can save many lives."

"Save lives? By helping you capture the town? Do you take me for a fool?"

When Ragnar and Ivar left to return to their ships, Hastein, who'd seen me standing nearby, had sent me to fetch Wulf from the *Gull*, where he'd been left tied and under guard. The Frank looked haggard. His hair was matted with dried blood, and his face looked pale above his short gray beard.

"We will take Ruda with or without your

help," Hastein told him. "Though without your assistance, it will be a hard fight, and we are likely to lose many warriors."

"I do not care if your warriors die," Wulf said. "I hope they do."

"I do not expect you to care about my men's lives. But if they lose many of their comrades, our warriors will be angry. Their lust for blood and revenge will be high, and they will vent their rage on the people of your town. Were you in Ruda four years ago when it was sacked?"

"No. I was away," Wulf said.

"I was there," Hastein told him. "It was I who led the warriors who attacked the town. By the time we finally broke in, many of our men had died, and many more were badly wounded. Our hearts were filled with anger and the desire for revenge. Many in Ruda died that day who should not have. It is the way of war. Towns that resist capture pay a high price when they are finally taken."

"A high price?" Wulf said indignantly. "Those are just words to you. What do you know of the price Ruda paid? When your men took Ruda before, my brother was killed trying to protect his wife. Two of your warriors raped her. They hacked him to pieces when he tried to stop them."

Hastein shrugged his shoulders. "It is as I am

telling you. If our warriors suffer heavy losses when we take the town, their anger will bring a bloodlust upon them. When that happens, neither I nor anyone else can control them. Ruda's capture is not in question. We *will* take the town, and we *will* plunder it. You would be a fool to think otherwise. But the fate of the people of Ruda is in your hands. Help us take the town quickly, and with few losses. The people of the Ruda may lose some of their wealth to our army, but at least they will keep their lives."

I pitied Wulf. It was a bitter choice the jarl gave him. He stared into Hastein's face, as though trying to read the thoughts concealed behind his pale blue eyes. His gaze was met with a cold, unwavering look. Hastein remained silent, giving him time. Finally Wulf looked away and gave a heavy sigh. "You must guarantee the safety of my family," he said. "They must be protected from any harm. And if the people of the town know of my role in this thing, it will mean my death once you are gone."

"Done," Hastein said. He pointed at me, and then at Tore, who had wandered near. "When we enter the city, these two warriors will follow you to your home, and guard it against attack. And they will billet there for as long as we hold Ruda. You will feed and shelter them, and in exchange they will keep others from molesting the safety of your family."

Tore looked indignant. Wulf did, too. He pointed at me.

"I do not want this one living in my home," he protested. "He killed the second in command of my crew. Alain was like a son to me."

I shook my head. "I killed no one on your ship," I told him.

"You lie," Wulf said. "I saw you holding the bloody arrow in your hand, and I saw Alain fall, pierced by it."

"I did not shoot that arrow," I told him. "I merely retrieved it. Arrows are too valuable to waste."

"It is true," Tore added. "I was beside him on board our ship during the fight. He did not kill your man."

Tore and I glanced briefly at each other, then looked back at Wulf. It seemed best if we did not mention that Tore had been the one who'd killed Alain.

"I am offering these men to guard your family," Hastein told Wulf. "No others. It is not your choice how I command my men. If you do not want their help, protect your family yourself."

"You are pagan devils, all of you," Wulf muttered. "May God strike you dead for your sins against good Christian folk."

"Call on your God if you wish," Hastein said. "We do not fear him. And I do not think he will save you or your family. Only we can do that, for you are in our power now. Give me your answer. Will you help us, or no?"

"What do you want me to do?" Wulf asked.

Moving upriver required much work with the oars. Our journey was slowed even more by the pace of the captured merchant ship, which Hastein insisted was crucial to his plan. Inappropriately named the *Swallow*, it was broad of beam and, possessing only four pairs of oars, was clearly not built for swift rowing. Torvald told Wulf he should have named his ship the *Turtle*. "You insult the good name of swallows with this fat, slow tub of a ship," he said. "They are graceful birds, and swift of flight."

Our slow progress upriver provided ample opportunity for mounted raiding parties to ravage the countryside. The size of our mounted force grew daily, for with each day's foray, more horses were taken.

The crew of the *Gull* did not join in the raids, though, much to their discontent. On the journey upriver, Ragnar placed Hastein in charge of the captured merchant ship, since he had insisted on bringing it. Ten members of the *Gull*'s crew, including Torvald, Tore, and me, were detailed by

Hastein to crew the Frankish trader with Wulf. The rest of the *Gull*'s crew were needed to man her own oars.

Torvald in particular bemoaned the assignment. He had longed to lead the attack on a large Frankish monastery located halfway upriver between the sea and Ruda. "We captured that monastery on our raid here four years ago," he told me. "It was a very profitable undertaking. The high priests of the White Christ paid us twenty-six pounds of silver to free the priests we captured there, and six pounds more not to burn the monastery. I was looking forward to taking it again."

Hastein was unmoved by Torvald's wishes. "You will move this ship upriver a half day ahead of our fleet," he told him. "If any Franks report back to Ruda that they have seen her, I want it to appear she is fleeing ahead of our forces. Have patience. Your reward will come in Ruda. Our crew will be the first to enter the town, so you will be the first to partake of her plunder."

Finally Wulf advised Torvald that we were less than half a day's journey from Ruda. We tied up on the side of the riverbank, and Torvald sent a man downriver in a small-boat to carry word to the fleet.

A few hours later, a large band of riders approached, led by Hastein and Ivar. Ivar sent scouts to search the surrounding countryside and ensure that no Franks lurked nearby who might carry a warning to Ruda. The rest of the party rode to where the *Swallow* was tied at the river's edge.

Hastein and ten other warriors dismounted and clambered aboard. Hastein turned and called back to Ivar, who was sitting astride a mottled gray horse, letting it graze on the lush grasses along the water's edge while he watched us prepare to cast off.

"Do not move your men close to the town until darkness hides you," Hastein said. "I do not want the Franks to realize how close our army is. If we succeed in capturing the gate, we will shoot a fire arrow up into the sky. When you see that signal, you must ride like the wind. There will be too few of us to hold for long."

"We will come," Ivar said. He held up a horn that was hanging by a thin strap over his shoulder. It had been highly polished and was trimmed with silver around the narrow end and the mouth. "When you hear this horn, you will know we are near."

Our men took turns manning the *Swallow*'s oars. "I want no one to row until he is weary," Hastein told us. "We will all need our strength in the fight ahead."

Darkness had long been shrouding the river, slowing our progress even more, when in the distance we finally saw the first lights marking the town's presence. They seemed to float high above the water, as though the town had been built atop a cliff. I said so, provoking a harsh laugh from Wulf.

"Aye, there are cliffs at Ruda," he said. "But they were built by men. Ruda is surrounded by high, stone walls, taller than two men, one standing on the other's shoulders. Those lights you see, so high above the level of the river, are torches carried by guards atop Ruda's walls."

Hastein had told us Ruda was protected by strong walls, but I had not expected anything like this. Hedeby, the greatest town in all the kingdom of the Danes, was protected by only a ditch and an earthen wall topped with a wooden stockade. Building such massive walls of stone around an entire town seemed a task beyond the power of mortal men.

"How did the people of Ruda build such walls?" I asked Wulf.

"They did not," he answered. "The walls were built long ago, before the memory of any living men, by the Romans, who once ruled these lands."

I was glad we were only fighting the Franks,

and not the Romans. I wondered what had happened to them. I hoped it had not been the Franks who'd driven them from these lands.

As we neared the town, eight of us, including Tore, Odd, and I, made ready. We pulled rough, simple tunics, collected from raided Frankish farms and villages, over our armor to conceal it, and stowed all of our helms in a sack. Up on the raised bow deck, we built a makeshift litter out of four shields laid overlapping across the hafts of two spears, and wrapped the lot tightly with cloaks to hold it together. We piled our weapons on top of the litter, and covered them with another cloak to hide them. I stretched out atop all, playing the role of an injured crew member who had to be carried ashore—a role I'd won because I was the lightest member of our crew. Only Hastein actually carried more than just a knife on his person—he stuck his sword, scabbard and all, down one leg of his trousers and concealed its hilt under his tunic.

The rest of our warriors aboard the *Swallow* crouched low in the shadows on the center deck of the ship and draped themselves in their cloaks to conceal any glint from weapon or armor. Some squeezed up under the bow and stern decks, hiding in the spaces where Wulf's cargo of wine had been stowed before we drank it.

"Do not forget," Hastein told Torvald, whom

he'd placed in command of the men remaining on board. "When you hear my call, bring our helms and the rest of our shields. We will need them."

As the ship passed the edge of the cleared land surrounding the town, I heard shouts from the walls and saw torches moving toward the tower that formed the downstream corner of the town's defenses. By the torches' light, I could dimly see a quay along the shore below the walls. The edge of the bank had been shored up with timbers, and narrow piers—some with ships and smaller boats moored alongside—jutted out into the river.

Wulf steered the ship toward a vacant pier in front of the low wooden gate in the center of the wall. The torches above followed our progress, moving along the top of the wall from the corner tower until they stopped in a cluster above the gate. As we neared the pier, I could see the glint of spearheads and helms in the flickering torchlight, and a voice called in heavily accented Latin from the wall. *"What ship are you? Who goes there?"*

"It is the Swallow,*"* Wulf answered. *"It is I, Wulf."*

A different voice spoke this time from among the guards atop the wall.

"Wulf, is that you? It is I, Otto."

"He is a friend of mine," Wulf murmured to Hastein.

"Otto?" he cried. *"Yes, it is me."*

"How is it you come to be back here now, and in the middle of the night?"

Wulf did not answer for a few moments, as he concentrated on turning the *Swallow* in toward the shore, and letting the sluggish current drift her against the pier while the rowers pulled in their oars. He climbed over the rail and tied a line from the stern to a post, while Tore did the same at the bow.

Once the ship was secured, Wulf stood silently on the narrow pier, his hands on his hips, staring at the gate and the guards on the wall above it. Suddenly he began walking in the direction of the riverbank. I wondered if he planned to make a run for the gate and warn the Franks of our presence. The same thought must have occurred to Hastein, who stepped to the ship's rail and whispered as Wulf passed, "Go no farther. You cannot run faster than I can throw a spear."

For a few steps more Wulf kept walking. I thought he was going to risk Hastein's threat, but he finally stopped opposite the ship's bow and shouted up to the Franks watching from the walls.

"We never reached Dorestad," he said. *"The sea was filled with Northmen's ships. It was only by the grace of God that we saw them before they saw us, and were able to escape and regain the safety of the river."*

"The Northmen are on the river now," Otto said.

"Their ships have been seen not far from here. How is it they did not catch up with you?"

"The grace of God," Wulf said again. *"Surely it was He who protected us and hid us from their sight. Even so, it was a near thing. Just this day, at dusk, one of the Northmen's ships did see us and gave chase. Three of my men were hit by their arrows. I think we escaped only because the pirates feared navigating the river in the failing light."*

To support Wulf's claim, I let out a long, shuddering moan.

The Frank who'd first challenged us from the wall now spoke again.

"You will have to stay on your ship until morn," he said. *"The count has given orders. None of the town gates may be opened between sunset and sunrise, while the Northmen are so near. We know not how soon they will arrive."*

"What if they arrive this night?" Wulf demanded. *"I know they cannot be far behind us. They will slaughter us if they catch us here. You must let us in!"*

I could see Otto, Wulf's friend, arguing with the man who had spoken, but we were too far away to hear what they said. Wulf called to him.

"Otto, please, have mercy on us. Do not leave us to die here, in sight of safety. Help us! Let us in!"

I moaned again, this time a high shriek, ending with what I hoped were heart-wrenching sobs.

Tore, who'd climbed back aboard the *Swallow* after tying off the bow, muttered, "You sound like a woman giving birth. I hope you will not act this way if you are ever truly wounded."

Up on the wall the sentry relented. *"Come then,"* he said. *"But hurry."*

Hastein climbed onto the pier beside Wulf. He walked with a stiff-legged limp, caused by the sword in his trouser leg, and put one arm around Wulf's shoulders, as though he was injured and needed Wulf's assistance to cover the distance to the gate. Tore and Odd carefully eased the litter over the ship's rail and lined up on the pier behind Hastein and Wulf. As the five of us headed toward the gate, the remaining three of our pretend Franks climbed onto the pier and fell in behind, and our little army of eight marched to capture Ruda.

When we neared the wall, I saw the helmed heads of three Franks peering down at us from the rampart above. Two were holding torches out beyond the wall to light our way, or perhaps to get a clearer look at who approached. One of the Franks pointed down at us and said something to the man beside him. He beckoned the third guard to come closer, and gestured at us again. I was sure they saw through our ruse. None of the rest of our men could see what the guards were doing, for they all had their faces averted, trying to prevent the Franks from seeing them. I wanted to warn Hastein, but we were too close to the wall now to speak without being overheard.

The gate, a single door built of heavy timbers, was just wide enough for a small cart to pass through. With a screech of hinges, it swung open. A single Frankish warrior holding a torch stepped out. Another stood just inside the doorway, a spear held loosely in his hand.

When the Frank who'd come out to meet us spoke, I recognized him by his voice as Otto.

"Wulf, where is Alain? I do not see him. And who is this?" he added, pointing at Hastein. *"I have never seen him before."*

Wulf grasped Otto's sleeve, and urged him back toward the open gate. *"Let us get inside quickly,"* he said. *"I will explain everything when we are safe. Alain is dead."*

Wulf and Otto passed through the open gate, followed closely by Hastein, and entered the short tunnel leading through the base of the massive wall. Only a few more steps and I would be inside, too, safe from the spears of the guards above us.

Tore entered the passage carrying the front end of the litter. The Frank standing in the doorway pressed back against the wall to let us pass by. Then Odd, who was carrying the rear of the litter, tripped on the stone threshold of the doorway. He staggered to one side, the litter tilted sharply, and I grabbed wildly at the edge of one of the shields, trying to keep from being thrown to the ground. I could feel the pile of weapons sliding beneath me. A sword and a small-axe clattered onto the stone floor of the tunnel directly in front of the Frankish guard.

He stared down at them, not comprehending. *"What's this?"* he said.

Tore released his grip on the front end of the litter and turned on the Frank. Grabbing him by his shoulders, he slammed the startled guard back hard against the tunnel wall, then swung his elbow and smashed it into the Frank's face. The guard's knees buckled, and Tore slung him facedown onto the stone floor. The Frank tried to rise back up onto his knees, but Tore straddled his back, grabbed his head with both hands, and wrenched it around. There was a sickening crack, and the Frank collapsed limply to the ground.

When Tore dropped the front of the litter, the ends of the two spear shafts bounced on the stone floor, jarring the shields loose and breaking the makeshift platform apart into a jumble of cloaks, weapons, and shields. I rolled off to one side, then scrambled back over the tangled mess, searching for my bow and quiver.

161

Otto, who with Wulf and Hastein had by now almost reached the far end of the tunnel, turned and began running back toward us. Hastein pulled his sword from the leg of his trousers, flung the scabbard aside, and drove the blade into Otto's back with such force that the point jutted out through his chest. With a choking cry, the dying Frank fell to his knees.

"He is my friend!" Wulf cried.

"You said no one must know your part in this," Hastein snapped. He put his foot against Otto's back and pushed his body off the sword's blade.

The Franks up on the wall were shouting now, asking what was happening. The rest of our men ran forward into the tunnel and began pulling their weapons from the wreckage of the litter. Hastein moved past them and stood just inside the open gateway.

"Torvald!" he shouted. "To me! Quickly!"

From up on the wall above us, a horn sounded, braying out an alarm to the sleeping town. *"To arms, to arms!"* a voice cried. *"The Northmen are attacking. They are at the river gate!"*

I found my bow and Tore's lying side by side. I threw his to him, then slung the strap of my quiver over my shoulder. Tore reached past me and pulled his own quiver from the pile. The fire arrow was in it. "I must signal Ivar," he said, and picked up the torch Otto had dropped, guttering now on the ground beside his body.

As Tore ran back to the open gate, a Frank appeared at the far end of the tunnel. He drew back his arm to hurl a spear at Hastein, who was kneeling to pull his shield from the jumble of weapons.

"Look out!" I shouted. Hastein glanced up, then threw himself forward. The spear skimmed over his back and struck the warrior behind Hastein in the belly. The man screamed and toppled across Hastein's back.

The Frank at the tunnel's mouth drew his sword and crouched behind his shield. Another guard appeared beside him, carrying a spear at ready.

"Odd, Halfdan, drive them out!" Hastein shouted as he pushed the body of the wounded man aside and staggered to his feet. "If they keep us trapped here in the tunnel, we are doomed."

Odd and I moved down the tunnel side by side, drawing arrows from our quivers and nocking them on our strings. Hastein pressed close behind us, followed by the rest of our men. Only Tore remained behind, kneeling just inside the gate. The burning torch lay on the ground at his feet, and the fire arrow, its tip now blazing, was nocked and ready on his bow.

Odd and I pulled our bows to full draw. The

two Franks, only a spear's length away, dropped into a crouch and jerked their shields up in front of their faces. I shot the man with the spear in his foot. He screamed and fell backward, clutching at the shaft, and Odd put a second arrow through his throat. The other Frank scuttled backward from his dying comrade. Howling like a wolf, Hastein ran past me, followed by two other warriors, and the Frank turned and fled.

I glanced back down the tunnel at Tore. Looking up, he stepped cautiously out of the gate, then darted back into the safety of the tunnel. A spear stuck, quivering, in the ground where he'd stood a moment before. Beyond, I could see Torvald and the rest of our warriors from the *Swallow* approaching at a run.

"Odd, Halfdan!" Tore shouted. "Clear the wall!"

Odd and I ran out of the tunnel's mouth and into the town, our bows at the ready. To our right, a stone staircase climbed the inside of the wall to the rampart above. Hastein was halfway up it, standing over the body of the Frank who'd fled from the tunnel. Above, on the rampart, a single Frankish guard remained. He was looking down at Hastein, and as I watched he raised a spear to throw. Odd and I shot together, and the guard staggered backward and collapsed, two arrows piercing his chest.

Odd ran back into the tunnel's mouth and waved to Tore. A moment later, the fire arrow streaked up into the night sky.

For now there were no more Franks to fight, though more were bound to come soon. We stripped off the Frankish tunics that had concealed our armor and adjusted our weapons. I'd stuffed my dagger and small-axe in my quiver, and used the brief respite to transfer them to my belt.

Torvald came trotting out of the tunnel, carrying a bundle of spears over one shoulder, followed by the rest of the *Gull*'s warriors who'd been hiding on board the *Swallow*.

"You lost only one man?" Torvald asked Hastein.

"Aye," Hastein answered. "Olaf. Is he dead?"

"Close to it," Torvald said. "The spear bit deep. He will not see the morning come."

"He may not be alone in that," Hastein replied. "So far fortune has smiled on us, but the real fight is yet to come. I hope Ivar does not tarry. Did you bring our helms?"

One of the men who'd come from the ship stepped forward with the sack of helms and handed Hastein's to him, then emptied the rest on the ground. While I was strapping mine on, Tore shouted, "Look, up on the wall!"

Three Franks armed with spears were running along the rampart, approaching from the left. Tore drew an arrow and loosed it, striking the leading Frank in the thigh. As he staggered sideways and fell, the man behind him hurled his spear wildly at us, then bent down and grabbed his wounded fellow under the arms. Odd shot at him and missed, but my arrow hit him high in the side of his chest. He bounced back against the wall, then top-pled off the rampart, dragging his wounded com-rade with him. The third Frank turned and ran. Tore caught him low in the back with a long shot.

"It's like knocking squirrels off a branch," he boasted, then jogged over to where the bodies of the first two Franks lay at the foot of the wall. The man I'd shot was still, but the other was groaning and thrashing on the ground. Tore drew his seax and cut the wounded man's throat, then pulled his arrow and mine from the bodies. "We'll need these before this night is over, I'll wager," he said, as he trotted back and handed me my arrow.

A clatter of horses' hooves echoed in the street leading to the gate, signaling the arrival of a coun-terattack. A group of Franks on horseback rode into view. When they saw us, the rider in the lead raised his hand and called out a command. The horsemen stopped and began forming into orderly rows, one behind the other, each composed of five men and stretching across the entire width of the street.

I had never seen warriors like these. Each man wore a helm, shield, and a brynie of ring-mail or scale armor, and many also had iron plates strapped over their lower legs to protect them. All were armed with swords and long spears.

"Form a shield-wall, quickly!" Hastein shouted, and our little band of warriors moved into a close-knit line in front of the opening to the tunnel.

"Aim your spear points at the horses' faces," Torvald cried to the men as they formed the line. "Make them turn aside. Do not allow them to run over us." In a quieter voice, he murmured to Hastein, who stood beside him, studying the Franks as they moved into formation opposite us. "There are too many of them," he said. "They will attack us in waves, and we have only enough men to form a single line. It will break too easily. Shall we take shelter in the tunnel?"

"We dare not," Hastein replied, shaking his head. "If we retreat into the tunnel, they can block and hold its entrance with only a few warriors, then send more of their men up to the rampart above the gate to keep us trapped inside the wall, and drive off any reinforcements. We must hold here until Ivar and his men arrive. Somehow we must keep them from charging."

Hastein turned and spoke to Tore. "Take Odd and Halfdan. You three are the only ones with bows. Bring down their front row and disrupt their ranks."

We moved forward and took positions out in front of the shield-wall. The Franks had finished forming into ranks by now, and the warriors in the front were positioning their shields and spears, readying for a charge. I looked for a target as I drew an arrow from my quiver and nocked it on my string. A Frank in the center of the front row had a banner on his spear, and was shouting commands to the other riders. I aimed my shot for his face, but he was too quick and caught my arrow with his shield. Tore chose him as a target, too, but sank his arrow deep into his horse's chest. Odd's arrow found the neck of another rider's horse.

"Their horses are easier targets," Tore called to me, "and dropping their mounts stops their charge as surely as a hit on the rider."

The two wounded horses reared, screaming in pain, as their riders jerked at their reins, trying to control them. The other warriors in the front row and in the ranks behind began backing their mounts away from the thrashing of the two wounded steeds.

"Shoot together on my mark," Tore said, "at the rest of the front rank. I'll take the horse on the right, Halfdan the one beside him, Odd the far left."

We nocked arrows and drew, three men challenging an entire troop of cavalry.

"Loose!" Tore shouted, and our arrows sped to their marks. At such close range, it was butchery. My arrow sank halfway to its feathers in my target's chest. The horse stood motionless for a moment, then its front legs collapsed and it keeled forward onto its knees. Its rider swung his right leg over the beast's drooping head and leaped clear as it collapsed onto its side.

Tore's target staggered sideways and fell heavily against the wall of a house abutting the edge of the street. Its rider screamed as his leg was crushed by the weight of his dying mount's body. On the opposite side of the street, the horse Odd had hit was standing stock-still, its head hanging down with long strings of blood draining from its mouth. In front of it, the horse Odd had wounded with his first arrow was still bucking wildly.

The leader's horse, though mortally wounded by Tore's first shot, was also bucking and kicking. Its rider, clinging desperately to the reins with his left hand, drew a long dagger from his belt and stabbed it into his horse's neck. Blood spurted and the horse reared up on its hind legs, pawing at the air with its front hooves and screaming in pain. The

Frank, a magnificent horseman, somehow hung on and stabbed again, this time striking the great artery in the beast's neck. The horse's front hooves thudded back down onto the ground and it stood still now, trembling as great spouts of blood pumped from its neck. In an instant, the Frankish leader slid off and ran back into the ranks of the troops behind.

The rider mounted on Odd's first target, who had been sawing at the reins and beating his wounded mount's flanks with the haft of his spear, somehow brought the injured beast under control. Suddenly the horse launched forward, charging us at a gallop, its rider howling a war cry and waving his spear.

"Run!" Tore shouted. Behind us, Hastein called out, "Quickly, come inside!"

Tore, Odd, and I turned and ran back to the shield-wall. Our warriors opened up, let us through, then swiftly closed ranks again, their spears presenting a hedge of gleaming steel tips. Only moments after we passed through the line the rider was upon them.

Even crazed by its wound, the horse would not throw itself against the spear thicket. At the last moment, it pulled up, and the Frank on its back stabbed down with his lance at the men in our line. One warrior dropped his spear and staggered back, his hand to his face. Beside him, another crouched low, his shield held overhead to ward off the Frank's thrusts, and lunged forward, stabbing the blade of his spear deep into the belly of the horse. The dying animal screamed in pain and staggered backward onto its haunches. Torvald and another warrior sprinted forward, dragged the rider from his horse, and flung him onto the ground. More men surged forward around him, stabbing with their spears. Others surrounded the horse and speared it again and again, finishing it to stop its thrashing.

"Reform!" Hastein shouted. "Reform the line!"

In front of us the rest of the Franks, acknowledging the vulnerability of their horses in such tight confines, were beginning to dismount. A few ran forward, finished off the dying horses with their spears, and pulled the wounded rider back to safety. Their leader trotted out and retrieved his spear from where he'd dropped it, then waved the banner overhead and shouted a command. The rest of his men moved forward and formed a dense wedge-shaped formation around him, in front of the bodies of the dead horses.

"Tore, take Odd and Halfdan up on the wall!" Hastein ordered. "Try to even up the odds, and buy us time."

I turned and ran up the stairs to the top of the wall, Tore and Odd following closely behind. When I reached the rampart, I looked out into the darkness. No riders were visible yet, but from somewhere beyond the darker line of shadow marking the woods encircling the town, I heard a horn blowing.

Below us the Frankish commander raised his spear. *"For God and King Charles!"* he cried. As Tore, Odd, and I drew and fired, the Franks charged, echoing their leader's war cry.

The Franks held their shields high as they ran, and none fell to our first volley of arrows. Before we could shoot again, the front ranks of their warriors crashed into our line, pushing its center back with the sheer weight of their numbers. The wings of our line wrapped forward around the sides of the Franks' wedge, and the Franks' formation and ours merged into a maelstrom of stabbing, hacking warriors, making it impossible to target the Franks' front ranks without endangering our own men. Instead Tore, Odd, and I aimed our arrows at the Frankish warriors milling in the back ranks of their wedge. I ceased to think. It was just focus, draw, and release, then choose another target, arrow after arrow, as quickly as I could find a face showing white beneath its helm, or a bared throat, or a chest or shoulder unprotected by a shield. It was short-range shooting, and our fire was deadly.

"They come upon the rampart!"

Odd had shouted the warning. I turned and looked. A party of Frankish warriors edged toward us from our right, their lead man crouched and holding his shield angled in front, his eyes barely peering over the rim. The warrior behind him carried a bow with an arrow ready on its string.

I was closest to the approaching Franks. "Tore!" I cried, as I knelt so he could fire over me. "I will shoot low at the front man's legs. You aim high."

From behind me, Tore answered, "I am ready. Odd, keep shooting at the Franks below."

"Now!" I called out, and skimmed my arrow low toward the leading Frank's feet. He reached down and caught it with his shield, but when he did, Tore's arrow, launched but a moment after mine, struck his exposed face. His body jerked straight upright, then fell back into the arms of the man behind him, knocking the bow from his grasp.

Swiftly I drew another arrow and readied it on my bow. The second Frank heaved his comrade's body off the rampart. As he did, my arrow found his chest. The third Frank reacted more quickly. No sooner had my shot struck the warrior in front of him, than he shoved the dying man sideways off the wall and charged, pulling his spear back to hurl it as he ran. Shooting from behind me, Tore stuck an arrow through the Frank's thigh. He stumbled, dropped his spear, and clutched desperately at the stone edge of the rampart, but rolled off the wall, screaming. Behind him, the remaining Franks on the rampart turned and fled.

As I stood, something moving out beyond the town walls caught my eye, and I turned and looked. Riders were pouring from the tree line now, racing toward the gate.

Below, Hastein and his men still held the entrance to the tunnel, though barely. Only half of our men still stood, and those had been driven back until they stood shoulder to shoulder just in front of the tunnel's entrance, with Hastein and Torvald anchoring the center of what remained of our line.

The Franks, who had withdrawn a few paces to regroup for their final attack, had abandoned their wedge formation. They now surrounded Hastein and his men in a semicircle, with their leader in their center. As I watched, they began edging forward again, their line bristling with spears and swords.

"Hastein!" I cried. "Ivar comes!" Even as I spoke, a clatter of hooves outside the wall signaled the arrival of the first of our reinforcements. I drew an arrow—the last one in my quiver—and launched it at the Frank's commander.

My shot hit the Frank on the top of the shoulder of his shield arm, but at an angle. The arrow glanced off his mail shirt and thudded harmlessly into the shield of the warrior behind him. The impact of the blow startled him, though, and he turned and looked up at the top of the wall where I stood.

When the Frank's leader turned to look at me, Hastein hurled his spear. It caught the Frank just below his chin and ripped out his throat. The man slumped backward, and the men around him reached out to catch him as he fell.

Hastein jerked his sword from his scabbard and waved it overhead. "With me!" he shouted. "Take them now!" He and Torvald threw themselves against the Franks' center, hewing and stabbing at the hapless warriors holding their fallen leader. The rest of his men followed, roaring their rage and defiance in the face of what had seemed just a moment before to be certain death. Behind them, the first of Ivar's warriors emerged from the tunnel and joined in the attack.

Our reinforcements' arrival—and the death of their leader—broke the Franks' spirit. They turned and ran back up the street, our warriors at their heels, hacking and stabbing. The battle became a slaughter, and moved rapidly away, a trail of

Frankish bodies marking its progress. As the sounds of fighting grew fainter, a new sound—screams of fear—began to fill the night air.

Tore and Odd ran down the stairs leading from the rampart and joined the stream of warriors pouring from the tunnel's mouth into the town. Tore called back to me over his shoulder as he reached the ground. "Come, Halfdan. The richest plunder is taken first!"

I followed them down the stairs, but, by the time I reached the bottom, I realized I had neither strength nor will to join in the sack of Ruda. A wave of weariness washed over me, and I slumped down onto the bottom step, staring at the dead and wounded who littered the ground before me. I had survived.

Wulf emerged from the shadows and tugged at my sleeve, an anxious expression on his face.

"We must go," he said. I looked at him uncomprehendingly. "My family," he explained. "Your jarl said you and the other warrior, the one with the chest like a barrel, would come with me and protect my family. The other man has gone with the battle, but you must come. The looting has already begun."

I sighed. "I will come," I said. "But first I must retrieve some arrows. I will do you little good if I have none."

I prowled among the dead and wounded, searching for my arrows. My bow was strong, with a heavy draw, and most that had hit their targets had sunk deep. It was grisly work. Even when they were undamaged, it took hard pulling and sometimes cutting to free the shafts from the bodies of their victims.

Thrice I found arrows embedded in Franks who still lived. The first time it happened, I drew my dagger and approached the wounded man cautiously. He was whimpering and clutching at the arrow sticking out of his chest. He coughed, causing blood to trickle from his mouth, and looked up at me with pleading eyes. If he had been a wounded deer, I would have cut his throat and thought little of it. He was a man, though, and I found I could not kill him as he lay there helpless. I left my arrow in him and moved on.

Wulf followed me around the battlefield, wringing his hands and urging me to make haste. While we were searching, Ivar strode out of the tunnel's mouth, surrounded by a heavily armed group of his housecarls. Seeing me, he called out. "You are Hastein's man, are you not—the young hunter? How goes the battle?"

"The Franks broke and fled," I said. "Hastein's ruse succeeded, though once inside the gate, we were hard pressed to hold it until the first of the reinforcements arrived. The *Gull*'s crew will be short many men after this night's fighting."

"Why are you still here if Hastein and the rest of his men are gone?" Ivar asked. "You do not look to be wounded."

The meaning behind Ivar's question seemed clear. He wondered if I was a coward who had fled from the fight. I was too tired to feel offended.

"Hastein ordered me to stay with this Frank. He pledged that we would protect his family in exchange for his help. But first I must recover some of my arrows."

Ivar cocked his head and listened. Sounds of battle, the clash of steel on steel, could no longer be heard. The screams and weeping had swelled, though, till they seemed to fill the night.

"If the Franks ran from the battle here at the gate," Ivar said, "then they are broken, and Ruda is ours. Fear spreads through an army even more swiftly than the plague."

Wulf lived on a narrow side alley not far from the main street leading to the river gate. He cried out in dismay as we approached his house. The door was open, and as we drew nearer I could see it had been kicked in and was hanging from only one hinge.

"We are too late," Wulf cried, and tried to rush

past me. I put my arm out and held him back. "Let me enter first. Wait here and hold my bow." I knew it would be of little use in the close quarters inside.

As I approached the open doorway, I slipped my small-axe from my belt and tightened my grip on the handle of the shield I'd picked up from the battleground. The room beyond the door was dimly lit by a torch someone had carelessly laid on a table, and by the glowing embers of a low fire in a small hearth against the far wall. Two warriors—men I did not recognize, though clearly they were Danes—were in the room, rummaging through Wulf's possessions. They had gathered the corners of a cloak to fashion a makeshift bag in which to carry their plunder. No one else was visible, though behind them, to the right of the hearth, I saw another doorway. From the darkness beyond that door came the soft sound of crying.

Both men turned when I entered the room, and one drew his sword from its scabbard. The warrior with the sword stared at me with cold eyes. He was tall, with long blond hair woven into two plaits that hung below his shoulders, and a mustache that drooped down almost to his chest.

"This house is ours," he said. "Go elsewhere."

"I have been sent by Jarl Hastein," I replied. "I am one of his men. This house belongs to the Frank who helped us gain entry into the town. It and all who live here are under the jarl's protection."

The blond warrior glanced at his companion and flicked his eyes sideways. The second man, who had brown hair and was wearing a jerkin of black fur, stepped back and grasped a spear and shield that were leaning against the wall of the room.

"I am not accustomed to being told what to do by a beardless youth," the blond man said. "I am not inclined to become accustomed to it now."

The man with the spear began edging sideways, so he and his comrade could come at me from different angles. I stuck my axe back in my belt and stepped back through the doorway, reaching my hand out toward Wulf for my bow as I did.

I had felt numb from fatigue in the aftermath of the battle at the gate, but now anger flooded over me.

"You have made two mistakes this night," I told the men who faced me. "Either could cost you your life. Your first mistake was to refuse to leave a house under Jarl Hastein's protection. The jarl gave his word to this Frank. If his oath is broken by your actions, you will have to die to cleanse the stain from his honor.

"Your second mistake was to insult me. While you sat safe atop a horse outside the walls, I was in the fight to win the gate. I have already killed more men this night than you have fingers on your hands. I had thought to kill only Franks, but your arrogance urges me to change my mind. Still, I will give you one more chance. Leave now, taking nothing with you, and I will let you live."

As I backed farther out into the street, I handed my shield to Wulf, drew an arrow from my quiver, and readied it on my bow.

"Wait!" a voice called from inside. The brown-haired man stepped into the doorway. "We did not know this house was under the jarl's protection. I am leaving."

He skulked away down the street. For a few moments there was only silence, then a woman's scream ripped out from inside the house. Wulf gasped and stumbled toward the gaping doorway. "Bertrada!" he cried.

"Stay back," I snapped, and pulled my bow to full draw. "Do not block my view. I can save her. You cannot."

The blond warrior stepped into view, lit by the flickering light of the torch that was burning on the table. He was holding a woman dressed only in a thin white shift. One arm was about her waist, pinning her tightly against his body, and the other held the blade of his sword across her throat.

The blond man laughed. "So this is what the

Frank bargained with the jarl to save? Her and her brats in the other room? Hear me now, boy, if you want her to live. You have offended me. You know not how to talk to your betters. Lay down your bow or I will cut her throat as you watch. You and I will fight man to man, and I will teach you manners before you die."

He watched me, looking for a reaction, with his cold blue eyes. I stared back, unblinking, into them. Into his right eye. And released.

9

THE WAR-KING'S IRE

"Wake up! Men are outside again."

Wulf was shaking me by the shoulders. I knocked his hands aside and staggered to my feet, struggling to remember where I was and what had happened.

Earlier, knowing that other looters would surely come, I had dragged the body outside and positioned it next to the door as a warning. With his legs splayed out in front of him on the ground, and his back against the wall of Wulf's house, the dead man looked almost like someone who had sat down to rest and fallen asleep. Almost. The gaping socket of his ruined eye and the stream of blood that had run down his face and onto his chest told anyone who came close that this man was in the sleep from which no one awakens.

Whenever looters had approached, I'd stood in the doorway, an arrow ready on my bowstring, and warned them away. "This house is under the protection of Jarl Hastein," I'd told them. "Pass it by." Some looked at the body and muttered angrily, but no one had challenged me.

As dawn approached and the street gradually filled with gray light, men passed the house less and less frequently. Finally, as the first rays of the sun lit the rooftops, I could no longer see anyone, Frank or Dane, moving through the town. The sounds of shouting, laughter, and screaming had tapered off, too. Even looters must eventually tire, and when they do, their victims find some respite.

I'd found myself unable to stay awake. "Wake me if anyone comes," I told Wulf, and curled myself in a ball in a corner of the front room of his house.

Wulf had taken me at my word. Three times earlier he'd shaken me awake, and I had resumed my position in the doorway. Each time it had been harder and harder to force myself out of my exhausted sleep. Fortunately, the men who'd passed had been stragglers, wandering aimlessly through the captured town, and had shown little interest in the house or the dead man.

This time was different. As I rubbed my eyes, trying to wipe the blurriness from them, I heard

angry voices outside. I snatched my bow up from
the floor and readied an arrow on it as I edged up
to the open doorway and peered out.

"There he is! There is the man who murdered
Sigvid!"

It was the brown-haired looter, the comrade of
the man I'd killed. He was pointing at me and talking to a group of men standing in the street in
front of Wulf's house. They were all wearing helms
and bearing shields and looked angry and eager for
a fight.

"Stay back!" I shouted. "This house is under
the protection of Jarl Hastein. He has sworn that
all who live here will be safe. I will kill any man
who acts to break the jarl's oath."

A stocky warrior with traces of gray in his
beard, one of the few in the crowd who was wearing a mail brynie, stepped forward.

"Who are you," he demanded, "that claims to
speak for Jarl Hastein?"

"My name is Halfdan," I replied. "I am one of
the jarl's housecarls."

The warrior stared at me silently for a few
moments. "You look very young," he finally said,
"to be in the service of the jarl. His housecarls are
all experienced warriors and chosen men."

I shrugged. I could not change my age or my
looks. These men could believe me or no. "I serve

the jarl," I told them. "I am here at his command."

The gray-bearded warrior pointed at the corpse.

"That man's name is Sigvid. He was a member of my crew and from my village. Are you claiming that the jarl ordered you to kill a fellow Dane?"

"I told your man that this house is under Jarl Hastein's protection, but he refused to leave and threatened to kill the wife of the Frank who lives here. Had I not stopped him, the jarl's oath would have been broken."

The brown-haired looter spat on the ground. "We did not come here to talk," he snapped. "Sigvid was our comrade. We came to avenge his death." The men standing around him nodded their heads and muttered their agreement.

"I have been ordered to defend this house," I repeated. "I will not allow you to enter it. There may be enough of you to kill me, but I will not die alone." I backed deeper into the room and raised my bow.

"Hold!" the gray-bearded warrior shouted, and turned to face his men. "I am still captain here. I will decide whether we fight or not. Or do any among you wish to challenge that?"

No one answered. The brown-haired man looked away.

The captain pointed back over his shoulder at me.

"This warrior claims he is a housecarl serving Jarl Hastein, and was following the jarl's orders. What if he speaks true? If you slay him, will the jarl not be angered? Will he not avenge the killing of his own man?"

"How will he know?" the brown-haired warrior said. "How will the jarl know we killed him? I will not tell him."

"I will not conceal a killing," the captain answered. "That is the work of a Nithing. We are not murderers who skulk in the dark and kill when no one sees. I must know the truth before we act." He turned back to face me.

"This matter is not over," he said. "We will find the jarl and learn whether you are truly his man. But whether you serve Jarl Hastein or no, I do not believe you should have killed Sigvid. My name is Gunulf. Remember it. You will hear from me again."

Pointing at the dead man's body, he spoke again to his men. "Bring Sigvid. He was our comrade. It is our duty to bury him."

Torvald and Tore found me in the afternoon.

"We have been searching the town for Wulf's house," Torvald said. "You have stirred up trouble.

We are to bring you before Ragnar at the palace of the Count of Ruda."

"Will Hastein be there?" I asked.

"Yes," Torvald replied. "And Ivar and most of the captains. The fleet has been brought upriver to Ruda."

"You have been accused of murder," Tore said. "Is it true?"

Tore's question infuriated me. It was his fault I was in this predicament. Had I truly been a murderer, at that moment he would have been at risk. I ignored him and spoke to Torvald.

"Someone must guard Wulf and his family if I am to leave. Hastein promised they would be protected. He entrusted their safety to me. And to Tore," I added, glaring at him.

Torvald looked over at Tore and smiled. Tore's face flushed red. "Do not expect *me* to stay here playing nursemaid to a Frank and his family," he blustered.

I turned on him. "It is your *duty*," I snapped. "Jarl Hastein ordered you to protect them, as he did me. If you had remembered last night, I might not have had to kill the man."

"So it is true," Torvald said, shaking his head. "You did kill one of our warriors."

"It was not murder," I told him. "I had no choice."

"You will have to convince Ragnar of that," he replied.

The Count of Ruda had fled the town as soon as he'd learned Northmen had broken through the town's gate. His palace, which Torvald led me to, was the largest building I had ever seen. We entered through massive double doors of oak, crossed a huge entry hall that our army had already converted into a stable for its captured horses, and climbed a broad, winding staircase of stone. At its top was a second level as large as the first, also constructed entirely of stone. I could not understand how its weight did not cause it to collapse onto the level below.

We entered a long open room illuminated by the afternoon sun shining in through tall windows. A narrow table stretched across one end. Hastein, Ivar, and some other warriors—chieftains all, I suspected, since Hastein's captains Stig and Svein were among them—were also seated at the table or talking in small groups scattered across the room.

Ragnar was pacing back and forth in front of the table. His raven was perched on his left shoulder.

"Do any of you know how many warriors we lost in the attack?" Ragnar was asking as we drew near. "Do any of you know?"

No one answered. Ivar looked bored and

picked his teeth with the nail of his little finger. Hastein appeared to be giving all of his attention to two bolts of cloth spread out on the table in front of him.

"Ah, Torvald," he said, looking up as we approached. "You are back, and you found Halfdan. Excellent. Look what Stig took from a merchant's storehouse last night. These are silk. I bought them from him."

One roll of fabric was a brilliant crimson and the other a deep blue. "These colors are very fine, don't you think?" he continued. "I am going to have two new tunics made from them."

Ragnar ignored Hastein.

"I know how many died," he said. "I know, because I am the war-king of this army, and I am responsible for it. Twenty-seven of our warriors died, and fifteen more have serious wounds."

"It was a remarkable victory," Ivar volunteered. "Hastein's plan was clever and worked well."

"The crew of the *Gull* paid a heavy price for it, though," Hastein said. "Eight of the dead are my men, as are four of the wounded."

Ivar shrugged. "Men vie for the chance to sail with you because you are bold. They know there is often great risk, but there is also greater chance for glory."

I thought Ivar's words sounded callous. How

many of the dead had wives who were now widows, or children left with no father? These were men who'd served Hastein with loyalty and courage. I did not believe he would so easily dismiss their deaths.

Hastein turned to me and spoke. "Halfdan," he said, "you can speak the Franks' tongue. Before you leave the palace this afternoon, I want you to question the count's servants and slaves. Ask who among them sewed the garments for the Count of Ruda. I shall have the same person make my new tunics."

"A remarkable victory?" Ragnar said to Ivar. His voice had a dangerous edge. "I'll tell you what was remarkable about it. Of our twenty-seven dead, only fifteen died during battle with the Franks. Seven more were cut down from behind while they were too busy looting and raping to even see the Franks who killed them. And five were murdered by our own men, their comrades, in arguments over plunder or women."

As he said this last comment, Ragnar turned and glared at me. I swallowed nervously and looked at Hastein, but he was busy examining the bolts of cloth. Did he not know what I was accused of?

Ragnar waved his arms at the walls of the huge room we were standing in.

"Look at this palace. Look at the walls of this town. Wondrous structures, constructed all of stone. The Romans built them many hundreds of years ago, yet still they stand, grander by far than any longhouse or palace of our greatest leaders. And these same Romans conquered countless kingdoms and peoples. For a time they ruled the world."

Ragnar paused in his pacing, and turned to face Hastein and Ivar.

"What do you think the Romans possessed that we do not?" he demanded. "Does anyone know? Do any of you care?"

Ivar looked around at the huge room's walls and high ceiling. "Many slaves?" he suggested. "It would take the labor of hundreds of thralls to build such structures as these."

"Discipline!" Ragnar shouted. The raven on his shoulder squawked and flapped its wings at the noise. "The Romans possessed discipline. Our army does not. Even before this town was cleared of Frankish troops, our warriors scattered and began looting. It was fortunate the Franks did not regroup and counterattack. Our men's greed was so strong, some killed their own comrades over plunder. But I suppose that should be no surprise," he added, "when even the greatest of my leaders is more interested in preening like a peacock than in enforcing discipline among our warriors."

"I, too, know something of the Romans," Hastein said. "Their soldiers were little more than thralls who were forced to serve in their armies for years—or until they died. We are not Romans. We are Danes. Our warriors are all free men. Each chose of his own free will to risk all and come to fight with this army deep within the land of the Franks. You know as well as I that they did not come here to avenge some ancient wrong the Franks committed against our people. They have come because they hope to better themselves and their families, and because they hope to win wealth that could never be theirs if they stayed at home on their farms."

"You make looting sound like a noble thing," Ivar said.

I was shocked at Hastein's words. He'd told us, on the shore that night below the king's long-house, that we were warring against the Franks to make our homeland safer. Did he not truly believe so? Were we really just attacking the Franks for personal gain?

"I think you make us sound as though we are no better than the cattle-raiding Irish chieftains who call themselves kings and spin heroic tales about stealing sheep," Ragnar said. "The Irish do nothing, and console themselves with glorious tales about it. The Romans conquered the world, and their exploits live on in legend and in these monuments of stone. We, too, could win an empire. Man for man, no warriors can match ours. Yet our people will never be great if they do not learn discipline."

"And if we *did* win an empire, I wonder who would rule it?" Ivar asked. "Perhaps the war-king who led the conquering army?"

"You carry your insolence too far," Ragnar snapped. "Were you not my son . . ."

"Yes," Ivar said, nodding and leaning forward in his seat. "And were you not my father . . ."

"Enough!" Hastein said. "We are the leaders of this army. We must not fight among ourselves. After all, Ragnar," he added, smirking, "it would be undisciplined to do so, and would set a bad example for the men."

Ivar gave a harsh laugh and slouched back in his chair. Hastein ignored him and continued.

"Do not try to make us what we are not, Ragnar. This day we are the victors. Why are you dissatisfied? What is it that you want?"

"We have brought a great army deep into the homeland of the Franks," Ragnar replied. "We have a chance to wound them in their heart. I do not want to plunder a few of their churches and towns, steal a few of their women, and be gone. I want the Franks to long remember this year as an axe-age, a sword-age, as a time of the wolf. I want them to so fear the might of the Danes that they will never again dare to attack our lands. We cannot do this, though, if we waste our strength. We cannot tolerate our warriors killing each other. We must bring discipline to the army now."

At least Ragnar had not forgotten why we were here. But his last words worried me.

"What do you propose?" Hastein asked.

"We must make an example. We must show our warriors that we will not tolerate them killing each other. We should hang someone. That will put a stop to it."

I did not like the turn this argument had taken.

"Do we know who the killers are?" Ivar asked.

"Not all of them," Ragnar answered. "Four of our dead were killed by other Danes, according to their comrades, but the killers fled and were not recognized. We know who one killer is, though. And I think one is enough. If we hang one man as an example, all in the army will know and take heed."

"This talk of hanging is premature. You are assuming the killing was murder," Hastein said. "We do not know that it was."

"It was a Dane killing a Dane," Ragnar answered. "We cannot afford to lose warriors this way."

"We cannot just hang someone," Hastein protested. "A case must be presented and proved."

"We do not have the time to waste on that!" Ragnar exclaimed.

"Perhaps Father is right," Ivar said. "It is just one man, after all, and we are at war and in a foreign land. Perhaps making an example would be a good thing. Who is the killer, anyway?"

"It is one of my men," Hastein replied. "It is Halfdan, who stands here in front of you."

Ivar turned and looked at me. "Ah," he said to Hastein. "Now I understand your sudden respect for the law."

Hastein pushed his chair away from the table and rose. "If you would execute one of my men for murder, the case must be heard and judged properly. We chose you to be war-king of our army. That is all. I did not agree to give you the power of life or death over my men. They would not follow me if I did. You must follow the law."

By now Ragnar's face had turned a dark red. The raven on his shoulder squawked nervously and pecked at his ear. He cursed and swatted at it, and it screeched in protest.

"The Franks do not need to attack us," he said. "They need only wait, and we will tear our army apart from within. We are little more than a rabble. We do not deserve greatness."

"We are free men," Hastein replied. "We do not give our kings absolute power. Even they must obey our laws. That is our greatness, and we will not surrender it."

Hastein and Ragnar stood glaring at each other. I feared that if the argument continued, they might come to blows. I feared our entire campaign against the Franks might collapse right here . . . and it would be my fault.

"I did not murder anyone," I blurted out. "There is no need to argue. Even Ragnar, when he hears the facts, will agree it was not murder."

As soon as I spoke those last words, I wished I could take them back. In his current state of rage, I suspected Ragnar would be happy to kill anyone at all, for almost any reason, and hanging me would satisfy that need nicely.

Ragnar, Ivar, and Hastein all turned and looked at me. It was Ivar who spoke.

"Well then," he said. "Let us hear the facts."

Ragnar turned to a small group of men standing in one corner of the hall. "Gunulf," he cried. "You and your man come forward."

Gunulf, the gray-bearded chieftain I'd confronted at Wulf's house that morning, walked forward until he stood beside me in front of the long table. With him was the brown-haired warrior.

"Tell Jarl Hastein and the rest of the captains

why you have come," Ragnar said.

"I have come because this boy," Gunulf said, pointing at me with his thumb, "murdered Sigvid, one of my men. He claims he is one of your followers," he added, looking at Hastein.

Hastein turned his head and looked at me for a moment, then faced Gunulf and spoke.

"Indeed he is one of my followers," he said. His voice was soft at first, but grew louder as he continued. "And despite his youthful appearance, he is not a boy. He is a warrior. He was with me when my men and I won the gates of Ruda for our army, and he fought well. Why do you accuse him of murder? I hope you are not wasting the war-king's time and mine with a baseless accusation."

I felt pleased at Hastein's words, but surprised by the tone with which he'd spoken them. Chieftains tend to be proud men, quick to feel their dignity has been insulted. From the color rising on Gunulf's face, it was obvious he had taken offense. His anger caused him to press his accusation even more hotly against me.

"It was murder!" Gunulf retorted. "Cowardly murder. He shot my man down with a bow."

"We are waiting to hear the facts," Ivar said. Gunulf glared at him, took a deep breath, then continued.

"I and half my crew, including Sigvid, were among the mounted force you led against Ruda last night. By the time we arrived and made our way through the gate . . ."

"A gate which I and my warriors, including Halfdan here, captured while you were waiting safely downstream," Hastein interjected.

"Let him finish," Ragnar snapped.

Gunulf continued. "By the time we entered the town, the battle at the gate was over, and from the sounds there was only scattered fighting continuing about the town. My crew scattered to find plunder."

"It sounds like a lack of discipline to me," Ivar said sardonically. Ragnar glared at him.

"Did you see Halfdan kill your man Sigvid?" Hastein asked.

Gunulf shook his head. "I was not with Sigvid last night after the looting began."

Ivar rolled his eyes. "You did not witness the killing?" he asked. "Where are your facts to support an accusation of murder?"

"I did not see it, but this warrior did," Gunulf said, indicating the brown-haired man standing at his side. "Stenkil here found me this morning and told me Sigvid was dead—killed by another Dane. Stenkil led me to a house in the town and we found Sigvid's body there, out in the street. This one"— Gunulf pointed at me—"was there. I asked him if he'd killed Sigvid, and he boasted that he had. As Sigvid's chieftain, I demand that this warrior be punished, and wergild be paid, that I may take it back to Sigvid's family."

Ragnar turned to Hastein. "You see? Your man admitted it. We need waste no more time on this. Send someone to fetch a rope."

"Killing is not always murder," Hastein said to Ragnar. "I have killed many men, but have murdered none. Nothing Gunulf has told us proves Halfdan murdered Sigvid."

Hastein turned a cold stare toward Stenkil. "Your chieftain says you saw the killing. Tell us your tale, that we may judge it."

Stenkil told Ragnar what had occurred the night before. To my surprise, his account was more truthful than not—he admitted I'd told him and Sigvid that the house was under Hastein's protection, and that I'd ordered them to leave.

"I did leave," he said, "but Sigvid remained behind."

"The words of this youth persuaded you to leave?" Ragnar asked, sounding surprised. Ivar, who seemed quick to see cowardice in other men, was looking at Stenkil with disgust.

"He was threatening to shoot us with his bow."

"If you left, then you did not see the killing, did you?" Hastein demanded. "You do not know how it occurred."

"No," Stenkil admitted. "I did not see the killing. But later that night I passed by the house again and saw Sigvid's body outside. And this boy admitted to Gunulf this morning that he'd killed him."

Hastein looked at Ragnar. "We have heard no evidence of murder," he said. "Do you still believe we should hang Halfdan?"

Ragnar glared at Hastein, then turned to face me. "Do you have anything to say?" he demanded.

"I admit that I killed Sigvid," I said, "but I did not murder him. Jarl Hastein gave his oath of honor to the Frankish sea captain that if Wulf helped us gain entry into the town, he and his family would be protected. I was only following my captain's orders."

"How did the killing occur?" Ragnar asked.

"Sigvid told me he would kill Wulf's wife unless I laid down my bow and fought him hand to hand. He was holding his sword to her throat when he made the threat."

"Why didn't you fight him?" Ivar demanded. "Were you afraid of him?"

"No. I was not afraid, but I was not certain I could defeat him, either, fighting hand to hand," I answered. "I knew I had to protect Jarl Hastein's oath to Wulf. I did what I had to do to uphold the jarl's honor. Had I chosen to fight Sigvid, I would have been placing my own pride before my duty to the jarl."

Ivar slouched back in his chair, an amused look on his face. "I see," he said, nodding his head. "You killed Sigvid because it was the surest way to obey an order your captain had given you." He turned and looked at Ragnar. "This sounds to me like the act of a disciplined warrior. Would you not agree, Father? Surely you do not want to punish such discipline and obedience? Think of the message it would send to our army."

For a moment Ragnar looked as if he would retort angrily. Then he let his breath out in a long sigh and nodded his head.

"You are right," he said to Hastein. "This was not murder." He waved his hand at me. "Go," he said. "You are quick to kill—perhaps too quick—but in this instance you have done no wrong."

Gunulf looked indignant. "What of Sigvid's family?" he demanded.

"Halfdan did no wrong, but he did kill your man," Hastein said. "I will pay the wergild, and you will take it to his family."

Ragnar waved his hand again. "So be it," he said.

"My men will not like this," Gunulf said. "Sigvid was their comrade."

"I do not care if they like it," Hastein replied.

"The matter is settled. Our war-king has agreed, as you have heard. If any of your men break the peace over this now, they risk his wrath, and mine."

I turned to leave. Hastein called after me. "Halfdan, do not forget to question the servants." I looked back at him, confused.

"The Count of Ruda's servants," he explained, and pointed at the bolts of silk on the table in front of him. "Ask them who sewed his clothes. For my tunics."

Torvald walked with me back to Wulf's house. I was silent for a while, mulling over what had happened. Torvald seemed content, for once, to walk in silence, too.

Finally I spoke. "Why does Ragnar have such a hatred for the Franks?" I asked.

Torvald looked surprised. "He does not," he said. "They are our foes. He is our war-king. He wishes our army to win, and theirs to lose."

"I thought he seemed filled with anger today," I said. "Anger at Hastein. Anger at Ivar. And anger at the Franks. It sounded as though he does not merely wish to defeat them; he wishes to destroy them."

"Ragnar is always filled with anger," Torvald said. "It is just his way. He is of royal blood, and all men know he is the greatest war leader among the

Danes. It eats at him that Horik is king and he is not, for he does not believe Horik is the better man. But Ragnar is above all else a man of honor, and when Horik was acclaimed our king upon the death of his father, Ragnar swore an oath to accept and honor him. He will not break his word, no matter how great his ambition. Ragnar would rather be a king without a throne than a man without honor."

I, too, had once felt a desire that had gnawed at my spirit, and poisoned my heart. I had been a slave, and had longed to be free—and a warrior. I finally found my dream, though, or it found me. I wondered if Ragnar would ever find his kingdom.

10

BLOOD OR ALE

Three days after we took Ruda, Torvald came to Wulf's house again looking for me.

"Bjorn Ironsides is coming," he said, "with the rest of our fleet from the Limfjord. One of our raiding parties saw them and sent a rider back to report to Ragnar. He and Hastein are on their way now to the river gate to greet them when they arrive. I am going down to watch. Do you wish to come?"

I did, but Hastein had ordered me to protect Wulf and his family, and he had never released me from the order. How long would I have to guard them? I'd never been responsible for the safety of others before, and the duty was weighing heavily on me. I'd grown tired of Wulf, tired of his family, and tired of being cooped up in his small, airless house. I had not left it for even a moment since I'd returned from the palace two days earlier. Why wasn't Tore sharing this duty?

I watched with regret as Torvald strode off down the street, his long legs quickly carrying him out of sight. Then I turned back from the doorway into the dim interior of Wulf's house.

Bertrada, Wulf's wife, was bending over an iron pot slung over the low fire in the hearth, beginning her preparations for the evening meal. The firelight shone on her face, and as I watched, a strand of her shiny, dark hair slipped out from under her cap and dangled in front of her eyes. She tucked it back under her cap, annoyed. In the three days I'd spent in her home, I had never seen her smile. Her oldest child, a girl of nine named Adela, knelt on the floor near the hearth. She rarely ventured far from her mother's side, and occasionally I caught her staring at me with a frightened expression in her eyes.

Wulf was seated at the small table with his youngest child, an infant, in his lap. Like the rest of his family, he had not left the house since the night Ruda had fallen.

"Ale," I said to Bertrada. "May I have some ale? I am thirsty."

Bertrada stood up straight, looked at me fearfully, then glanced nervously over at Wulf. I cursed, remembering that unlike Wulf, she did not understand the tongue of the northern folk.

I felt a sudden surge of anger. I had saved her life, and probably her children's, too, yet they were afraid of me. What sort of gratitude was this? *"Ale,"* I snapped, this time in Latin. *"I want ale."*

Wulf looked up, hearing the tone of my voice.

"Bertrada," he said, speaking over his shoulder to her, *"pour a cup of ale for Halfdan."*

"You wish me gone, don't you?" I said to him. "Gone or dead."

"You are a Dane," he replied angrily. "Would you expect sheep to welcome the wolves into their fold?"

Bertrada set an earthenware cup filled with ale on the edge of the table, then backed away from me. I took a swallow. It was a weak brew that tasted like it had been mixed with water. Was this the best Wulf's household could offer, or was it special fare they'd prepared for their uninvited guest?

I could feel anger welling up in me. I tried to quell it, though it was as difficult to force down as Wulf's bad ale. Perhaps if we got to know each other better, he could come to see me as a man— not just as a Dane.

"Your wife is much younger than you are," I

said to Wulf, trying to make conversation. "And your children are young, too, for a man whose beard is as grizzled as yours."

"She is my second wife," Wulf answered. "And only the baby is my child. Bertrada's first husband was killed the last time the Danes took Ruda. He was one of the Count of Ruda's soldiers. I lost my first wife then, too, and our two daughters. They were both older than Adela."

"Your wife and daughters were killed?"

"I did not say that. I said I lost them. The Danes took them. Had I been here, perhaps I could have ransomed them back. But I was away at Dorestad. By the time I returned, the Danes had left the town."

No doubt Wulf's family had been sold as slaves. It was no wonder the man's heart was so filled with anger toward Danes.

"I was not with the fleet that captured Ruda before," I told him.

"You are a Dane," he sneered.

And he was a Frank. Should I hate him for what his forefathers had done when they'd attacked *our* land? I'd had enough. I needed to be with people who did not despise me. I walked over to the corner where I'd made a makeshift bed, and picked up my small-axe from the pile of my weapons and gear.

"What are you doing?" Wulf asked. I could hear the fear in his voice. Did he think I was going to murder them? I stuck the axe in my belt, next to my dagger, and turned back to him.

"I am going out," I said. "Do not touch my things. I will be back later."

"You are leaving? Who will protect us?"

"That seems a strange question for the sheep to ask a wolf," I replied. "Bar the door when I leave, and protect yourselves."

I caught up with Torvald as he was walking down the last stretch of street leading to the river gate. This was where the Frankish cavalry had formed, and Tore, Odd, and I had shot their horses down. The only signs now that a battle had been fought here were some dark stains on the road.

"I thought you were not coming," Torvald said.

"I changed my mind."

He turned and looked down at me. "You are angry," he said.

It irritated me that he could tell. "I am not," I retorted. "Why do you say that?"

"The look on your face gives it away. That, and the sound of your voice."

We walked on in silence for a few moments, then Torvald spoke again.

"Blood or ale."

"What?" I asked.

"Blood or ale," he repeated. "It is how I deal with anger. It is not good for me to hold anger in. When I do, it is like having a splinter so deep I cannot get it out, that festers and generates poison. It clouds my thoughts and constipates my bowels."

I was unsure whether Torvald meant that anger or splinters had the latter effect on him, but I was grateful neither caused the same effect on me.

"What do blood and ale have to do with it?" I asked.

"I am an easygoing man," Torvald explained. "It usually is difficult for someone to anger me. But if another does manage to, I rid myself of the anger by spilling his blood."

"And the ale?"

"Sometimes it is not possible to purge my anger with blood. Occasionally, for instance, Hastein angers me. I cannot shed his blood, for he is my friend and my jarl. Instead, I drink. Ale affects my anger like water poured on a flame. After enough, I almost always feel better. Who has angered you?"

I shook my head. "I am just angry," I said. "At Wulf, at his family, at Tore—even at Hastein."

"Clearly blood cannot purge this anger. I think you need ale," Torvald said.

As we approached the opening of the tunnel leading through the wall to the river gate, I saw that at the far end the gate was standing open. Three guards—Danes, of course—stood watch over it from the rampart above.

I had not been back to the river since the night we'd attacked the town. In three days, the area outside the walls had been transformed. Just upstream, a long island, curved along one side and straight on the other like a strung bow, split the river into two channels. Most of the ships of our fleet were moored along its banks, and tents crowded the interior. A number of ships' small-boats were tied up at the downstream end of the island, and as I watched, one pushed off and headed toward the quay in front of the river gate.

A few ships, among them the *Gull* and Ragnar's black *Raven*, were moored along the riverbank below the town wall. No encampments for the crews of these ships had been set up, though their sails had been tented above their decks. To complete our army's transformation of Ruda into a military stronghold, deep defensive ditches extending from the town wall to the water's edge had been dug to protect the quay area, and our ships moored there, from attack. The rock and soil removed to create the ditches was being shaped into an earthen wall on the inside perimeter of each ditch by Franks from the town, laboring under the watchful eyes of armed Danish guards.

"The island looks a more comfortable place to camp," I remarked. "Why is our ship moored on this side, and why do we have no encampment?"

"Only a few of the leaders' ships are moored here," Torvald explained. "Ragnar's, Hastein's, Ivar's, and a few others. Most of the men from these ships are staying in the count's palace. We are the new garrison of Ruda. Only a small guard is staying aboard the ships." Torvald grinned. "Tore is in charge of guarding the *Gull*. It is his punishment for not helping you protect Wulf and his family on the night the town fell."

I was pleased to learn that Hastein had realized Tore had ignored his order. I suspected, though, that being punished would strain relations between Tore and me even further.

"Look," Torvald said. "They come."

A longship appeared from around the bend in the river below Ruda, its oars rising and falling in a steady rhythm. Two long red horns jutted above the gold-painted carved head decorating the stempost in the bow. A moment later, more ships rounded the bend behind it, moving up the river two abreast.

"It is the *Golden Bull*," Torvald said. "Bjorn's ship."

While Bjorn and the new arrivals made their way to the shore below the town wall, Torvald and I boarded the *Gull*. "There will be ale here," Torvald assured me. "Hastein sent a cask out from the town for Tore and the others standing guard duty." He was correct. A keg was propped up on the raised stern deck. Tore, who had obviously been sampling its contents, was propped up beside it.

"Did Hastein send you?" Tore asked Torvald, his voice a bit slurred. "Am I being relieved?"

"Yes," Torvald assured him, nodding his head vigorously. "He did send me, and Halfdan, too. He wanted us to sample the ale and make certain it was of decent quality, since you will be here for a long while."

Torvald and I filled a cup and passed it back and forth between us. It took us several refillings to fully evaluate the quality of the rich brown drink. It was far stronger than what Wulf had offered me. Some Franks, at least, understood how to brew good ale.

"You were right," I told Torvald, and burped. "I do feel better now."

"I heard that Ragnar wanted to hang you," Tore said. He, too, was continuing to assess the quality of the ale. It seemed to have mellowed his usually prickly disposition. I was glad. I'd expected him to be angry about the way I had spoken to him the last time we'd met, but he seemed to have forgotten about it—or washed it from his mind with drink.

"Only for a little while," I assured him. "Once he became satisfied that I am a disciplined warrior, he changed his mind."

Tore nodded, looking a little confused, and refilled his cup and mine.

By now a crowd of warriors had disembarked from the arriving longships and was milling around on the narrow strip of land between the town's wall and the river.

"Look," Torvald said, pointing at the gate. "Here come Hastein and Ragnar. Ivar is with them, too." He strode down the deck toward the bow. Tore and I followed more slowly, walking carefully to avoid spilling our brimming cups.

"Well met, brother. How was your journey from the Limfjord?" Ivar was saying as we reached the bow. He, Ragnar, and Hastein were not far from where the bow of the *Gull* rested against bank of the river.

Bjorn was standing in front of them, hands on his hips, staring at the walls of Ruda. The growing crowd of warriors from the newly arrived ships had gathered behind him. I would not have guessed

Bjorn and Ivar were brothers. Where Ivar was tall and lean of body and face like their father, Bjorn was of only average height, with a thick chest, heavy shoulders, and a belly that bulged out below as if he was trying to conceal a small keg of ale beneath his tunic.

"I've had worse journeys, but better ones, too," Bjorn replied. "We were slowed by contrary winds, and were hit hard by a storm off the coast of Frisia. We lost one ship, but managed to rescue more than half her crew."

"How many ships did you bring me?" Ragnar asked.

"Twenty-nine," Bjorn answered. "Including mine. By the Gods, these walls are high. How did you take the town?"

"A ruse," Ivar said. "It was Hastein's idea."

Bjorn grinned and clapped his hand on Hastein's shoulder. "You always were a clever one," he said.

About twenty of the men standing behind Bjorn turned away and headed for the gate. Hastein and Ragnar exchanged glances.

"Hold," Ragnar called. "Do not enter the town."

"Why should they not?" Bjorn asked. "These men have been long at sea and are ready to feel dry land underfoot, and a roof overhead. And we are also ready for the Franks to share some of their wealth with us. We did not stop to raid along the way."

"That is probably just as well," Ivar said. "I doubt our raiding parties left much downriver from here for you to find."

"Our army is encamped on the island," Ragnar told Bjorn. "Move your ships and men there. The town was looted the night we took it, but it is calm again now. I wish to keep it that way, for we may be based here for a while. The town will be easier to hold if its folk are left in peace."

Ragnar's decision was clearly unpopular with the newly arrived warriors. A low rumbling noise, indistinct like distant thunder, began to swell as they grumbled to each other.

A voice from somewhere in the crowd shouted, "I thought we came here to harry the Franks, not to protect them."

"Who said that?" Ragnar snapped. No one answered, but a dozen voices growled their agreement with the sentiment.

"Bjorn, control your men," Hastein murmured.

"These are not my men," he replied. "I merely led them here. And in truth, I do not think their feelings are unjust."

Ragnar raised his voice and addressed the

crowd of warriors. "This is a large and rich kingdom," he said. "No army has attacked its interior
for hundreds of years. There will be more than
enough plunder for all."

"When?" someone shouted, interrupting him.
By the sound of it, it was the same man who had
shouted before.

"I see him," Torvald said, pointing. "Skulking
over there. I do not think a man should hide his
face that way when he is addressing his betters."
He rested a hand on the top strake of the hull and
vaulted over the side, landing between two warriors standing on the shore below. They staggered
back, startled to have a giant suddenly appear in
their midst.

Torvald looked back at Tore and me. "Aren't
you coming?" he asked, then turned and began
pushing his way through the crowd.

"You must have patience," Ragnar roared.
"Patience and discipline."

I carefully set my cup of ale down on the deck
and climbed up onto the top strake, balancing
myself with one hand on the neck of the *Gull*'s
carved dragon head while I looked for a clear
space to land. As he staggered forward to follow,
Tore's foot hit my cup and sent it flying. The ale
in it sprayed us both, and the cup bounced off
the ship's side, clattering across the deck. Tore

cursed and lunged in a vain attempt to catch it. When he did, he lost his balance and stumbled, hitting me in the back of my knees with his shoulder.

For one horrified moment I stood there, both arms flailing wildly as I tried to regain my balance, then I pitched forward off the bow. A tall, black-haired warrior was right below me, looking up. He must have turned around to see where Torvald had come from. I hit him full-on, my knees against his chest and his face in my belly, and we fell together to the ground and lay there for a moment, him on his back and me facedown across him. He was more stunned by the impact than I, though, for although I quickly regained my senses enough to raise myself up on my hands and knees, he continued to lie there, his mouth opening and closing soundlessly as he struggled to recover the breath I'd knocked out of him.

He was a truly ugly man, with a big, hooked nose and a coarse, wild beard that looked as if small animals might live in it. A long scar ran diagonally across his face from one side to the other, making a deep furrow through his left eyebrow and down his cheek, leaving a ragged gap in his mustache where it crossed his lip below his nose. His upper front teeth were missing and his left eye, the one the scar crossed, was a milky white.

I realized with a shock that I knew him. I scrambled to my feet. When I did, he pushed himself to a sitting position, coughing. "Murderer!" I shouted, and kicked him in the face, knocking him flat again. I threw myself back onto him, straddling his chest, and began choking him and pounding the back of his head against the earth.

Hands grabbed me and dragged me off, flinging me sideways onto the ground. Men crowded in, kicking and punching. I grabbed someone's belt and pulled myself back up to my knees, but a fist smashed into the side of my head, knocking my grip on the belt loose and making my vision blur. The fist hit me again and I fell forward onto my stomach. Someone stepped on the back of my head, grinding my face into the dirt, then two men grabbed my arms, dragged me to my feet, and turned me around. The man I'd attacked was standing in front of me, a long, wide-bladed seax in his hand.

"I have been looking for you, boy," he said. "For a long time now. I heard a youth had joined Jarl Hastein's followers and hoped it might be you. I never dreamed you'd come to me and make it this easy, though. Toke has promised a rich reward for proof that you are dead."

I heard a roar like an angry bear, and Tore threw himself off the bow of the *Gull* and crashed into the back of one of the men who held me, breaking the man's grip on my arm. As he and Tore fell to the ground I turned and kneed the other man holding me in the crotch.

"Halfdan! Behind you!" Torvald shouted the warning.

I grabbed the shoulders of the man I'd just kneed and spun around, swinging him in front of me as I did. The one-eyed man was lunging with his seax as I turned, and its blade stuck into the side of the man I was holding.

Hastein and Ivar pushed through the circle of men around me, their swords drawn. The one-eyed man backed away, and I pushed the man I was holding after him. He took a few steps then sat down heavily, clutching at his groin with one hand and his wounded side with the other.

Hastein looked furious. "You have much explaining to do," he snapped, glaring at me.

Ragnar appeared, shoving men out of his way with both hands. His face was an even deeper red than it had been at our last meeting. When he saw me, he stopped, and his mouth fell open.

"You! Again?" he shouted. His eyes darted wildly from side to side, as if searching among the crowd for a rope to hang me with on the spot.

I looked at Hastein with alarm, then pointed at the one-eyed man.

"Hastein," I pleaded. "He is Toke's helmsman. His name is Snorre."

"What is he babbling about?" Ragnar demanded.

"This man helped kill my brother," I exclaimed.

My ribs felt bruised in several places, one eye was beginning to darken and swell, and I still had traces of dirt in my mouth and nose. My clothing looked disreputable, too, stained with mud from the river-bank. For now these problems were insignificant. What worried me was that once again I had been haled into the count's palace to appear before Ragnar Logbrod to answer for my conduct.

Fortunately this time I had not killed anyone, so he could not hang me. At least I did not think he could. On the other hand, this time Hastein was angry, too. Ragnar and the jarl were seated beside each other at the long table. Bjorn and Ivar, the other top commanders of our army, were also present, seated to Ragnar's left. Bjorn seemed to be irritated to have to be there. Ivar, surprisingly, seemed to be amused. He leaned over and whispered in Bjorn's ear, in a voice loud enough that even I could hear it from where I stood in front of the table.

"I'll wager you three silver pennies to one that Father talks about discipline at least once before we're through here today."

Ragnar pretended not to hear, but his face slowly turned a deep, dark red. It seemed a shade that frequently colored his visage.

"How much have you had to drink?" Hastein asked me. "I can smell it on you from here."

"Halfdan did not drink that much," Tore interjected. He, Torvald, and Snorre were also standing, as I was, in front of the table. "He just smells that way because I tripped over his cup and spilled it on him."

I appreciated Tore speaking up for me, and was even more grateful for his rescue earlier. I suspected, though, that he would have carried more weight as a witness if his voice was not still slurred from the amount he'd drunk.

"Are you saying Halfdan drank less than you?" Hastein asked him, in a soft voice.

"Oh, yes," Tore said, nodding his head vigorously. "Much less. I'd been drinking for a while before he and Torvald arrived."

"I left you in charge of guarding my ship," Hastein said through gritted teeth. Tore took a step back.

"The *Gull* is safe," he said.

"And obviously in good hands," Ivar added.

"We are not here to discuss how much your men do or do not drink," Ragnar said to Hastein. "We are here because there has been another breakdown of discipline in the army . . ."

Ivar nudged Bjorn with his elbow.

"And once again this member of your crew was involved." As he finished speaking, Ragnar shook his finger at me.

"I can solve your discipline problem, Lord Ragnar," Snorre said. "This boy attacked me without provocation. I demand my right to challenge him to a duel. I will kill him, and he will not trouble your army any more."

"Well that seems a tidy way to resolve this," Ivar said. "And it will provide us with entertainment, too."

"There will be no dueling," Ragnar snapped. "Not while we are deep within the heart of Frankia and surrounded by enemies. One killing always leads to another and another. I do not want petty differences tearing our army apart."

"I have been struck and insulted," Snorre protested. "I have the right to defend my honor."

I turned on him. "You have no honor to defend. You murdered my brother. You murdered innocent women and children. You and Toke."

"I knew a Toke," Ivar said. "A chieftain from Dublin. Is this the same man?"

Snorre put his hand on his sword hilt, but Torvald stepped forward and clamped his hand on Snorre's wrist, preventing him from drawing.

"I will kill you, boy!" Snorre shouted.

"Silence!" Ragnar roared.

Torvald released Snorre's arm and pushed him away. Snorre looked at Ragnar.

"Do you see, Lord Ragnar? Did you hear? I have a right to challenge him to a duel."

"Not here," Ragnar answered. "Not now. I do not care if you both kill each other after we leave Frankia. But while we are here, our warriors will not fight each other, and will not kill each other. If you cannot abide by that, then take your ship and leave."

Snorre stared at each of the chieftains in turn, as if hoping someone would contradict Ragnar. No one did. Ivar smirked at him.

"I will not break the peace," Snorre finally said. "I will stay." As he turned to leave, he murmured to me, "Your time will come."

"Snorre," Hastein said. "What is the name of your ship? And how many men do you lead?"

"Why do you ask?"

"I am just curious. I would like to know what you've brought to our army."

"My ship is the *Sea Steed*," Snorre replied. "My crew numbers twenty-six, including me."

Ivar slapped his hand loudly on the table. "The *Sea Steed*," he said. "It *is* the same Toke I knew in Ireland. That was the name of his ship. Is he here, too?"

Snorre shook his head. "Toke has a larger ship now," he said. "The *Red Eagle.*" He looked at me and gave an evil smile. The *Red Eagle* had been my father's ship, then Harald's after my father had died. It was bitter to think of her in Toke's hands now.

"I captain the *Sea Steed* for Toke," Snorre continued. "He is my chieftain. But he did not come on this voyage. He had other matters to attend to." He inclined his head toward Ivar. "When next I see Toke, I will tell him you spoke of him." Then he wheeled and strode from the hall.

"Yes, I do remember Toke," Ivar said. "A big man. Very strong, and with an evil temper, though a good warrior to have with you in a fight. What is this talk of murder?"

"This is not the time or place to discuss it," Hastein told him. He turned to Ragnar. "Are we through here? May my men leave?"

"Are you going to deal with this one?" Ragnar asked, pointing at me.

"I will deal with him," Hastein replied.

"Then we are finished."

In the corridor outside of the great hall, Hastein told Tore, "Go back to the *Gull.* You will remain on guard duty there until you hear otherwise from me. Torvald, go with him and fetch the cask of ale. From now on, my men will drink only water while on guard duty."

When they had gone, Hastein turned to me, looking angry. I opened my mouth to explain to him who Snorre was and what he had done, but before I could speak he snarled at me.

"Had I known you were prone to behave as rashly as you did today, I would not have offered you a place on my crew."

Hastein's words hit me as hard as if he had struck me with his fist. Suddenly I saw my behavior as it must have appeared to him—the newest member of his crew engaging in a drunken brawl before the war-king.

"I am sorry," I said. "I have shamed myself this day and I have embarrassed you. I regret the latter the most."

Hastein stared at me silently for a long time. I wanted to look away, but I kept my head up and met his gaze.

"It does you credit," he finally said, "that you do not offer excuses for your conduct. I cannot abide a man who will not admit when he has done wrong."

I said nothing. There seemed no words to add that would not, at this point, sound like an excuse.

"Tell me more about this Snorre," Hastein commanded.

"He was Toke's helmsman and second in command on the *Sea Steed*."

"Can you swear he was among the men who attacked and killed Harald and the others?"

"He had to have been," I answered. "At that time, Toke had only the one ship. And Snorre was with him on it just days before the attack."

"Hmmm," Hastein replied. "Well, for now, it is not our concern. Your vengeance must wait. We are at war. But remember this. You seek to claim a great blood-debt, which will be satisfied only by the deaths of many men, including a renowned and dangerous chieftain. You will never achieve it if you lose your head again like you did today."

"I will not," I promised him.

"I hope not," Hastein replied. "Yet even if you are able to master your own temper, I do not trust Snorre to control his. I want you to stay out of his sight. I do not want you meeting him again. Go back to Wulf's house and stay there until I summon you. It will cost you to stay away from the rest of the crew, because it will mean you cannot accompany us when it is our turn to use the captured horses to go raiding in the countryside. But it is right that you should pay a price for embarrassing me."

My heart sank. In truth, I did not mind missing the chance to go on raiding parties. Though I hoped to win some wealth on this campaign, I had no taste for doing so by stealing from poor farmers and folk like Wulf. But I dreaded the thought of once more being cooped up in the merchant's house.

Perhaps my disappointment showed on my face, or perhaps it was just the dirt and damage showing on my body and clothes, but when I reached Wulf's house, he took one look at me, and said, "What has happened? You look terrible. Would you like some ale?"

I was sorely tempted, but I told him no.

11

INTO FRANKIA

My exile to Wulf's house was cut short after only five days, when Torvald appeared early one morning to summon me.

"Hastein has work for you," he said. Despite my questions, he would not explain further. "Hastein will tell you all," was his only answer.

Torvald took me to a large room at one end of the second floor of the count's palace. It was furnished with a bed, two tables, a number of ornately carved wooden chairs, and several large chests, each big enough for a grown man to hide in. One of Hastein's sea chests—he had two, and as he was captain, no one protested the amount of space they took up on board the ship—was also there, at the foot of the bed. Two shields, both painted in the three-colored pattern Hastein favored, leaned against a nearby wall.

"Welcome to my quarters," Hastein said as we entered. He was seated at one of the tables with a wooden platter in front of him. On it was a loaf of bread, a thick block of ivory-colored cheese, and a roasted chicken. One leg had already been ripped off of the chicken and was now in Hastein's hand.

"Have you eaten?" he asked me, and gestured at the platter with the chicken leg. "Help yourself if you have not."

I had eaten, but only porridge. In Wulf's home, the night's fast was not broken with such fine fare. I used my dagger to cut the other leg from the bird.

"Thank you," I said.

"Cullain," Hastein called. "Fetch two more cups of ale. I have guests."

Torvald used his seax to carve off a thick slice of cheese, and sawed the end off the loaf of bread to accompany it.

"I thought you ate before you left to fetch Halfdan," Hastein said to him.

Torvald shrugged. "I am still hungry."

Hastein shook his head. "You are always hungry," he said. Turning back to me, he added,

"You should eat your fill, and then some. You will not have food like this, nor ale, where you are going."

In light of our last parting, I had been pleasantly surprised to be greeted in such friendly fashion by Hastein. His last words had an ominous ring, though. I glanced down at the chicken leg I'd been contentedly enjoying a moment before, and suddenly felt like a pig being fattened for the slaughter.

"Where am I going?" I asked.

"Into Frankia," he answered. I did not understand. I thought we were already in Frankia.

"Ragnar believes the Frankish king may finally have mustered his army and be on the move," he continued. "A number of our raiding parties have seen solitary riders following them, probably Frankish scouts. And one raiding party has failed to return to Ruda. Twenty men and their horses are missing.

"The Franks' mounted troops are a force to be reckoned with. They are heavily armed and armored, and they ride as though they were born on horseback. If large units of Frankish cavalry are moving against us, it is time to change our tactics. Our raiders will stand no chance against them."

It was gratifying for Hastein to explain all of this to me, but I still did not understand my role in it. "But where am I going?" I asked again.

"We are sending out eight scouts to try and locate the Frankish army. You will be one of them," Hastein replied. "You will each travel alone, and on foot. Ragnar and I believe that way you will have the greatest chance of avoiding detection by Frankish patrols."

"Why did you choose me?" I asked. What I wondered, but did not say, was whether my selection was further punishment for embarrassing Hastein by my conduct. It sounded to me like this mission might be a way for Hastein to rid himself of an unwanted member of his crew. I did not relish the thought of wandering alone through this foreign land, where everyone I met would be my enemy—and likely wishing to kill me.

"You told me that after Toke attacked the farm on the Limfjord and killed your brother, Harald, and his men, you eluded the men who hunted you and even turned the tables and killed them. If you could do that, you, more than most men, have a chance to find the Frankish army and live to tell us where they are. Our army is blind, and Ragnar and I need to know where our enemies are."

If I could do that? Did Hastein now doubt what I'd told him? Was this a test to see if I could truly accomplish what I'd claimed to have done?

"What of Wulf and his family?" I asked.

"They will be safe—safe enough. The town is calm now, and most of our men are encamped on the island."

We left that same morning, heading upriver in two ships. Ivar's, the *Bear*, carried four scouts for the left bank of the river. I was on the *Gull* with the other three men selected to scout the right bank. One of them was Einar.

"I am glad to finally see you again," he told me when he came aboard. "Hrodgar asked me to give you his greetings, too. We have looked for you since the fleet came to Ruda, but it was as though you had disappeared from the army. When I heard they were asking for warriors to go out scouting for the Franks' army, I hoped you would volunteer."

I was glad to see Einar, too. I wished we could scout together.

"You *volunteered* to be a scout?" I asked.

"Of course," Einar answered. "We all did. Much honor will be won by whoever finds the Frankish army."

Unless, I thought, the Frankish army finds the scout.

"I have important news for you," Einar continued. "I saw one of Toke's men just two days ago on the island where our army is camped. He is a big man with a scar on his face. His name is . . ."

"Snorre," I said. "We have already met."

Einar's eyes widened. "I am surprised blood was not shed between you."

"It was," I said. "Or almost. He boasted that Toke promised him a rich reward if he brings back proof that I am dead. He wanted to challenge me to a duel, but Ragnar has forbidden dueling while we are in Frankia."

"There are other ways a man can die besides in a duel," Einar suggested. "Accidents can happen. Sometimes men even die in their sleep." I was not sure whether Einar was warning me to take care, or suggesting that we might secretly murder Snorre. From what I'd seen of Einar, he could mean either—or both.

The crew of the *Gull* rowed up the Seine River for well over half a day before the first scout was put ashore. Hastein insisted that none of the scouts take a turn at the oars.

"Once you are ashore," he told us, "you will need all of your strength to move fast and cover as much ground as possible. Rest now while you can."

While the remainder of the crew rowed, I pulled my sea chest to the center of the deck and chose the gear I would take with me. I stuck my dagger and small-axe in my belt, then squatted in front of my chest, staring at its contents and trying to decide what I might need. If I hoped to survive this mission and return, I would need to travel swiftly and unseen. Armor would only slow me down. If a Frankish patrol discovered me, alone and deep within their territory, my leather jerkin, helm, and shield would not be enough to keep me alive. I chose only one quiver—after the battle for Ruda's gate, I had only enough good arrows left to fill one, anyway. I rolled my thickest cloak lengthwise, tied the ends together, and draped it over my shoulder. A skin filled with water and a worn leather pouch containing dried salted pork from the ship's stores, plus a loaf of bread and some cheese I'd taken from Wulf's larder, completed my gear. That, and my bow.

Tore watched me sorting through my sea chest as he rowed.

"You have not taken any plunder yet, have you?" he asked. I shook my head. If my luck continued as it had so far, I was certainly not going to make my fortune on this voyage.

"If you are killed," he added, "who do you want your possessions to go to?"

It was a question I had not thought to consider. Now that I did, I realized with a pang that I had no one—no family, no close comrades—to leave my few belongings to.

"It does not matter to me," I answered. "If I am dead, I will not care."

"You have no one?" Tore asked. "There is no one at all?"

His questions made me think of Harald and my mother, and how much I missed them. I shook my head and turned away so Tore could not see my face. When I did, I saw Einar, seated with his back against the mast, sharpening the head of one of his arrows with a whetstone.

"Give them to him," I said, pointing at Einar. "If he returns and I do not, give my possessions to him. He is my friend." The closest thing to a true friend that I had, anyway.

One by one, the scouts were put ashore, till only I remained. Hastein was taking me far deeper into the Frankish countryside than the others.

Dusk was approaching. As the *Gull* glided upstream, she passed more and more frequently through long stretches of deep shadow, cast by stands of trees along the river's bank.

"This will do," Hastein finally said. Torvald steered the ship out into the middle of the river, then ordered the rowers on the steer-board side to back oars, while the port-side rowers pulled forward. The *Gull* slowly pivoted in place. When she was facing downstream, Torvald steered her over to the bank. Two men leaped ashore with ropes and tied her fast.

Hastein approached. "We are deep within the

Frankish heartland here," he said. "I purposely chose you to search this area for the Frankish army. The danger will be greatest here, and help farthest away. I believe you, more than any of the other scouts, are most likely to survive and return."

If Hastein's words were intended to cheer me because of the honor he paid me, they missed their mark. I would rather have felt less honored, but more likely to live.

"Two days from now, Ivar and I will be back on the river," he continued, "searching for our scouts. We will stay on the river for five days, unless Frankish forces harry us and force us back to Ruda. If all goes well, you will have up to seven days to search for the Frankish army and make your way back here. But if you do not reach the river before we return to Ruda on the seventh day, or if we are driven away before that time, you will be on your own."

Before darkness fully cloaked the land, I went ashore and climbed the tallest of the nearby trees to view the ground I would be crossing. The branches were just beginning to bud into leaves—spring was awakening the land here in Frankia. Beyond the river, the countryside was mostly open, grassy plain, dotted with scattered clumps of trees and brush. Far in the distance, almost to the horizon, I could see a long band of solid darkness that marked, I suspected, a line of trees—perhaps the edge of a forest.

After I lowered myself through the tree's branches back to the ground, Hastein and I walked together to where the growth along the river ended and the edge of the plain began. Night was approaching swiftly now. A breeze had sprung up, and the high grass ahead of me swayed and rustled. If anyone was watching from afar, when I left the shelter of the trees hopefully the darkness would hide me and I would appear to be nothing more than another windblown shadow rippling through the grass across the plain.

"Good speed and good fortune," Hastein said. "And may Ragnar's words be true."

I frowned. "What words?"

"That a fylgja guides you and protects your path."

I left the woods and moved out at an easy trot across the plain. The grass, thigh-high at its deepest, was brown and brittle from the winter, but new shoots, fresh and green, were beginning to sprout from the earth and provided a soft cushion underfoot.

A rising half-moon painted the plain with its pale light, giving the countryside a strangely dead and colorless appearance. High clouds blew rapidly across the sky, their shadows causing the gently rolling plain around me to shift from dark to light as the moon was alternately hidden then revealed.

I knew the pace I'd set covered distance rapidly. After a time I paused to rest and looked back. I could no longer see the line of trees bordering the river that hid the *Gull*. I was all alone now in the heart of Frankia, and I felt it. I drank a swallow of water, and set off again at a faster trot. I did not want to be caught on this open plain in daylight.

It was past midnight when I smelled fire. The breeze, blowing from my left now, carried a faint but distinct odor of wood smoke mixed with the bitter stench of burned flesh.

It was the latter smell that caused me to change my course. Where there was death, perhaps there would be signs of the Frankish army. I turned and headed into the wind, following the smell.

The harsh odor grew stronger as I traveled, until finally, ahead of me, I could see a dark wall of shadow against the sky marking a line of trees. There was a gap in the tree line directly ahead of me. Indistinct shapes were scattered across the ground there. The acrid stench was coming from them.

I stopped and strung my bow, then moved cautiously forward, an arrow nocked on the string. The ground changed underfoot, and I found myself walking across the uneven surface of a plowed field. As I drew nearer, I realized that the dim shapes ahead of me must be the remains of buildings from a small village, perhaps ten or twelve houses. They were much smaller than the great longhouse I'd grown up in, smaller even than the compact dwellings in Hedeby. Some must have been little more than hovels.

The village was situated along the bank of a small river. All of its buildings had been burned. Now there were only mounds of ash, with low charred stumps marking where the structures' corner and door posts had once stood. When I touched the ashes no warmth still lingered. The remains of a single hut still smoldered, the coals from the long, center ridge beam of its roof having been banked by the collapsing structure's own ashes. The beam lay across a body. I could not tell if it was a man or a woman. Whatever clothing had once covered it had been burned away by the fire, and the corpse's skin was black and charred.

I knew this village must have been attacked by one of our raiding parties. The ground in and around the village was covered with the prints of horses' hooves. I was surprised they had ranged so far from Ruda.

As I wandered through the remains of the village, I passed another body, this one clearly a man.

Two dogs feeding at his carcass bared their teeth
and growled at me, but when I did not molest
them they put their heads down and resumed their
meal. Other bodies lay scattered about, too, all
showing signs that they had fed the dogs or carrion
birds. I passed the body of an old woman lying on
her back. Her skull had been split, no doubt by a
sword or axe, and the ground around her head was
stained in a dark halo. Her eyes, now empty sockets picked clean by the ravens, stared sightlessly up
at the sky.

Why had she been cut down? I could not picture this old woman as an enemy who threatened
the land of the Danes. None of these simple farmers, lying slain among the ruins of their homes,
could have posed any threat to our people. Were
these the foes we had traveled so far to fight?

A noise to my right startled me out of my
thoughts. Something or someone was moving
among the ruins. Was it a man, a beast, or a spirit of
the dead? My stomach knotted and sweat sprang out
on my forehead as I spun and brought up my bow.

A chicken strutted forward around the corner
of one of the burned houses. How it had escaped
the raiders, I could not imagine. Perhaps in the
confusion of the attack it had flown away into the
fields. I wondered if it approached me now out of
loneliness for human contact, or if it just saw me as

less threatening than the wild dogs that now roamed the village.

Alas, it had misjudged me. I was a predator, too. I needed more than the dried salted pork in my food pouch to give me strength to travel. I shot the poor bird, gutted it, and tied its body by its feet to my belt. I laid the chicken's entrails in a small pile on the top of a charred post at the corner of a hut, and said a prayer of thanks to whichever God or spirit had sent the bird my way. Perhaps it was the fylgja.

Leaving the ruined village, I followed the tracks of the raiding party for a short distance. Just beyond the village, they had forded the little river at a rocky shallow where the water was no more than ankle-deep, then headed north and west, cutting across country toward the Seine and Ruda. In the soft, damp earth on the far side of the ford, I could see, even in the dim moonlight, that interspersed among the hoofprints of the raiding party's mounts were the tracks of cattle, sheep, and swine, plus a number of human footprints. The latter were mostly small in size, probably women and children. These tracks, I realized, represented the raiders' plunder from their attack on the village, being driven in a mixed herd toward our army's base at Ruda.

Like the Seine, the small river I'd just crossed was lined with a belt of trees. But beyond, the land again reverted to mostly open plain. I stood at its edge wondering where to head now.

Looking down, I realized I was standing astride a single set of tracks left by a shod horse. They came from the direction of the open plain, and behind me merged into the broad, muddled track left by the party of raiders. Who had this solitary rider been? Stooping low to follow the thin trail left by his mount's hooves, I backtracked along his path.

I'd traveled less than the distance of a spear's throw when I found the answer to the mystery. The single rider's trail led back to a wide, trampled track left by a second large group of mounts. These riders had remained across the river from the village, and a little distance away from the path left by the retreating Danes. Their trail led off across the plain, parallel to the course the raiding party had traveled.

My pulse quickened. This second group of horsemen had to have been Franks. I felt sure of it. The single rider who'd ridden away from their group was following the trail left by the raiders' passing. The rest of the mounted force of Franks were traveling off to the side, so as not to damage the spoor he followed.

I hesitated. With Frankish cavalry abroad upon the plain, by the time daylight lit these open lands

I needed to have reached cover. Yet here was the first hard evidence I'd found of the Franks' forces. If I followed the trail of this troop of cavalry, they might eventually lead me to the main army. Reluctantly, I set out after them, moving at a brisk trot across the plain.

Because they were driving prisoners and livestock, the pace of the raiding party must have been very slow. The Franks, unencumbered, would have moved far more swiftly. Even so, the Danes must have had a long lead, for the hunters did not catch up with their prey quickly. I wondered whether the Frankish patrol would have found the track of the raiding party at all, had they not burned the village, announcing their presence by the smoke that had no doubt been visible for miles around.

The sky was already beginning to lighten in the east by the time I first saw signs that the Danes had realized they were being hunted. The tracks on the ground bore mute witness to what had happened. Once they caught sight of the pursuing Franks, the raiders had wisely chosen to abandon their plunder and try to save their own lives. Their horses had sped away from the huddled captives and cattle at a gallop. From the chopped and trampled turf, I could see where the main body of Franks in hot pursuit had swept past the huddled cluster of livestock and freed prisoners.

The sky was rapidly growing brighter now. I hurried along the track of the fleeing Danes and their Frankish hunters, increasing my pace to a loping run.

Most of the horses our army had captured were farm animals, bred more for pulling plows than sustained speed. They must have been badly outclassed by the Franks' mounts. I had not traveled much farther along the path of their flight before I began to pass the bodies of Danes. Most were pierced by spear thrusts, usually in the back—grim evidence of the Franks' skill and deadliness on horseback.

As with most pursuits, it was a one-sided slaughter. Only once did I come upon any sign of a Frankish casualty, and that was but a horse—clearly a Frankish cavalryman's mount by its trappings—slain by a sword cut to the head. It was slim and well-muscled, much taller than the horses bred in the land of the Danes.

The sun was edging above the horizon when I reached the site of the raiders' final stand. Ahead of me on the plain I could see a dark mound. As I drew nearer, I saw that the Danes, no doubt realizing they could never outrun their pursuers, had chosen to make a fight of it. They'd dismounted and slain their horses, cutting their throats or stabbing them so their bodies fell in a rough circle.

Their final shield-ring had been formed inside the low barricade of dead mounts, in the hope that the bodies of the horses would be enough of an obstacle to keep the attacking cavalry from charging over them. The hacked, bloody corpses of eighteen Danes lay there. The Franks had made no effort to bury their enemy's dead.

These last members of the raiding party, in their final stand, appeared to have taken some of the Frankish cavalry with them into the afterworld. No bodies of Frankish warriors had been left behind, but several patches of grass outside the circle of dead horses and men were heavily stained with blood, offering mute witness. Four of the fine Frankish mounts lay dead. Also around the outskirts of the ring I found a Frankish helm, cloven through and soaked with gore, and a Danish spear, its shaft snapped but its sharp head covered with blood. Two abandoned Frankish shields had been shattered by mighty blows.

The eyes of the dead Danish warriors were gone, eaten by carrion birds, and the flesh of their faces was pecked and torn. They had died far from their homes and their families, and their bodies would never be buried or burned. I wondered if their spirits were doomed to forever wander this foreign land.

Beyond the site of the battle, perhaps three bowshots away, stood a small copse of trees. I wondered if the raiding party had been trying to reach it. The tracks of the Franks led in that direction. Had they had camped there after the fight, to tend to their wounded? I wondered if they were still there now.

For a moment I considered throwing myself to the ground and lying among the dead, hoping to hide myself among the bodies. I realized as soon as the thought came to me it would be a foolish plan. If they were still within the circle of trees, the Franks would surely have posted sentries. Anyone watching would have seen me standing here beside the pile of dead, for the grassy plain was fully lit now by the rays of the rising sun.

The copse of woods was the only cover in sight. I had to go there. I had to find a place to hide during the daylight hours. If Franks lurked hidden in the undergrowth, waiting—if that was the fate the Norns had woven for me—there was no way to escape. I laid an arrow across my bow, nocked it on the string, and began a slow, cautious walk toward the trees.

12

DANGEROUS
SAUSAGES

The Franks had been there, but they were gone. The ground in and around the small stand of trees and brush had been heavily trampled by horses and men. Three charred circles surrounded by stones marked where they'd built their cook fires.

I was exhausted, but ravenous, too. My hunger won out over my fatigue. I plucked the chicken I'd brought, cut it into pieces, and roasted them one by one over a tiny fire. I made certain to add only a few twigs at a time to the flames, to prevent creating a telltale plume of smoke. I did not intend to repeat the mistake that had cost the raiding party their lives.

I ate half of the chicken while it was fresh and

warm, together with a thick slab of Wulf's bread. The other half I saved for my evening meal. I washed my food down with a few swallows of water, and thought longingly of ale—the fine ale Hastein had offered me in his quarters, or even the weak ale Wulf had served.

My waterskin was getting dangerously light. I should have filled it when I crossed the river by the ruined village. When night came and I traveled again, I would need to find water.

After I ate, I climbed a tree and surveyed the plain around me. The only movement I saw was back where the Danish raiders had made their final stand. With the coming of day, carrion birds had returned to their grisly feast at the site of the battle.

When I climbed down, I wrapped myself in my cloak, crawled under a bush whose low, overhanging branches would at least partially conceal me, and tried to rest. But although I was weary from my long trek, I chased sleep with little success far into the morning. Every time I began to doze off, some small distraction—the chirping of a bird, the buzzing of a bee, the tickle of a fly landing on my face—startled me awake again.

Exhaustion finally overwhelmed my nerves. But even then, my sleep was not restful. I was visited in my dreams by the spirit of the old woman whose body I'd seen in the village. With the eye of my mind I saw her standing at the edge of the grove where I slept. Though I remained motionless under the bush, hoping she would pass by, she entered the circle of trees and drew closer until she stood over me. Her hair was caked with blood and brains that had leaked from her split skull. I longed to run, but could not move.

"I know you are there, but I cannot see you," she said, her empty eye sockets gaping as she turned her face toward where I lay. "I cannot tell. Are you a good man, or are you evil? Why are you here? Why have you come to this land?"

I tried to speak, to tell her I was sorry for the attack on her village, but no words would come. Finally a low moan escaped my lips.

The sound woke me. I was gasping for air and drenched with sweat. It was still hours before darkness would fall, but I abandoned further efforts to sleep. I feared the ghost of the old woman would surely come again if I dozed, for even in the bright afternoon sun I could not drive the image of her face from my thoughts.

While I waited for night to arrive I ate the rest of my chicken, and finished my bread, too. The remaining contents of my food pouch—the block of hard cheese, and some slices of dried, salt-cured pork—were all the food I had left. Soon both hunger and thirst would become problems.

As I ate, I made plans. Hastein and Ivar would be back on the river tomorrow, keeping watch for the scouts. I wondered if any had been captured or killed yet by the Franks. I wondered where Einar was, and what he was doing.

I stood and began pacing the length of the copse, pondering what I should do. When I passed the site where I'd plucked and cooked the chicken that morning, a swarm of fat black flies, disturbed by my passing, flew up from the small pile of feathers, bones, and skin. I should have buried them, but I'd been too tired that morning to dispose of the rubbish from my meal.

Suddenly I turned and looked around me, searching every inch of the ground within the grove of trees. Nowhere had the earth been dug or disturbed. The same was true of the grassy plain immediately around the grove. I still felt certain, from the split and blood-soaked Frankish helm I'd seen, that at least one Frank, and perhaps more, had died in the final fight. But there were no graves. What had the Franks done with their bodies? And what of the Frankish wounded? Surely there had been some.

After climbing a tree again to scan the plain for danger, I ventured out and examined the trail the cavalry troop had left when they'd headed out across the plain. When I did, I found the answer to my questions.

Among the numerous hoofprints marking the horsemen's trail, I found four pairs of shallow grooves running in long, unbroken lines. And I'd seen stumps in the patch of woods where the Franks had chopped down saplings—I'd mistakenly assumed to burn on their cook fires. I had been wrong. The Franks had built four horse-drawn litters to carry their dead and wounded.

If these Franks were carrying dead and seriously wounded with them, they would be returning to their camp—hopefully to the main army. Their trail would lead me there.

I set out at dusk. The broad track they'd left was easy to follow, even in the dark. I traveled all night like a silent shadow in their wake.

About midway through the night, the tracks led me to a small river. The Franks had turned there, and followed the river's course. I hoped they would hold to it. Along the river I would have water and cover to hide in during the day. I might even find game to supplement my dwindling supply of food.

The Franks' trail was still following the course of the river when dawn forced me to seek shelter in the trees and undergrowth that lined its banks. I stayed awake as long as I could, my bow strung and ready, in the hope that some beast or fowl might make an early morning visit to the river. None did. My fylgja—if indeed I had one—did not provide me with the fresh meat I craved and needed. Perhaps it was as tired as I was, too tired to send good fortune my way. At least I had no difficulty sleeping. The many miles I'd covered over the past two nights had exhausted me beyond dreaming.

I awoke as evening was approaching, and ate sparingly of my small store of dried meat and cheese. Looking out across the plain in the fading light, I realized that the land was becoming hillier, and patches of trees and undergrowth more frequently broke up the expanse of plain. What would this night's journey bring?

It was still well before midnight when I topped a low ridge crossing the tracks I was following. The grassy plain ended ahead, at a solid line of trees. From my vantage point atop the ridge, I could see the dark line of a road angling across the plain. The Franks' trail veered over to the road. I followed, and the rough, dirt track led me into the woods. It was too dark under the shelter of the trees to read the ground for spoor, but it no longer mattered. The road itself was the trail I followed now.

After two nights on the open plain, I found it

disorienting to travel through the dark forest with the light of the stars and moon blotted out and the trees pressing in around me. Unable to measure how far I had traveled or how much time had passed, I was uncertain whether it was still early in the night, or if midnight had come and gone unnoticed.

Suddenly, in the distance ahead, I saw the flickering light of a fire—and then another. I ducked off the road and into the trees, strung my bow, then moved ahead again more slowly, slipping from trunk to trunk toward the lights.

Soon I realized that the flames were torches, carried by men pacing back and forth. As I drew nearer and details became discernible, I could see that they were Frankish warriors, for the light from their torches gleamed on the helms and armor they were wearing. Only the upper parts of their bodies—their chests and heads—were visible. The rest was hidden by a barricade built of felled trees. The crude wooden wall spanned the road, leaving only a narrow passageway in its center, just wide enough for a single man or horse to pass through. The ends of the log wall curved away from the road and into the darkness on either side.

Why had the Franks built this fortification here, on this rough roadway through the forest? Did the Frankish army lie beyond? I slipped through the trees, moving farther from the road, and dropped to my hands and knees to creep closer.

The simple fort protected the end of a low, stone bridge. The river I'd been following earlier had veered toward the west, and the road crossed it here.

On the other side of the river, just beyond the far end of the bridge, more lights shone through the darkness. I crawled forward to the river's edge to investigate.

A village lay on the far bank of the river. Through gaps between its buildings, I could see a bonfire blazing in an open square in its center.

This village was much larger than the one the raiding party had burned. A number of tents had been pitched in the square, and horses were tethered to a picket line along one side. Many men—some in armor, others not—wandered about. Others were seated around the fire.

Did the trail end here, at nothing but a small garrison? This was clearly not the main army. It was not what I'd been sent to find.

The bridge was blocked to me, but there was more than one way to cross a river. After moving far enough upstream that the lights from the village and fort were no longer visible, I stripped off my clothes, wrapped them around my weapons, and—holding the bundle overhead—stepped into the chilly water. At its deepest, the water never rose higher than my chest.

The road that had led across the bridge and into the village continued beyond. When I eventually reached it again, I saw its surface was covered with tracks. Wherever this road went, it appeared to be heavily traveled, so I set my course parallel to it through the woods and forged on.

Fatigue, made worse by the hunger that gnawed at my stomach, prevented me from continuing until dawn. My feet ached and my legs felt stiff and heavy. My thoughts kept wandering to memories of meals I had eaten. More than once I trod clumsily on a fallen branch, announcing my presence with a loud snap of dried wood had anyone been close enough to hear. It was too dangerous to continue in this condition.

A hill, steeper than most I'd passed, rose up through the trees off to my right, overlooking the road. I staggered up it, wormed my way into a dense thicket of underbrush near the summit, and stretched out thankfully on the ground, wrapping myself in my cloak. After a few bites of cheese to stave off the worst of my hunger, I slipped into a deep, exhausted sleep.

A loud boom that seemed to shake the ground under me startled me awake. I sat up suddenly, sticking my head into the midst of a bush. I batted at the branches scratching my face, my mind still fogged with sleep, wondering where I was. Another boom, louder than the first, rattled the trees, and a flash of lightning lit the sky. Rain began falling, a few fat, scattered drops at first, but soon turning into a steady, relentless downpour.

Though I stretched it overhead like a tent, my cloak did not protect me for long. The force of the beating rain was too great. Even the arrows in my quiver took on a forlorn look, the feathers of their fletching limp and bedraggled from their soaking. I sat, miserable and shivering, wondering how much of the day had passed while I slept, for the dark clouds that filled the sky concealed the sun's location and hid the hour.

Finally the rain slowed, then stopped. I wrapped my cloak tight around me, for its thick wool offered some warmth even though wet, but I could not stop shaking. Recklessly I ate all of my remaining cheese and dried pork. I needed the energy the food could give me now.

A clatter of noise on the roadway roused me from my misery. I crawled to the edge of the thicket and peered out. A small unit of cavalry, ten men at most, was passing on the road below, headed at a fast trot toward the village and bridge I'd seen the night before. Their leader was wearing a brilliant scarlet cloak, cut short so it barely hung below his waist. It flapped and fluttered out behind him as he rode, like a banner hanging from his shoulders.

Suddenly what my eyes had seen broke through the chilled stupor clouding my mind. The Frank's cloak was flapping behind him. It was dry, not soaked through by the rain like mine. These men—or their captain, at least—had been under shelter during the storm. And their shelter could not be very far away, for only a brief time had passed since the storm had ended.

Perhaps there was another village or military encampment nearby. If so, when night fell I might be able to sneak close enough to steal food there. At the moment, the thought of getting my hands around a fat chicken seemed far more desirable than finding the entire Frankish army. At any rate, movement would at least warm me. If I sat here shivering in the mud, waiting until night cloaked my movements, I feared I would not have strength left to continue on.

I crawled out of the thicket, brushed as much of the mud and wet leaves as I could from my clothing, and headed off down the hillside, following a course through the woods parallel to the road in the direction the cavalry had come from.

I heard the encampment—men shouting, horses whinnying, cattle lowing, and the chunk, chunk of axes hitting wood—long before I got close enough to see it. That alone told me it was probably large.

The narrow road I was following ended at a junction with a much larger and more heavily traveled one. From my concealed vantage, I could see an ox-cart plodding down the road, coming from the west, and behind it, a drover herding five head of cattle. Trudging down the road from the east was a double column of Frankish footsoldiers that stretched as far as I could see.

All of the traffic on the road seemed to be headed for the same destination: a vast, fortified encampment that was being built just beyond the crossroads in a great clearing the Franks had carved out of the forest. A deep ditch had been dug around its perimeter, and the trees felled to clear the land were being trimmed to make a palisade atop the earthen wall inside the ditch. It was still far from finished—numerous gaps in the ditch and wall remained—but the sound of countless picks and axes told of the size of the force working to bring it to completion. Seeing the encampment's size, I knew I'd found what I had been seeking. Concealed within this forest, the army of the Franks was gathering.

The encampment was enormous. The army it was built to house must surely be, too. Had Ragnar and Hastein misjudged our ability to challenge the might of the Franks?

I had seen enough. Now it was time to escape with the information I had gained. I still had five days to make my way back to the river; five days to retrace a distance it had taken me only three nights to travel. I could afford to take time to search for food. I feared, though, that in the forest I would be unlikely to find any, despite my skill at hunting. There were too many men on the move in this area, too much noise and activity. Any game would have moved on or gone to ground.

I thought about the ox-cart I'd seen traveling along the road from the west. It had been piled with goods of some nature—supplies, I suspected, being transported to the vast army that was assembling. If I could not replenish my stores by hunting, perhaps I could do so by theft.

I set off toward the west, following the main road but staying concealed from view just within the trees. I'd been traveling long enough without having encountered anyone at all to have become tired and discouraged, when I noticed the smell.

Someone was cooking sausages. It was a dangerous thing to do, when one as desperately hungry as I was in the vicinity.

I paused to string my bow, drew and readied an arrow, then crept forward through the trees. They grew so thickly here I could see nothing ahead, save more trunks. After a time, I heard an indistinct murmur of voices. Trying to gauge how far away the speakers were—and more importantly, the sausages—I stepped to the edge of the roadway and cautiously peered out.

Not more than twenty-five paces ahead, a two-wheeled cart, with a canvas canopy tented over its square wooden body, was stopped at the side of the road. The two horses that were hitched to it were helping themselves to the grass and low shrubs growing along the border of the woods. Two additional horses, saddled for riding, were tied by their reins to one of the cart's wheels. No one was in sight.

I ducked back into the trees and continued forward, slipping from trunk to trunk. When the voices became clear enough to understand, I lowered myself to my hands and knees and crept toward the sound on all fours.

A man was speaking, in the mangled style of Latin used by the Franks.

"I hope you do not intend to keep this slow a pace for the entire journey, Genevieve. At this rate, it will take us a week to reach Paris."

"We will get there when we get there," a woman

answered. *"What does it matter how many days the journey takes?"*

By now I had crawled forward—the last few feet flat on my stomach, wriggling along the ground like a serpent—to where I could see the speakers. My body was concealed behind the trunk of a thick ash tree. My bow, the single loose arrow, and my quiver lay on the ground beside me. I edged forward just enough to be able to peer around the base of the tree with one eye.

Two women were seated on a cloak that had been spread on the ground in the shade of a large oak. A young man, fully armored in the Frankish cavalry style—mail shirt, helm, and iron greaves strapped to his shins—was pacing back and forth in front of them.

A few feet farther off the road, a second man was squatting beside a small fire. He'd driven two forked, iron rods into the ground on either side of the fire, and spanned them with an iron spit. A string of thick sausages was looped around it. Fat dripping from them was sizzling when it hit the flames. My stomach convulsed at the sound and felt as though it would begin to consume itself if I did not put food into it soon.

"What does it matter?" the young man exclaimed. *"You know very well! Father has ordered me to escort you back to Paris. He has told me I may*

not join the army until I do."

"*A few days will make no difference, Leonidas. I am certain the Northmen will not have fled in that time. Even your father and his men have not joined the army yet.*"

The woman who spoke was wearing a simple gown, woven of gray, undyed wool, cut like a long tunic that came to her ankles. A hood and mantle of a lighter, white fabric—possibly linen—covered her head. I could not see her face, for she was seated with her back toward me.

"*Father and his men ride to join the army tomorrow,*" the young man she'd called Leonidas replied. "*Because we are from this part of the country, Father believes his scara will be sent out to hunt for raiding Northmen. I will not be able to go with them because I am stuck with you.*"

"*Stuck with me? How charming. Since we were children, you have had the manners of a pig,*" the woman said. "*Age has not improved you at all.*"

"*Forgive me, cousin, if I offended you,*" the young man said, bending forward in a mocking bow. Then he turned and stomped over to the fire. "*Are the sausages not ready yet?*" he snapped at the man tending them.

The second woman, who was partially reclined with her back against the bole of the oak tree, had not spoken until now. When the young man walked away, she leaned forward and spoke quietly to the first woman.

"It is my fault that Leonidas is angry, my lady Genevieve," she said. *"We should not have stopped."*

"Nonsense, Clothilde," the woman called Genevieve responded. *"You were feeling ill. You looked quite weak and almost green in the face. It is no doubt because of your condition. The best way to treat an uneasy stomach is to put food in it. Have some bread and cheese, while the sausages are cooking."* As she spoke, Genevieve took a loaf of bread from a basket in front of her, broke off a large piece, and offered it to her companion.

I found it difficult to picture the woman Clothilde as looking either weak or green in the face. She was quite robust of build, with fat, round cheeks that were ruddy from exposure to the sun. Her deferential manner suggested she was the smaller woman's servant. If that was the case, I was surprised at the simplicity of Genevieve's garb.

Taking her mistress at her word, Clothilde accepted the bread, then reached into the basket and removed a small knife and a cloth-wrapped bundle. She unwrapped the bundle, revealing a flat, round cheese. Slicing a large wedge from it, she began spreading the cheese on the bread. It was soft and creamy, almost the texture of butter. My mouth watered as I watched her.

"Where has Hugh gone?" Leonidas asked. *"How long does it take the man to relieve himself?"*

As I watched Clothilde tear off a huge bite of the cheese-smeared bread, I wondered who Hugh was. My thoughts were interrupted by the sharp point of a sword pressed into the back of my neck.

"Stand up slowly," a voice said. *"Very slowly, or I will skewer you like the skulking dog you are. And do not touch your bow."*

13

A RICH PRIZE

My brother, Harald, had taught me that with a sword, as with most weapons, maintaining proper distance is everything. His lesson saved me now. I raised myself slowly to my hands and knees, looking back cautiously as I did. The man behind me, a Frankish warrior wearing a brynie of scale armor but no helm, was standing close, holding his arm extended straight out. The sword's tip was now resting lightly between my shoulder blades.

He'd have been wiser to have stepped back and cocked his arm and the sword, prepared to strike.

I closed my right hand into a fist, filling it with loose dirt and resting most of my weight on it, then swung my left arm back and up. The thick leather bracer I wore on my forearm to protect against the slap of the bowstring hit the sword's blade and knocked it aside. Spinning around, I hurled the handful of dirt into the Frank's face and scrambled to my feet.

He staggered back, wiping his eyes with his left hand while he belatedly raised his sword with his right. I moved with him, frantically grabbing his sword arm and trapping it above our heads. He seized my shoulder with his free hand and tried to swing me away so he'd have room to strike. I lunged forward, crashing against him, and butted my forehead against his nose, breaking it with a loud crack.

The Frank cried out in pain and stumbled backward as I hung on to his sword arm desperately. Blood was gushing from his nose, and fear was showing now in his eyes. I reached behind me with my free hand, clawing my small-axe from my belt, and punched it forward into his face.

"Help me!" he screamed, as blood spurted from a gash in his forehead. I swung my axe again, this time a full arcing blow, and buried its blade in the top of his skull.

Behind me, both women screamed. "*Hugh!*" a man's voice cried. As the dying Frank toppled back, I turned and scrambled over to where my bow and quiver lay on the ground.

The Frank who'd been tending the fire was running toward me, a long knife in his hand. He was wearing no armor. The other Frank, the young warrior named Leonidas, was just disappearing from sight around the back of the cart.

I snatched up my bow and the loose arrow I'd been carrying with it when I'd first approached the campsite. Holding the bow horizontal, I slapped the arrow across it, fitted its nock to the string, and drew and launched toward the charging Frank in one swift motion without aiming. It was a sloppy shot, but the range was short. The arrow hit him in the shoulder. He dropped his knife, staggering backward as he clutched at the shaft with a surprised look on his face, and sat down hard.

"Gunthard! Gunthard!" the servant woman, Clothilde, screamed, then slumped over in a faint.

Leonidas reappeared, crouched behind a shield. He had drawn his sword and was moving toward me slowly and cautiously. He should have run. He should have charged to the attack. Instead he gave me time to sling my quiver over my shoulder and fit another arrow to my bow.

"Lay down your sword and I will not kill you!" I shouted. He looked surprised to hear me speak Latin, but his expression quickly changed to a sneer.

I pulled my bow to full draw and the Frank

crouched lower, covering more of his body with his shield. His eyes barely peeked above the top rim. The shield was metal. I did not think my bow would shoot through it, even at this close range.

The Frank continued his slow progress toward me. My arms were beginning to tire from holding my bow at full draw while I searched for an open target. His shins, showing below the shield, were protected with metal greaves, but his feet were covered only in black leather boots. I aimed down at his left foot, the one in front. Seeing the movement of my bow, he dropped lower, into a squat, as I loosed my arrow. The bottom rim of his shield touched the ground a moment before my arrow would have pierced his foot. Instead, it clanged against the shield and bounced back.

"Be careful, Leonidas!" Genevieve screamed. Again—whether from inexperience or fear—the young Frank moved toward me slowly, when he should have run.

I drew another arrow and readied it on my bow. One of us would have to take a chance—would have to risk his own death to kill the other. I drew my arrow back to full draw and began advancing toward the Frank, a single step at a time, keeping the arrow aimed at the top edge of the shield, and his eyes behind it.

The Frank stopped his own advance, looking

surprised. I continued moving slowly toward him, stepping, stopping, stepping, stopping, staring into his eyes and keeping my bow aimed at them. With each step, I lessened the amount of time he would have to react when I shot. But if he blocked my arrow again . . .

Suddenly I lunged forward, twitching my shoulders in an exaggerated jerk and shouting as I did. He flinched and ducked, raising his shield to hide his face. When no arrow came, he realized I had tricked him with a feint, and now, huddled behind his shield, he could not see me. Drawing his sword arm back ready to strike, the young Frank leaped toward me, screaming a wordless roar of anger mixed with fear.

My arrow struck him in the mouth. He was dead before he hit the ground.

"Leonidas!" Genevieve screamed. She stood and took a few tentative steps toward where he lay sprawled on his back. Even to her, though, it was obvious he was dead. She turned toward me with a terrified look on her face.

"No," she said. *"Please. Do not kill me."*

I would not kill a woman. What did she think I was?

I needed to calm my thoughts. I had not planned this fight, but the Norns had woven it into my fate. I had survived. But what would happen when someone found the bodies of the men I'd slain? What would happen when these women told them a single warrior had fought with their escort, then had fled into the forest? The entire Frankish army was only a short distance down the road. I would be hunted. The woods would be filled with Frankish warriors searching for my trail.

"Who are you?" the woman asked. *"Are you a deserter from the army? Are you an outlaw?"*

Her questions startled me. She thought I was an outlaw? I looked down at myself. Perhaps it was not surprising. My clothes, my face, my hair were all filthy from my days of travel and sleeping on the ground. My hands were spattered with the blood of the man I had killed with my axe. I wondered if my face was, too. I must have looked like a desperate fugitive, someone who'd been living in the wild.

"I am a Dane," I said.

"Sweet Mother of God," she murmured, making the sign of a cross over her heart. *"Mother of Jesus, be with me now, for I am surely lost."*

I was beginning to realize what I had done. I needed to make plans, but I could not force my mind to think. Instead, it kept reliving scenes of what had occurred. I saw the fear in the first Frank's eyes, heard him cry out for help, and felt my axe smash into his head. It was not the same as shooting arrows from a distance.

My knees suddenly felt weak, and my legs started to tremble. I staggered forward and sat down on the woman's cloak.

Genevieve backed away, looking alarmed. *"What are you doing?"* she asked.

I did not want to admit my weakness. *"I am hungry,"* I told her. I picked up the loaf of bread, tore a piece off, and stuffed it in my mouth. It was freshly baked, and tasted delicious. I picked up the cheese and took a bite out of it, too.

"He attacked us, he killed Hugh, he killed Leonidas, all for food," Genevieve murmured. I looked up at her. Her eyes were unfocused. I do not think she even realized she'd spoken aloud.

This woman talked too much. I needed her to be quiet. I needed to clear my head and think.

"I attacked no one," I said. *"I was just watching from the trees. Your man attacked me. They all did. I take no blame for their deaths."*

"You are a Northman," she said, as though that was an answer to my statement. *"You are a pirate and a murderer."*

This discussion was pointless. Fortunately, the food had made me feel better. My legs, at least, had regained their strength. I stood up, walked over to the fire, and cut a sausage from the spit. As I ate it, I surveyed the scene of this disaster.

Two men lay dead, and a third was wounded. He was still sitting on the ground, watching me warily. The woman called Clothilde was still unconscious.

I turned to Genevieve, then pointed at the unconscious woman with my half-eaten sausage.

"Wake her up," I said.

Genevieve took a few steps backward, putting more distance between us. She looked down at Clothilde, then glanced behind her at the road. Surely she would not be so foolish as to try to run.

"What do you want with us? Just take our food and leave."

Her voice was quivering with fear. What she suggested was tempting. I wished I could just go. I could not afford to, though. Someone would pass this way before long. I was surprised it had not happened already. I could leave no one to tell the Frankish warriors what to hunt for. I could not even leave the dead. The cart would be found—it was too large to hide. But let what had happened to these people be a mystery to the Franks. Solving it would buy me precious time.

I picked my arrow up off the ground—the one that had bounced off Leonidas' shield—then stepped over to where his body lay. Genevieve was staring at me, horrified.

"Do not watch this," I told her. I feared she,

too, would faint. I did not need another unconscious woman to deal with. I pointed to where
Clothilde still lay sprawled on the ground. *"I told
you to wake her. Do as I say, and you will not be
harmed. But if you disobey me . . ."* I left the threat
hanging in the air. Let her imagination and fear
complete it.

Genevieve turned and scurried over to
Clothilde. She knelt beside her and began shaking
her by the shoulders.

"Clothilde," she said. *"You must wake up."* The
fallen woman groaned, but did not open her eyes.

The sharpened head of my arrow had passed
completely through the young Frank's neck, severing his spine. His eyes were still open. I thought
they had a startled expression. I wondered if he had
lived long enough, after the arrow hit him, to be
aware of his own death. I pulled my arrow free,
wiped it clean on the bottom of his tunic, and
returned it to my quiver.

"Do you intend to kill me?"

It was the wounded man who spoke.

"Not unless I have to," I told him. *"What is your
name?"*

"Gunthard," he replied.

*"Do as I tell you, Gunthard, and you will live.
Do not try to escape, and do not attack me again."*

"What are you going to do with us?" he asked.

274

"What are you going to do with Lady Genevieve and Clothilde?"

"We are going into the forest," I said. *"All of us. The living, the dead, and the horses. If we are discovered, more will die. Perhaps you will be one of them. Perhaps the women."*

The last was a bluff. I would not kill defenseless women. But he did not need to know that.

"What do you want me to do?" he asked.

First, I had to draw my arrow from his shoulder. He was a brave man, and did not cry out at the pain. Fortunately, because I'd had to snap off so quick a shot, I hadn't pulled my bow to full draw. The arrowhead had hit the bone in his shoulder, but had stopped there instead of breaking it and continuing on through. He was losing blood, though.

He helped me unhitch the two horses from the cart, and we draped a dead body over each. I lashed them down tightly with rope I found in the cart, then made lead ropes and tied one to each horse's reins.

By this time, Gunthard was looking pale, and the sleeve of his tunic was soaked with blood. I sighed, exasperated at the delay. He could not wait to have the wound bandaged. Drawing my dagger, I cut the sleeve from his tunic, exposing the wound.

"Go over to the women," I told him. *"Get them*

to bandage you while I finish."

Genevieve was still trying to rouse Clothilde. The big woman was uttering soft moans regularly now, but still had not opened her eyes. There was no time for this. I strode over to them, pulled the stopper from my waterskin, and dumped water over her face. She sat up suddenly, opened her eyes, and began screaming when she saw me.

"Help me! Genevieve! Gunthard!"

"Calm her!" I snapped to Genevieve. *"Or at least silence her. If you do not, I will."*

"Hush, Clothilde," she said in a frightened voice. *"Do not anger him. He is a Northman. He will kill you. He will kill us all."*

The screaming stopped. There are some advantages to a bloodthirsty reputation.

"My baby," Clothilde whimpered.

I looked toward the cart in dismay. *"Is there a child in there?"* I asked Genevieve.

"It is in her belly," Genevieve replied. I glared at her and at Clothilde. I did not need this.

"Get her up and ready to travel," I snapped. *"And put a bandage on his wound. Bind it tightly so it will stop the bleeding. Hurry. We must leave soon."*

I stuffed the rest of the half-eaten cheese and bread into my food pouch. A quick search of the cart revealed two full waterskins and a pottery jug with a cork stopper in its neck. I opened it and sniffed. It was wine. I placed all three into the women's large food basket and added the sausages. There were other cloth-wrapped parcels in the basket, hopefully more food, but I did not take time to investigate them. I lashed the basket to the saddle of one of the riding horses, then led both around to where the two cart horses—now serving as pack animals, bearing the dead—were standing patiently.

There was little more to do. I kicked the fire apart, scattering the coals, picked up the shield and the dead men's swords, and lashed them onto the packhorses. Blood stained the ground where the two men had died. I scattered loose dirt and leaves over it. If the Franks brought a skilled tracker, he would not be fooled for long. But it would take time to bring a tracker here.

I walked over to where my three prisoners were sitting. Genevieve and Clothilde had wrapped a strip of white cloth—torn from the bottom of Clothilde's under-shift—around Gunthard's shoulder. Bright red blood was already starting to seep through.

"Stand up," I commanded. *"We are leaving."*

I brought one of the horses over, and handed the reins to Gunthard. *"You two will ride on this horse,"* I told him, nodding at Clothilde. To her I added, *"You ride behind him. He is weak from his wound, and will get weaker. Do not let him fall off the horse."*

The Frankish saddles had no stirrups. Gunthard tried to climb onto the horse's back, but was too weak. I stepped forward and crouched beside him.

"Put your foot on my knee," I said. When he did, I straightened, heaving up on his belt while he pulled on the saddle with his good arm, and between us we managed to swing him up onto the horse's back. He swayed for a moment, then nodded down at me.

I turned to Clothilde, and cupped my hands, lacing my fingers together. She looked alarmed and took a step back.

"Put your foot in my hands," I snapped. *"Now."* She did, and I heaved her up onto the horse behind Gunthard. She was a large woman. If one had to boost her up onto a horse many times during a single day, it would be tiring work.

I took the reins of the remaining horse and turned to Genevieve. *"You will ride with me on this horse,"* I told her.

"I do not wish to ride with you," she replied.

I rolled my eyes. What was wrong with this woman? Did she not understand that she was a prisoner?

"I do not care," I told her. I cupped my hands,

but she backed away.

I straightened up angrily and glared at her. She was a very small woman. I had not realized until now how little she was. I reached out suddenly, grasped her waist with my hands, and swung her up and onto the saddle, straddling the horse's back. Her long gown rode up when I did, revealing slender legs. She shrieked and tugged at the fabric, pulling it down to cover herself.

"Do not touch me!" she shouted. *"Do not touch me again!"*

I bent over, picked up my bow from where I'd laid it on the ground, then vaulted up onto the horse behind her. She gasped when I leaned forward against her back and reached my arms around her to take the reins.

I turned the horse until I was facing Gunthard and Clothilde, then addressed them all in a loud voice.

"Listen to me, all three of you, and heed my words well. When I tell you to stop, you will stop. When I tell you to ride, you will ride. If I tell you to be silent, you will make no noise. Do not disobey me, and do not anger me. Remember, I am a Northman. If I have to, I will kill you. I will kill you all, starting with your mistress here."

Genevieve gasped, and Clothilde closed her eyes and began muttering a prayer. Gunthard just stared at me, looking into my eyes. Perhaps he was wondering if I would really carry out my threat.

Our trail would not have been difficult to follow. Fortunately, little of the day remained. With luck, even if the Franks discovered the cart before night-fall, they would not have time to bring a tracker to the site before night's sheltering darkness hid our path.

We headed north by west. I hoped to cross the river, upstream from the fortified crossing at the bridge, before we stopped to rest.

After darkness fell, though, it became more and more difficult to take bearings and choose our course. Although the forest canopy overhead was still not fully leafed out, it was thick enough to hide the stars. And as the night progressed and we rode deeper into the forest, the darkness seemed to grow thicker, until at times I could swear it had become a physical thing that brushed lightly across my face and hands as we rode. If I had not tied all of our horses together with the lead ropes I'd made, we would surely have become separated in the dark.

Because I could see nothing, I eventually let the reins hang limp, and allowed my horse pick its own way among the trunks of the trees. I hoped it would not carry us in a circle back to the road.

An owl hooted nearby. Genevieve jerked in my arms, and sat upright—over time she had slumped back more and more against my chest, and her head had drooped forward.

"Where are we?" she whispered, sounding frightened.

"We are in the forest," I answered. More than that, I myself did not know.

Hearing our voices, Clothilde spoke up.

"Mistress Genevieve, I am worried about Gunthard. He has been unconscious for some time now. And my back and legs—they are hurting so."

"Can we not stop?" Genevieve pleaded. *"At least briefly, to stretch and rest?"*

The forest seemed thinner here, and the darkness with it. The ground had been rising for some time, and I could dimly see, off to the right, the crest of a hill. A patch of night sky was visible above it. The hill would give me a vantage point from which to watch for pursuers. And in truth, I was tired and sore, too.

I pointed toward the hilltop and answered Genevieve, but in a voice loud enough for Clothilde to hear, also.

"We will ride up there. We can stop and rest on top of that hill."

As we climbed the slope, a vague shape loomed out of the darkness ahead of us, as if it had suddenly risen up from the ground when we neared. It was taller than a man, and ran across the side of the hill as far as I could see in either direction, barring our progress. At first I thought it was a massive outcropping of rock, forming a cliff around the top of the hill, but when we drew nearer I saw it was a man-made stone wall.

"*What is this place?*" Genevieve murmured. This was her land, not mine. Why did she ask me?

"*I do not know,*" I answered. Whatever it was, it looked very old, and there was no sign that men lived here now.

We turned and rode left, circling the hilltop just below the wall. Behind me, Gunthard moaned. As if in response, something rustled through dead leaves on the other side of the wall. My horse's ears pricked up suddenly, and I could feel its muscles twitching nervously beneath my legs.

"*Did you hear that?*" Genevieve whispered. "*What was it?*"

"*Just an animal. Probably a fox,*" I answered, to reassure myself as much as her, for the hair on the back of my neck was standing on end. I wondered if ghosts inhabited this ancient place. Perhaps they had smelled Gunthard's blood.

We reached a gap in the wall. I hesitated, wondering whether to enter. Within these walls would be shelter, a place to hide. From within I could watch for hunters on our trail, while remaining unseen. But what if there were ghosts?

I shook my head, disgusted at my own fear. I had never seen a ghost, except in the sleep-world of my dreams. And those I had seen there had never actually harmed me. I had been hunted by men before, though, and I knew the Franks would be hunting me soon. That was a real danger, one that could kill me. I kicked my heels in my horse's sides and urged him forward through the gap in the wall.

I awoke to the sound of birds chirping. The sun, high in the sky, was shining on my face. It was almost noon. I had slept much longer than I'd intended.

I stood up and rubbed my eyes. A few feet away Genevieve sat, her back against the trunk of the small tree I had tied her to, glaring at me with a bleary expression. Behind her, on the other side of the tree, Clothilde was slumped down on her side, snoring noisily. Gunthard was cradled in her arms.

Before I'd fallen asleep, I had seated the two women against opposite sides of the tree, bound their hands and feet, and looped a rope around their waists and the tree's trunk. I had not bothered to bind Gunthard. He had not regained consciousness even when I'd dragged him down from the horse and stretched him out along the ground. Clothilde had insisted I position him so his head could be pillowed by her lap. He had lost much blood. Whatever skills Genevieve possessed, bandaging wounds was apparently not among them.

Seeing that I had awakened, Genevieve spoke. *"These ropes are too tight. I can no longer feel my feet. And I need to get up."*

It was easy to picture her as one who owned slaves. She was used to giving orders, and having them obeyed without question. I stood up and began walking over to where I'd tethered the horses in the shelter of the stone wall. The basket of food was there, still lashed to one of the saddles.

"Please," she said, desperation in her voice now. *"I need to get up. I cannot wait much longer."*

I turned back toward her, suddenly understanding.

"Do you need to relieve yourself?" I asked. She blushed, looked down, and nodded.

"Do not go far," I told her, as she stood up unsteadily on numb feet, after I had untied her bonds. *"Stay where I can see you."*

"You are going to watch?" she asked, a shocked expression on her face.

Now I felt embarrassed. *"No,"* I said curtly, and turned away.

I busied myself by searching the contents of the

food basket. Besides the two waterskins, the bottle of wine, and the sausages I'd added to its contents, it contained four more cheeses—one soft, like the cheese I'd already sampled, and three others that were hard—plus two more loaves of bread and a half-dozen apples. The greatest prize, though, was a plump chicken, already roasted, wrapped in cloth and bound with twine. That would not keep. We would eat it now.

Genevieve approached. Her face looked tired—I guessed she had slept little, if at all. For a fine Frankish lady, sleeping out of doors on the ground was no doubt a new experience. As I looked at her, I realized she was far younger than my original impression had led me to believe. She was probably no older than me.

"What are you staring at?" she asked nervously.

"I am not staring," I told her. *"Wake the others. We will eat now."*

Gunthard looked to be developing a fever, but at least Genevieve and Clothilde were able to wake him. He had little appetite, but eagerly drank from the bottle of wine when I offered it to him. Between the four of us, we finished the chicken, plus the rest of the loaf of bread and round of cheese that had been partially eaten yesterday. Clothilde wanted more. I gave her an apple, but packed the rest of the food back in the basket. I did not know how long it would have to last.

As I packed up the food I glanced up and saw Gunthard staring at me.

"You are alone, aren't you, Northman?" he said. I ignored him, and continued with my work.

"I thought you were with a raiding party. I thought you were taking us to join them," he continued, *"but I was wrong. There are no others. You are alone."* Genevieve turned and looked at me with a surprised expression on her face. *"You are doomed,"* Gunthard added. *"You will never escape on your own."*

He sagged back against Clothilde's shoulder, panting from the exertion of talking.

Gunthard could not continue. He was far too weak. That much was obvious. For that matter, there was really no reason to bring any of them with me now. I had gained as much advantage as I could by removing them from the scene of the fight, and leaving the Franks who found the abandoned cart to wonder what had become of them. With the coming of daylight, though, hunters would be able to find our trail and begin pursuing us. Now I needed to move more swiftly than the men who would be hunting me. From here on, these prisoners would only slow me down.

I walked the short distance to the peak of the hill. It was flat on top, as though it had been lev-

eled at some time in the distant past. I wondered if
a chieftain's hall had stood here long ago. In the
daylight, it was obvious the stone wall had once
been a fort. Hundreds of years must have passed
since it had been used, though, for a scattering of
mature trees grew within the perimeter of the wall
now, as the forest slowly but relentlessly worked to
reclaim the land men long ago had cleared in its
midst.

Looking down into the forest, I saw that we
had traveled farther during the night than I'd
dared to hope. Through the trees, below the steep-
est side of the hill, I could see sunlight glinting on
water. It had to be the river.

I strode down to where the horses were tethered. I'd been too exhausted, when we'd stopped
the night before, to unload them. I unlashed the
two bodies now, dragged them onto the ground,
and began searching them to see if they bore anything I could use.

The Frank I'd killed with my axe had obviously
been a common soldier. His brynie was made of
metal scales sewed onto a leather jerkin—effective,
but heavier than mail—and his sword was unre-
markable.

The gear belonging to Leonidas, the young
nobleman, was a different matter. His mail shirt
was very fine. It was longer than most worn by

warriors of the northern lands—the sleeves reached to just below the elbow, and its bottom edge to mid-thigh. It was very supple, too, for the mail links were smaller than any I'd seen before. His sword was fine, also. The blade was pattern-welded, like Harald's sword, Biter, had been. The hilt was decorated with inlays of silver wire, and it balanced well.

The dead man looked close to my size. I began stripping the mail shirt and padded jerkin underneath off of him. It was not easy, for during the night his body had taken on the stiffness of death. I thought it worth the trouble, though. I hoped to reach the safety of the *Gull* before my pursuers could catch up with me. But it was only a hope, and probably a vain one. I had chosen to bring no armor when I'd set out on this mission because I did not plan to fight. But now I was being hunted, and the odds had greatly risen that I would have to. If I did, this dead man's armor and sword might help keep me alive.

After donning the jerkin and mail shirt, and strapping the sword belt around my waist, I lashed Leonidas' helm and shield behind my saddle. Then I led the two packhorses to the gap in the wall, where the gate to this ancient fortress once had stood, and sent them through with slaps on their rumps. Perhaps whatever trail they laid would confuse my hunters briefly.

I returned to where my three prisoners were seated, watching me nervously.

"Hand me the basket of food," I said to Clothilde. It was on the ground between her and Genevieve.

"I suppose if we are dead we will not need food. Or horses," Gunthard said, eyeing me.

"What do you mean?" Clothilde demanded.

"You do not intend to take us any farther, do you?" he asked, watching my face closely.

"You are correct. I do not," I agreed. Genevieve gasped.

"Please do not kill us," she said. *"If you will spare me, my father will pay well for my return. He is a wealthy and powerful man."*

"So your father will pay to ransom you?" I asked in disgust. *"What of Gunthard and Clothilde? Are their lives worth nothing? Shall I kill them?"*

Clothilde let out a wail, then clutched at Gunthard's arm, pulling him towards her and burying her face, sobbing, against his shoulder. He winced in pain, but put his uninjured arm around her to offer some comfort.

He was a decent man. I felt ashamed of my cruel jest.

"Do you think I would have wasted food on you if I was going to kill you?" I asked, shaking my head.

To Genevieve, I said, *"Who is this wealthy and powerful man who is your father?"*

"He is a count, one of King Charles' strongest. He rules many towns, and the lands around them, for the king."

She was a rich prize. A very rich prize indeed. I had found, since our army had come to Frankia, that I had no stomach for robbing poor folk of their few possessions. Now, though, it seemed the Norns had offered me a different way to profit from this voyage—if I could survive to claim it.

"What are you going to do with us, if you are not going to kill us?" Gunthard asked.

"I am going to leave you here," I replied. *"The daughter of so great a count will surely be missed. Warriors from your army will hunt for her after they discover the abandoned cart. No doubt they already follow our trail. Eventually they will find you here. Or, if you do not wish to wait for them, the river is down there,"* I added, pointing down the hill. *"If you follow it downstream, it will lead you to a village. Some of your army are there."*

"Thank you for sparing our lives," Genevieve said. *"Thank you for leaving us here."*

"I am only leaving them," I told her. *"You are coming with me."*

14

TRAPPED

" I want you to deliver a message for me."

I was seated on my horse, holding the reins to Genevieve's mount. She was sobbing quietly now, an improvement over the pleading, arguing, and wailing she had filled the air with earlier. I'd finally had to threaten to gag her and bring her strapped across a horse's back like one of the bodies we'd hauled the night before to silence her and persuade her to cooperate.

Gunthard was standing below me, leaning on Clothilde for support. She, too, was sobbing.

"Tell her father that she has been taken by the Danes," I continued. *"Tell him I will return her in exchange for a payment of ransom. Assure him she was unharmed when you last saw her, and that I will do my best to keep her that way, so long as*

she does not try to escape."

"How much will he have to pay for her release?" Gunthard asked.

I had no idea what she was worth. I had never collected ransom before.

"He will hear from me," I said, then turned my horse and rode through the gap in the wall, leading Genevieve behind me.

"They will hunt you, Northman," Gunthard called after me. *"You will not escape. Have faith, Lady Genevieve. They will find you."*

We needed to move fast, or Gunthard's prediction would likely come true. Even if the Frankish army had been unable to begin tracking us until this morning, hours of daylight had passed while I slept. If they had a skilled tracker and were pressing hard, by now the Franks would have greatly reduced the lead I'd gained on them. If we merely ran ahead of our pursuers, I feared they would almost certainly catch up with us. A trail left by two horses would not be difficult for an experienced tracker to follow. I had to find some way to throw them off.

We waded our horses across the river at a shallow bend. I paused mid-stream, studying the channel. Once before when men had hunted me, I'd run my trail through water as frequently as possible, each time costing my pursuers delay while they'd searched for where I'd returned to land. Then I'd been on foot, though, and alone. I did not think that tactic would work here. Traveling up this riverbed would be treacherous footing for the horses. It would slow us too much, and wherever our mounts eventually did leave the river, the spoor they'd leave in the damp soil of the bank as they climbed out would be easy to find. I kicked my heels in my horse's sides, urging him forward, and we splashed on across the river and up the far bank, heading off through the forest.

I set a course north by west, hoping to stay well within the cover provided by the forest and avoid open ground as long as possible. Eventually we would have to cross the plain in order to reach the Seine River, but I wanted to delay that danger as long as I could.

Genevieve stopped crying not long after we'd left the hilltop fortress behind. She was obviously not an experienced rider, and merely staying on the horse required all of her concentration. In the late afternoon, however, she began whimpering again.

"What is the matter?" I asked her.

"I am exhausted," she answered. *"My back is aching, and my legs feel as though the flesh on them has been worn to shreds. I cannot go on."*

I could well imagine that she felt that way. I was tired and aching, too. Being able to ride, instead of having to walk, was a mixed blessing.

"We will rest," I said. *"But only briefly."* I hoped to continue riding the rest of the day and through the entire night, or at least most of it. I did not tell Genevieve that, though. I did not wish her to despair.

After I helped her off the horse, Genevieve hobbled painfully over to a large oak, lowered herself gingerly to the ground, and leaned back against its broad trunk. She sat there, breathing in and out slowly, her eyes closed. She looked pale and drawn. I was struck again by how young she looked under the dirt and fatigue.

I untied the basket of provisions from my saddle and carried it over to where she sat. Uncorking the jug of wine, I handed it to her.

"Here," I told her. *"Drink some of this. And eat some food. It will give you strength."*

She looked at the fat bottle dubiously—perhaps, being a fine lady, she had never drunk directly from one before—then tipped it cautiously to her lips. After a brief initial taste, she took two longer swallows. When I sliced bread, cheese, and sausages and shared them with her, she ate hungrily.

"Why can you not let me go?" she asked, sighing, after the worst of her hunger had been eased. *"You could travel much faster without me. I*

cannot keep up this pace."

"You are coming with me," I told her firmly. *"I would be a poorer man at my journey's end without you. It was you who suggested your father will pay a generous ransom for your return."*

"I was afraid you were going to kill me. That is why I said it." She glanced up at me, but when her eyes met mine, she would not hold my gaze, looking away quickly. Surely, I thought, she had not lied about the ransom.

"Is your father a count?" I pressed her.

She nodded. *"He is."*

"And he will pay a ransom for your return?"

She looked up briefly, then averted her eyes again. Her answer was long in coming—so long, I began to fear I had indeed been wasting precious time by bringing her with me. Was I risking my life for the hope of a ransom that would not be paid?

"He will not wish to," she finally said, *"but I am certain he will pay. It would reflect badly on him if he did not, and my father is very particular about his honor."*

I thought it a strange answer. Why would her father not wish to pay ransom for her return? I asked her.

"I do not wish to speak of this," she replied. *"It is a private matter. It is enough for you to know that he will pay. Though if I am harmed—harmed in any*

way at all—he will not pay as much. And you should know this, also. I am a holy woman. I have dedicated my life to the service of my God, the Lord Jesus Christ. If you harm me, you will be cursed. Do not . . ." she paused here for a moment, as if searching for the correct words to say, then continued, her voice quavering and her eyes averted, *"Do not try to force yourself on me, or I will call upon my God for vengeance, and He will strike you dead."*

I stared at her, dumbfounded for a moment, then began laughing. She looked up at me then, and tears filled her eyes. By my laughter, it seemed, I had just confirmed her worst fears.

"I am sorry," I told her. *"I do not mean to mock you. You should know this about me. My mother was not a Dane. She was captured by my father in a raid on her people's land. She told me of the fear she felt, how she was terrified she would be raped. You do not need to fear that from me."*

Genevieve looked skeptical. *"I have heard stories,"* she said, *"about women who were captured by the Northmen."*

I did not doubt that she had. Though my father had not raped my mother, women taken in the same raid by other warriors had not been so fortunate.

"The women you have heard tales of were not captured by me," I told her. *"All I wish from you is the*

wealth your ransom will bring me."

She still looked skeptical. "*Why did you laugh?*" she demanded.

"*My mother was a worshiper of the White Christ all her life,*" I explained. "*Her prayers did not protect her. You were trying to frighten me with empty threats. I have seen no evidence that your God has the power to protect his own, and certainly not to strike men dead.*"

Her face flushed scarlet, and she looked down at the ground again. It surprised me that she should feel embarrassed to be caught lying to an enemy. I did not feel there was any dishonor in what she had done.

"*How long have you been a priestess?*" I asked her.

"*I am not a priestess. I am a nun,*" she answered.

"*What is that?*"

"*We—nuns,*" she said, "*devote our lives to prayer, and to serving God. We are brides of Christ, rather than of men.*"

If you are wed to a God, I thought, surely you are a priestess, whether you call it that or not. I wondered how one wed a God, when you could neither see nor touch him.

"*What was it like?*" I asked her. "*The ceremony where you wed your God?*"

She hesitated. *"There has been no ceremony,"* she finally said. *"Not yet. I am still preparing to become a nun."*

At least what she'd told me explained the strange, plain clothing she wore. It must be the garb of a priestess. I'd thought it odd that the daughter of a count would not be more finely dressed.

"You said you serve your God. How do you serve him, and where? Do you live in a temple? Is there a particular high priest whom you serve?"

She shook her head vigorously. *"You do not understand,"* she said. *"Christians do not have temples, we have churches. And nuns do not live in our churches. No one—no man nor woman—lives there. A church is the house of God."*

"But where do you live? Where do nuns live?" I asked.

"We live away from the world, in our own communities," she answered. *"We serve our God there by leading lives of devotion and prayer."*

She was correct. I did not understand. What use were priests or priestesses, if they did not live among the people? How else could they intercede for their people with the Gods?

A thought occurred to me—if nuns lived in their own communities away from the world, what had she been doing traveling on the road in the company of soldiers?

"*Where is this place, this community, that you live?*" I asked her.

"*At the Abbey of Saint Genevieve, in Paris,*" she answered.

"*Why were you traveling on the road?*"

"*My uncle's wife, my aunt Therese, was ill. She is very dear to me—almost like a second mother. For a time my uncle feared she would die. He asked me to come, to comfort her and help nurse her. The abbess allowed me to go.*"

"*Were you on the way to see her when I found you?*" I asked. She shook her head, looking surprised by my question.

"*No,*" she said, "*We were on the way back to Paris. That is where that road leads—from the town of Dreux, where my uncle lives, to Paris. My aunt recovered, and I was returning to the abbey.*"

I wondered if that information—where the road led, and where the towns along it were located—would be something Hastein and Ragnar would wish to know. Hopefully not. Surely they would not think of bringing our army so far from the safety of the Seine River and our ships.

Roads and the river—perhaps it was thinking about both at the same time that caused a plan to begin to form in my mind. Using my finger, I drew a line in the dirt on the ground between us.

"*This is the road you were on,*" I explained. "*You say you were traveling from your uncle's town toward Paris?*"

She nodded.

I placed small stones in the dirt at either end of the line I'd drawn.

"*This is Paris,*" I told her. "*And this is the town where your uncle lives.*"

She looked down at the stones, then back at me. "*If you say so,*" she said.

"*Is there a road that leads in this direction?*" I asked, pointing to the area above the line I'd drawn. "*A road that leads north?*"

She shrugged her shoulders. "*I do not know which direction north is,*" she said.

I stared at her with disbelief. Did she not see the sun rise in the east in the morning, and set in the west? How could a person travel if they did not know in which direction they were going?

She stared back at me with a blank expression on her face. "*What?*" she asked. "*Why do you look at me like that?*"

"*Are there any roads leading in any direction out of your uncle's town, besides the road that leads to Paris?*" I asked, in an exasperated voice.

"*I do not know,*" she replied, also sounding exasperated. "*Why should I know? I have spent most of my life in Paris. I have traveled on a few occasions*" *to Dreux to visit my uncle and his family there, but never beyond.*"

There must be some way to find out what I needed to know.

"*Do you know of the town of Ruda?*" I asked her. She frowned and shook her head. I muttered a curse under my breath. Ruda was the name we peoples of the North called the Franks' town on the Seine; it was not the Frankish name. I could not recall the name Wulf had called it.

"*The town on the Seine River where the Northmen are camped—surely you have heard your father or your uncle speak of it?*"

"*Ah,*" she said, nodding her head vigorously. "*You mean Rouen.*"

That was it. "*Yes, I mean Rouen,*" I agreed. "*Is there a road that leads between Dreux and Rouen?*"

She shrugged her shoulders again. I was getting tired of that gesture. "*I have never been to Rouen,*" she said. I knew she was going to say that.

"*But,*" she continued. "*After my aunt's health improved, and I began speaking of returning to Paris, she told my uncle that he must not allow me to leave because it would be too dangerous with Northmen abroad in the land. I remember he told her there would be no danger, because no Northmen had been seen south of the town of Evreux.*" She paused for a moment, then her eyes narrowed and she added, *"Why do you ask me these things?"*

"Do you know where Evreux is?" I continued, ignoring her question.

"No," she replied, sighing. *"I have never been there."* I, too, let out a sigh. *"But,"* she added, *"I believe it is between Dreux and Rouen. In fact, I am certain it is. The Count of Rouen stopped in Evreux after he fled Rouen on his way to Dreux. I heard him say so. He stayed at my uncle's home for more than a week, until the king's summons came and he went on to join the army."*

If only she had said that to begin with. Still, I had learned what I needed to know. These towns—Dreux, Evreux, and Rouen—would be connected by a road, one that ran north toward the river. Therein lay my best hope for throwing our pursuers off, and reaching the Seine and the *Gull* safely. That road would hide our trail. We would travel it by night. The traffic upon it by day would obliterate whatever tracks our horses left.

"You should try to rest now," I told Genevieve. *"Sleep, if you can. When darkness falls, we will ride again."*

As the sun was setting, turning a pale rose color just before it sank below the horizon, I noted its position, then closed my eyes and tried to fix it in my mind.

At dusk we set off, headed due west. I wanted

to find the road as quickly as possible.

As the night grew darker, my estimate of the direction we were traveling became more and more of a guess. Periodically I closed my eyes and tried to find, still lingering within my mind, the memory of where the sun had set. The Danes, my brother, Harald, had told me, were such fine sailors because they have a natural sense for direction, greater than other men. I hoped I had inherited my sense for direction from my Danish father, rather than from my Irish mother.

The earth underfoot was thickly matted with fallen leaves, and our passing made no sound, save for an occasional click when a hoof found a stone on the forest floor. In the distance behind us, a wolf howled. A few moments later it was answered by two others. I hoped the Franks who hunted us would find Gunthard and Clothilde before the wolves did.

It was still long before midnight when a road materialized across our path. This was more than a simple dirt track through the forest—it was broad enough for two carts to pass one another, and it followed a course that, for as far as I could see in the dim light, ran as straight and unwavering as the flight of an arrow. I wondered if it had been built by the Romans. The Franks' land seemed filled with great, ancient works by those once-powerful people.

I paused briefly among the trees along the edge

of the road, listening and watching. The forest was silent, save for the distant hooting of an owl. I could see nothing but the dim trunks of trees, one after another, fading into the dark along either side of the lighter strip of bare roadway. I gave a tug on the reins of Genevieve's horse, and we moved out onto the dusty surface and headed north.

As the night wore on, I found it increasingly difficult to stay awake. Though Genevieve had dozed restlessly for several hours during our afternoon halt, I had not slept. I'd remained awake and on guard, fearing the Franks on our trail. But now the monotonous, rocking motion of my horse's gait, and the fatigue that had been building through too many days and nights, wore away at my ability to remain alert.

I do not know how long I'd been dozing. A muffled gasp from Genevieve, whose horse had been walking alongside mine since we'd reached the road, startled me awake.

Ahead in the distance, just off one side of the road, the light of a fire was flickering between the trees. The figure of a man—he must have been a sentry—backed into the roadway, laughing. He was facing the fire and talking to someone I could not see.

"Quickly!" I whispered. *"Off the road."* I kicked

my horse ahead of Genevieve's and tugged on my reins, turning my mount to the right, crossing in front of hers and grabbing its reins as I passed. As we entered the woods, Genevieve looked back longingly toward the light of the fire, then glanced at me with a frightened expression on her face. I feared she would cry out. Just then I heard a voice calling in the distance, *"Halloo. Is someone there?"*

"Make no sound," I hissed at Genevieve. *"It will do you no good. By the time they could saddle their mounts and come after us, we will have disappeared into the forest. They will not be able to find us in the dark. But if you try to call to them, I will hurt you. I swear it."*

She remained silent, and no further sounds came to us from the direction of the Franks' campsite. Perhaps the sentry was uncertain he had seen anything. It was foolish of him to have been so close to the fire and looking toward it, when he was supposed to be standing watch. The fire's light would have made the darkness seem even deeper to his eyes.

As we traveled among the trees, moving deeper into the forest and farther from the road, I wondered whether the Franks we'd seen had been hunters pursuing us, or just a patrol we'd happened upon by chance. Did I dare return to the road, or should I keep from now on to the forest? I decided the latter course was safer.

My thoughts were interrupted by the sound of quiet sobbing coming from behind me. Turning in the saddle, I called back to Genevieve in a hushed voice.

"What is the matter? Why do you weep?"

She did not answer. I saw her raise one hand to her mouth, as if trying to muffle the sound. I pulled back on my reins, slowing my horse, and waited for her to come alongside me.

"Are you injured? Are you in pain?" I asked.

"I am ashamed. I am disgusted with myself. I am a coward."

"You would have been foolish to have cried out," I told her. *"It was not cowardice to choose the wiser course."*

She said nothing more, but the sound of quiet weeping continued for some time.

I must have dozed again as we rode on through the night, even though my eyes remained open, for suddenly I realized that the forest around us had grown much lighter. Morning was approaching. Individual trees were visible in all directions, where before they had been but deeper shadows that would loom suddenly from the dark as we passed, only to disappear again behind.

I glanced behind me. Genevieve was wide

awake and staring defiantly back at me.

Ahead, off to the right, the growing light seemed strongest. Perhaps there was a clearing there where I could see the sky and take my bearings.

It was no clearing. The light marked the edge of the forest. The plain beyond was bathed in the grayness that lies upon the earth just before the sun shines its first light across the land.

Part of me longed to head out now across the plain and to strike for the river and the safety of the *Gull*. I was weary of trying to remain ever watchful, of fearing that behind every tree might lurk a Frank seeking to end my life. But I knew we dared not. It would take at least half a day to cross the plain, if not more, even on horseback. Moreover, our passing would leave a clear trail—visible from a distance and easy to follow—through the tall, dry winter grass that covered the plain. It was too great a risk to travel in the open, in daylight, in an area that was likely heavily patrolled by Frankish cavalry. We would have to turn back into the forest and hide until nightfall.

The sun was shining brightly overhead, and the forest alive with the flutter and singing of birds greeting the new day, before I found a hiding place. A ravine, cutting a gash across the forest floor, opened up suddenly before me. Its edges screened by thickets of low scrub, it had been invisible until we were almost upon it. The merest trickle of a stream meandered along its bottom. I could not, at this late hour, prevent someone from finding us here if they were follow our trail, but the ravine was deep enough to hide our horses from the view of chance passersby.

I dammed the rivulet with stones and mud to form a small pool for the horses to drink from, and tied them with a long lead to a sapling by the water's edge, giving them room to move about the bottom of the ravine and forage as best they could. I wished I had food to give them in addition to water, for I intended push them hard once night came again.

I knew that this day I would be unable to stay awake. If the Franks found our trail where we'd turned off the road and into the forest, I would have to depend on my fylgja to wake me and warn me of their approach.

I kicked loose leaves together into a low pile, spread my cloak over them, and called to Genevieve, who was seated near the horses, eating bread and cheese.

"*Come here,*" I said.

She looked at the cloak, and then at me, with an alarmed expression growing on her face.

"*Why?*" she asked. "*What do you want of me?*"

"*I must sleep. I am too weary to stay awake.*"

"You wish me to lie with you?" she exclaimed.

"Only to sleep," I assured her. *"I have already given you my word that I will not molest you. I swear to you again I will not. Among my people, if a man breaks his oath, he has no honor. You can trust that you will be safe."*

"I do not wish to lie beside you," she said. *"I will sleep over here."*

"If you sleep here, beside me, I will not have to bind you so tightly. I will only tie your hands, and connect them with a cord to my wrist. If you get up, if you try to sneak away, it will be enough to wake me. If you choose not to sleep here, I will have to bind your hands and feet, tie you to a tree, and gag you. It will make for a long and uncomfortable day."

Still she sat there, across the ravine, staring at me suspiciously.

"I am offering this to you as a kindness," I told her. *"It matters not to me. It is your decision."*

Reluctantly, she stood and walked over to me.

I fell asleep beside a source of ransom, a hope of wealth. I awoke beside a woman.

It was late afternoon. At some point, while we both slept, we had rolled against each other, her back pressed against my chest, my legs curled behind hers, my arm draped across her body.

I climbed from the depths of sleep gradually.

Slumber gave way to the pleasant feel of Genevieve's warm body against mine, and the gentle rhythm of her breathing within my arms. She had removed her hood and mantle before falling asleep, and her hair now brushed softly against my cheek, like the lightest of caresses. The sensation of her body pressed against mine caused my body to stir.

We both started fully awake at the same time and rolled apart. I stood, keeping myself turned away from her, and fumbled at the cord around my wrist, until I untied the knot securing it.

"I must go relieve myself," I muttered, and stumbled away down the ravine.

We broke fast with the remaining sausages, slices of hard cheese, the last remnants of stale bread, and an apple each. Neither of us spoke, and we avoided each other's gaze. After we ate, as dusk began to fall, I pulled the padded jerkin and mail shirt on over my tunic, strapped my new sword around my waist, and saddled the horses. A small black toad crawled from a hollow under a tree root nearby, watching my preparations. I smiled at him, then bent down, scooped my hand into the pool I'd made for the horses to drink from, and dribbled water onto his back. He flicked his tongue at a droplet sparkling beside him on the leafy forest floor.

never seen this stretch before. I was certain of it. We were still upstream—how far I did not know— from where the *Gull* had put me ashore.

"Where is your ship?" Genevieve asked.

"That way," I lied hopefully, pointing down- stream.

We rode at a brisk trot until the sun rose above the horizon and lit the land. I had never welcomed the coming of morning less. It was no good. We could not stay out here longer, exposed upon the plain. Since dawn, I had already seen four separate trails left by the passing of groups of mounted men. We had to go to ground.

We rode past several stretches where wide bands of woods lined the river's bank, but I passed these by. Instead, I chose a long stretch of the river where the bank was mostly open save for occasional low, scruffy shrubs and a single, small thicket of trees and undergrowth—a huge, ancient grandfather of a willow in its center, and five smaller specimens spreading in either direction along the bank.

The cluster of trees and shrubs was no longer than three spears, laid end to end, and little more than half as wide. It would have to do. We could not stay out on the plain any longer. Hopefully, any passing patrol of Frankish cavalry would think this cover so slight that no one could be concealed within it.

I stopped our horses a good stone's throw out on the plain. Our peril was great enough without running their trail directly up to our hiding place.

"Get off your horse," I instructed Genevieve, *"and walk over there, to those trees."* She looked at me a moment, frowning, but said nothing. When she'd dismounted, I handed her the basket of food to carry.

I freed the helm and shield I'd lashed behind my saddle, jammed the helm on my head, and slid to the ground. My horse turned his head and looked back at me, blew his breath out in a snort, then reached down and tore a mouthful of dry, brown grass from the ground and began chewing it.

"I know you are weary," I told him. "You have carried me far and faithfully, though I have given you little rest, and no food. I am sorry, but I must ask still more of you."

A Frankish patrol would find these horses. It was inevitable. It might be possible, though, to make them misinterpret what they found.

Slinging the shield on my back, I strung my bow and eased two arrows from my quiver. Nocking the first on the string, I fixed my gaze on my horse's front shoulder, just ahead of the saddle, and drew. I pulled the arrow back to only half its length—I did not wish to kill this poor beast, or even injure it any worse than necessary—and released.

The horse screamed in surprise and pain at the arrow's impact. It raised its head, looking wildly around, trying to spy what had attacked it without warning.

"Hah!" I shouted, waving my arms and the bow. "Hah!" The horse ran two steps then stopped, bucking and kicking, neighing angrily.

I nocked my second arrow, drew—halfway, again—and launched it into the haunch of Genevieve's horse. Spooked already by its comrade's actions and my shouts, it turned and raced off across the plain at a gallop. My horse wheeled and followed in its wake.

I walked backward, one slow step after another, to the copse of willow trees. As I did, I bent down and with my hand fluffed and rearranged the grass wherever it was bent or flattened, trying as best I could to erase the scant trail left by our passing.

Genevieve stood at the edge of the trees, staring at me with disgust and horror on her face. I stepped past her, laid the shield and helm on the ground, and unstrung my bow.

"You are a monster!" she exclaimed. *"How can you be so cruel?"*

I knew she was speaking of the horses. I felt guilty for the pain I had caused them, even without her words.

"I did not wish to hurt them," I told her. *"And their wounds are not fatal. I did what I had to do."*

"What you had to do?" Her voice was filled with scornful disbelief.

I did not know why I felt a need to justify my actions to her. She was a source of ransom, nothing more.

"Your troops patrol this area regularly," I explained to her. *"I have seen their tracks. They will find the horses. When they do, my arrows may make them think they were the mounts of soldiers ambushed by Danes. It is better they think that than suspect these are the two horses you and I rode."* Better for me, anyway. I doubted Genevieve would agree.

I left her standing at the edge of the small wood, staring out across the plain, and turned to investigate our hideaway.

At one time, the large willow must have been growing at the very edge of the river, its roots reaching down into the current to drink from the passing waters. Over countless years, flotsam and silt had been caught in the tangle of roots, forming a low shelf of beach, only a few feet wide and several feet below the edge of the original river bank. The narrow strip of beach had been invisible from out on the plain. If we crouched low here, behind the trunk of the willow, we would be hidden from all but the closest inspection.

I carried the shield and helm down to the strip of beach, and laid my quiver and bow beside them.

"Come," I called to Genevieve. *"Bring the basket of food. We will wait down here for the ship."*

"There is no ship, is there?" she said, after she had joined me. *"It is gone. You are trapped now, with no way to escape."*

I did not answer her, for in my heart I feared her words were true. The *Gull* would not come. We were too far upstream.

The sun had reached its zenith, and my spirits a nadir, when we saw them. Fifteen warriors—Frankish cavalry—riding slowly toward us from upstream. They looked to be following the trail left by our horses, for periodically the rider in front leaned over, as if studying the ground. I guessed he was their captain, for a narrow pennant, striped blue and white, fluttered from the tip of the long spear he carried.

The patrol halted opposite the thicket of trees where we crouched, hidden on the low strip of beach. Could they see our foot trail? Had I failed to fully erase it? The captain and several of his men were engaged in a discussion. As I watched them, I strung my bow and pulled my quiver closer.

Finally one of the Franks kicked his horse into an ambling walk in our direction. He wasn't following our foot trail, for he did not look at the ground as he came. He did not appear to be expecting trouble, either—he left his shield slung across his back by its long strap, and held his spear upright, resting against his shoulder. The Franks did not realize we were here. This warrior was just checking the thicket before the patrol moved on.

Perhaps he would take only a cursory look from the edge of the woods and not see us. Perhaps.

"Stay low," I warned Genevieve in a whisper. She was staring intently at the Franks out on the plain. *"Do not move or make a sound."*

As the rider neared the border of low undergrowth that formed the outer perimeter of the thicket, Genevieve gave a sudden gasp.

"What?" I hissed.

"I know their leader," she whispered, more to herself than me. *"It is Captain Marcus. Those men are from my uncle's scara."*

Suddenly she darted away from me, down the little beach to its end, and scrambled up the bank.

"Help me," she cried, waving her arms. *"Captain Marcus! I am here!"*

Startled, the approaching Frank backed his horse a few steps, while he swung his shield around to the front and lowered the point of his spear.

Dropping my bow, I clambered up the bank and sprinted after Genevieve. I caught up with her in three steps. She screamed as I grabbed her from behind.

"It is Lady Genevieve!" the Frank cried, and spurred his horse forward through the fringe of undergrowth. I sidestepped and flung Genevieve to the ground behind me as the Frank sawed at his reins, wheeling his horse to the side to avoid her. He stabbed his spear down at me with an overhand thrust, aiming for my throat. I threw myself down, and his spearhead grazed over the top of my shoulder as I dropped, scraping across the rings of my mail brynie.

He wheeled his horse again and spurred it, trying to trample me as I lay on the ground, but I rolled clear and scuttled frantically out of reach of his spear.

The Frank turned toward the plain and raised his spear overhead, waving it back and forth. *"Captain Marcus! She is here,"* he shouted. Then slinging his shield around to his back again, he urged his horse toward Genevieve, leaning over and extending an arm to her. *"Come!"* he cried.

She staggered unsteadily to her feet and took a step toward him. I jerked my sword from its scabbard and ran forward, plunging its blade into the horse's belly.

The horse screamed and kicked at me. As I backed away, the Frank turned in his saddle and clubbed down at my head with the shaft of his spear. I raised my sword overhead and blocked the blow, then lunged forward again and slashed my blade across the back of his horse's hind leg, cutting it to the bone.

The horse staggered sideways, almost falling. Clutching frantically at the reins, the Frank dropped his spear and tried to urge the crippled beast forward and out of the thicket, out of range of my sword. The horse tried to place weight on its injured leg and staggered again, crashing against one of the smaller willows.

I slammed my sword back into its scabbard and picked up the fallen spear. Running up behind the struggling horse from its flank, I thrust the spear forward with both hands, ramming its long blade into the Frank's back.

"*No!*" Genevieve screamed. The Frank cried out in pain. I wrenched the spear free and he slumped forward, sliding off his horse as it staggered through the fringe of undergrowth and out onto the plain.

The rest of the Franks were nearing the trees, charging in a ragged line. I turned and ran to Genevieve. As the first rider, their captain, burst through the fringe of undergrowth, he raised his spear as if to throw it. Grabbing Genevieve by the shoulder, I spun her around so she was between the Frank and me. Holding her pinned tightly against my chest with my left arm around her waist, I lifted her feet off the ground and began backing away from the Franks' captain. She thrashed her arms and legs helplessly as I edged toward the riverbank, using her as a shield and holding the spear at ready with my other arm.

"*Stay back*," I shouted, as a second rider entered the grove, and then a third. "*Stay back, or if your spears do not kill her I will.*"

By now the entire troop of cavalry was ringing the grove. Most had stopped just outside of it, uncertain what to do. Only the first three riders, including the captain, had actually passed beyond the outer border of undergrowth. One of these now slid from his horse and ran to his comrade who lay moaning on the ground. Putting the wounded man's arm around his shoulder, he dragged him up to his feet. The second of the three who'd entered the grove walked his horse over, watching me warily, then slung his shield to his back and leaned over, extending his arm down to help pull the injured warrior up onto his horse.

I had reached the edge of the bank. Dropping the spear, I scrambled down to the strip of sandy beach and stepped behind the cover of the massive willow. Hurling Genevieve to the ground hard enough to knock the breath out of her, I snarled, "*Do not move.*" As she lay there, coughing and gasping for air, I picked up my bow and quiver.

I was seething with anger at what Genevieve

had done. She'd almost cost me my life. The Franks would pay with blood.

Nocking an arrow and pulling it back to full draw, I stepped sideways, out from behind the cover of the willow's trunk.

The captain had walked his horse forward, trying to see where Genevieve and I had gone. He was only a spear's length away. I saw his eyes grow wide when he saw me, and he opened his mouth to shout a warning to his men. I used his open mouth as my aiming point and put an arrow in it.

His body flopped backward against his horse, then began to slide sideways out of the saddle. Before it hit the ground, I had nocked and shot a second arrow into the chest of the Frank who'd dismounted to help his wounded comrade. As he crumpled to the ground, the remaining Frank within the grove, his arm around his injured comrade now seated in front of him, turned his horse and spurred it hard. Just as he cleared the thicket, my third arrow hit him between the shoulder blades. His horse continued running, but he and the man he carried fell off to the side.

The suddenness and deadliness of my attack panicked the remaining Franks. They wheeled their horses and galloped out onto the plain, out of range.

Four of the Franks, including their captain,

were down, dead or dying. Eleven still remained, though, and they could send for reinforcements. I was trapped. I could not leave this thicket. And the Franks had time on their side.

Genevieve had sat up now, and was brushing sand from her face. *"What has happened?"* she asked.

"The Franks have retreated," I answered, *"for now."*

A tear trickled down one of her cheeks, washing a path through sand she had missed.

I could not leave her free. That was clear. I had to make certain she did not interfere with my fighting when the Franks attacked again. But I had left the rope I'd tied her with earlier on my horse's saddle.

Pulling my spare bowstring from the pouch at my belt, I stepped over to her. She flinched and drew away. I pushed her back roughly against a thick root that drooped down from the base of the willow's trunk to the strip of beach. Over time, the wash of rain and high water had eaten away the earth behind it, so the root stood out now from the bank. I wrapped the bowstring several times around Genevieve's neck and the root, securing her tightly to it. If she did anything other than sit still, the cord would choke her.

"Do not touch me!" she protested, as I tied her

to the root. *"You are a pig. You are a coward. What kind of warrior hides behind a woman?"*

Her words made my anger burn even hotter, and made me cruel.

"The kind of warrior who kills Franks. And I will kill more before this day is ended. You said you knew these men's captain? You cost him his life. He lies dead on the other side of this tree. Had you not called out, he would still be alive."

She closed her eyes and began sobbing. Tears streamed down her face.

I picked up my quiver and slung it over my shoulder. Twenty-one arrows remained in it. Three more were out in the bodies of the fallen Franks. Hopefully none had broken. I suspected I would need all of them and wish for more before this day was ended.

The captain and the man I'd shot in the chest were dead. The third Frank, who'd fallen just outside the grove, still breathed. Thankfully, he was unconscious, and looked unlikely to ever awaken again. After I retrieved my shafts, I stood and looked out across the plain. The remaining Frankish cavalry sat on their horses, watching me from a safe distance. I counted them. There were only ten now. They had already sent one of their number for help.

Turning away, I surveyed the willow grove.

Frank was almost to the edge of the willow grove.

"Come no closer," I said. *"We will talk. What terms do you offer?"*

"Let me see the lady," he answered. *"I must make certain she is alive and unharmed."*

"Call to him," I told Genevieve. I had no intention of untying her just so this Frank could see her. *"Tell him who you are, and that you have not been harmed."*

"Can you hear me?" she cried. *"I am Genevieve. My father is Robert, Count of Tours, and Autun, and Paris."*

I had not thought to ask Genevieve what towns and lands her father ruled over. It sounded as though he was much more powerful—and hopefully, much wealthier—than the count who had ruled Ruda. She was a richer prize than I had realized.

"Are you in good health, Lady?" the Frank asked.

"I am tired and hungry, and I am frightened, but the Northman has not harmed me."

"I have not harmed her yet!" I interjected. *"If your men attack, I will cut her throat."* I heard Genevieve gasp.

"If you slay her, there will be nothing to hold us back," the Frank said. *"We will kill you."*

"You have many men, and I am but one. If you attack me, some of you will die, but we both know you will kill me in the end. What will her father say,

though, what will he do, if you cause her death by attacking me?"

I hoped her father would care, though from what Genevieve had told me earlier—that he would but grudgingly pay ransom for her—I was not certain he would. Hopefully this Frank did not know their relationship was troubled.

"Release her," the Frank said, *"And we will give you a horse and allow you to leave in peace. I give you my word that none of the men under my command will pursue you."*

I thought it an empty offer. I had no doubt that other patrols of cavalry would have been alerted by now, and would intercept me long before I reached Ruda.

"I have grown weary of riding your horses," I told him. *"Your offer does not appeal to me. Bring me a boat. A small one, with oars, that one man can handle. Then we will talk further. Until then, we have nothing to discuss."*

"Wait, Northman," the Frank protested. I picked up my bow, and drew an arrow from my quiver.

"I agreed to allow you to approach so we could speak. Our speech is finished now. Leave while you still can."

The Frank wheeled his horse and cantered back out onto the plain.

Genevieve was watching me with a frightened expression in her eyes.

"*You would kill me? You would cut my throat?*" she asked.

"*I would threaten to,*" I answered, "*to keep those warriors from attacking.*"

"*You killed Captain Marcus. You killed my cousin Leonidas. You killed the other soldiers, too.*"

I nodded. "*Aye, I did. They were warriors, as I am. They attacked me, and I fought them. It is the way of things. It is what warriors do. I did kill them, but had they not attacked me, I would not have. They chose the path that led to their deaths.*"

"*You are a killer,*" she said, "*a ruthless, cruel killer.*"

I shook my head. "*I am a warrior.*"

"*What is the difference?*" she said, her voice disdainful.

"*If I was a killer, I would kill you. But I will not. If those soldiers attack, I will fight them and kill as many as I can. Then they will kill me, and you will be free.*"

Dusk was beginning to fall. The Franks had posted sentries at intervals around the grove, safely out of range of my bow, while the rest of their warriors withdrew farther out onto the plain and set up camp. Cook fires were burning now. I was glad the breeze was blowing away from the river. The only food remaining in my dwindling supply was a single block of hard cheese—that, and water. I did not care to be tortured by the smells of fresh, hot food being cooked.

I would have to stay awake during the night, because the Franks might try to sneak close under cover of darkness and launch a sudden attack. It would be difficult, for I had been awake all day and all of the previous night. The last time I had slept was in the ravine, with Genevieve beside me. I closed my eyes for a moment, and remembered the way her hair had felt against my cheek, and the way it had smelled.

"Why do you smile?" she demanded. I opened my eyes to find her staring at me. I shook my head.

"I was just thinking of another place and another time," I answered.

There was a noise out on the plain. I stood up and saw a rider, a Frankish cavalryman coming from downstream, galloping hard toward the encampment. After he reached the Franks' camp, it exploded into activity, men saddling their horses and donning their armor.

"What is happening?" Genevieve asked.

"I do not know," I told her. *"The Franks out on the plain are arming themselves. I think they are going to attack."*

With a sinking feeling, I strung my bow, slung

my quiver over my shoulder, and strapped on the Frankish helm I'd taken from Genevieve's dead cousin. As I pulled its laces tight under my chin, I heard a faint sound from far downriver.

It was a horn. When it sounded again, louder this time, I realized I had heard this horn before. It was Ivar's.

Frantically I searched the ground for tinder, for anything that would burn. After I gathered together a small pile of dried grass and dead leaves, I drew my dagger and stepped over to where Genevieve sat, still tied to the willow root.

"What are you doing?" she asked, her voice shaking. *"You said you would not kill me."*

"I need a strip of cloth," I answered, then knelt down and cut a narrow strip of linen from the edge of her under-shift. I used it to tie the tinder to the end of one of my arrows, then lit it with my flint and steel. When it was blazing steadily, I laid it across my bow, raised it overhead, and shot it high into the sky.

The fire arrow arced above the river, trailing sparks, then stalled and dropped, like a star falling from the heavens. From downriver, the horn sounded again, three peals in quick succession.

"What is it?" Genevieve asked.

Tears were streaming down my face when I turned and answered her. I could not stop them, but did not care. Once again, the Norns had chosen to continue weaving the pattern of my life.

"*It is a ship,*" I said. "*I am saved.*"

Despair filled Genevieve's face, and she began to weep.

LIST OF CHARACTERS

Bertrada
The wife of Wulf, a Frankish sea-captain and merchant in the town of Ruda, or Rouen.

Bjorn Ironsides
One of the sons of Ragnar Logbrod, and a Viking chieftain who helps lead the Danish attack on Western Frankia.

Charles
King of the Western Kingdom of the Franks, which roughly corresponds in territory to modern France.

Clothilde
A Frankish woman who is the personal servant of Genevieve, the daughter of Count Robert of Paris.

Cullain
Jarl Hastein's personal servant, a former Irish monk captured and enslaved during a Viking raid on Ireland.

Derdriu
An Irish noblewoman captured by the Danish chieftain Hrorik in a raid on Ireland, who became a slave in Hrorik's household and, as his concubine, bore him an illegitimate son named Halfdan.

Einar   A Danish warrior and skilled tracker from a village on the Limfjord in the north of Jutland, who befriends Halfdan.

Genevieve   A young Frankish noblewoman; the daughter of Count Robert of Paris.

Gunhild   The second wife of the Danish chieftain Hrorik, and the mother, by a previous marriage, of Hrorik's foster son, Toke.

Gunthard   A retainer of Count Robert assigned to escort Genevieve, the Count's daughter, on her return to Paris.

Halfdan   The son of Hrorik, a Danish chieftain, and Derdriu, an Irish slave.

Harald   The son of the Danish chieftain Hrorik by his first wife; Halfdan's half-brother and Sigrid's twin brother.

Hastein   A Danish jarl who befriends Halfdan, and who is one of the leaders of the Viking attack on Western Frankia.

Horik   The King of the Danes.

Hrodgar   The chieftain of a village on the Limfjord in Jutland, and the captain of a ship of warriors that sails as part of the attack on Frankia.

Hrorik   A Danish chieftain, known as Strong-Axe; the father of Halfdan, Harald, and Harald's twin sister, Sigrid, and the foster father of Toke.

Ivar the Boneless   One of the sons of Ragnar Logbrod, and a Viking chieftain who helps lead the Danish attack on Western Frankia.

Leonidas   A young Frankish cavalry officer; the cousin of Genevieve, and a nephew of Count Robert of Paris.

Odd
A crewman on Hastein's longship, the *Gull*, and a skilled archer.

Ragnar
The Danish war leader of the attack on Western Frankia, known by the nickname Logbrod, or "Hairy-Breeches."

Robert
A high-ranking Frankish nobleman, the count who rules over a number of towns and lands in West Frankia, including Paris; Genevieve's father.

Sigrid
The daughter of the Danish chieftain Hrorik by his first wife, Helge; Harald's twin sister, and Halfdan's half-sister.

Snorre
A Danish warrior who is the second in command of the chieftain Toke.

Stenkil
A Danish warrior; the comrade of a man Halfdan kills.

Stig
A follower of Jarl Hastein, and the captain of the ship the *Serpent*.

Svein
A follower of Jarl Hastein, and the captain of the ship the *Sea Wolf*.

Toke
A Danish chieftain who is the son of Gunhild by her first marriage, the foster son of the Danish chieftain Hrorik, and the murderer of Harald, Halfdan's half-brother.

Tore
A crewman on Hastein's longship, the *Gull*, and the leader of the archers in the crew.

Torvald
The helmsman on Hastein's longship, the *Gull*.

Wulf
The captain of a Frankish merchant ship captured by the Danish fleet.

GLOSSARY

berserks: Warriors in Scandinavian society who were noted for their exceptional fierceness and fearlessness in battle, and for their moody, difficult dispositions in periods of peace.

Birka: A coastal town in Sweden that served as one of the main Viking-age trading centers. Birka formed the northern end of a long trade route running down several rivers through the lands of modern Russia, eventually reaching the Black Sea. Using the Eastern Road, as the trade route was called, the Vikings traded with the Byzantine Empire and with the Moorish kingdoms of the Middle East that lay beyond.

bracer: A long cuff of leather worn by archers on the forearm of the arm they hold their bow with, to protect against the slap of the bowstring when the bow is shot.

brynie: A shirt of mail armor, made of thousands of small iron or steel rings linked together into a flexible garment.

byre: A barn or animal shed.

carl: A free man in Viking-age Scandinavian society.

Danevirke: A great earthen wall built across the base of the Jutland peninsula of Denmark, from coast to coast, to protect the Danish lands from invasion by the Franks.

Dorestad: A Frankish port and trading center located near the convergence of the Rhine and Lek rivers, in the area now forming part of the Netherlands. Dorestad was one of the largest trade centers of early medieval Europe.

fletching: The three feathers at the back of an arrow, used to stabilize its flight.

Frankia: Also called Francia; the land of the Franks, roughly corresponding to most of modern France, Belgium, the Netherlands, and western Germany. By A.D. 845, the setting of *Dragons from the Sea*, the former Frankish Empire had split into three kingdoms: West Frankia, roughly corresponding to modern France; the Eastern Frankish Kingdom, stretching from the Rhine River eastward through the lands now comprising modern Germany; and the short-lived Middle Kingdom, which stretched from Frisia in the north to the Mediterranean coast of modern France, and also included parts of northern Italy.

Frisia: The coastal region of Frankia roughly corresponding to those lands comprising the present-day Netherlands.

fylgja: A beneficial spirit that attaches itself to a person and brings him or her good fortune. Some were visible and took the form of animals, often reflecting some aspect of the human they followed, such as a raven symbolizing wisdom, or a wolf representing ferocity. Others were invisible, but were generally considered to be female guardian spirits.

godi: A priest in pagan Viking-age Scandinavian society. The position of godi was usually held by a chieftain, and typically a godi would preside not only over religious festivals and sacrifices, but also over the Thing, or regional assembly. Godis also administered oaths, which were usually sworn on a special ring of iron or sometimes gold.

greaves: Armor, usually constructed of curved steel or bronze plates, worn to protect the lower leg from the knee to the ankle.

Hairy-Breeches: Hairy-Breeches, or sometimes Hairy-Breeks, is the translation for "Logbrod," the nickname of Ragnar, a famous ninth-century Viking war leader.

Hedeby: The largest town in ninth-century Denmark, and a major Viking-age trading center. Hedeby was located near the base of the Jutland peninsula on its eastern side, on a fjord jutting inland from the coast.

hnefatafl: A popular Viking board game, whose name roughly translates as "King's Table." The game was played on a board divided into regular squares, somewhat like a chess board. One player set his pieces up in the center of the board, and attempted to move his king to the outer rim. The other player started with his pieces surrounding his opponent's pieces, and attempted to capture the king before it could escape.

housecarl: A warrior in the service of a chieftain or nobleman.

i-viking: To go raiding.

jarl: A very high-ranking chieftain in Viking-age

Scandinavian society, who ruled over a large area of land on behalf of the king. The word and concept "jarl" is the origin of the English "earl."

Jul: The Germanic pagan midwinter feast, known in England as Yule.

Jutland: The peninsula that forms the mainland of modern and ancient Denmark, named after the Jutes, one of the ancient Danish tribes.

knarr: A general-purpose ship used in Viking-age Scandinavia for trade and other commercial uses. Though built of similar construction to longships, knarrs tended to be shorter and broader, had higher sides, and were designed to be propelled primarily by sail, though they could be rowed and typically had three to five oars per side.

Limfjord: A huge fjord that runs completely across the northern tip of the Jutland peninsula, providing a protected passage between the Baltic and North seas.

longship: The long, narrow ship used for war by the peoples of Viking-age Scandinavia. Longships had shallow drafts, allowing them to be beached or to travel up rivers, and were designed to be propelled swiftly by either sail or by rowing. They were sometimes also called dragonships, because many longships had carved heads of dragons or other beasts decorating the stem-post at the bow of the ship.

Niddingsvaark: Work of infamy; the dishonorable acts of a Nithing.

Nithing: Also Nidding; One who is not considered a person because he has no honor.

nock: The notch cut in the rear of an arrow, into which the bowstring is placed to shoot it. Also the notches cut into the tips of a bow's limbs, in which the bowstring is secured to the bow.

Norns: Three ancient sisters who, according to pagan Scandinavian belief, sat together at the base of the world-tree and wove the fates of all men on their looms.

Norse: The Scandinavians who lived in the area of modern Norway. During the mid-ninth century, large portions of the Norse lands were at least nominally ruled by the Danish kings. Non-Scandinavians sometimes used the term Norsemen, or Northmen, to describe any Viking raiders from the Scandinavian lands.

Odin: The Scandinavian God of death, war, wisdom, and poetry; the chieftain of the Gods.

pattern-welded: A process used to forge the blades of fine swords and other weapons during the Viking Age. Numerous small bars or strips of steel and iron were hammered together under high heat to form a solid piece of steel, in which the individual pieces could still be seen as a pattern. Blades produced through this labor-intensive method tended to be expensive, but very flexible, resistant to breaking, and often capable of taking and holding a very strong and sharp edge.

pig iron: Rough ingots of crude cast iron providing the raw material used for creating products of iron or steel by blacksmiths.

Ribe: A Viking-age town and trading center on the west coast of the Jutland peninsula in Denmark.

Ruda: The Viking's name for Rouen, a Frankish town near the mouth of the Seine River.

runes: The alphabet used for writing in the ancient Scandinavian and Germanic languages. Runic letters, comprised of combinations of simple, straight strokes, were easy to carve into stone or wood.

scara: A unit of Frankish cavalry. Each scara was composed of several smaller units called cunei, each of which numbered from fifty to one hundred men.

Schliefjord: A long fjord on the east coast of the Jutland peninsula, near its base, on which the town of Hedeby was located.

scot: A tax or duty, usually in the form of military service, owed to the king.

seax: A single-edged knife, often quite large, widely used as a weapon and tool in the Scandinavian, Germanic, and Anglo-Saxon cultures.

skald: A poet.

strake: A plank used to form the hull of a Viking ship.

strandhogg: The practice by Viking ship crews of acquiring cattle and other needed provisions by coming ashore and stealing them.

Thing: A regional assembly held periodically in Viking-age Scandinavian countries where citizens of an area could present suits to be decided by vote, according to law. Lawsuits heard at Things were the forerunner and origin of what became, centuries later in English culture, the concept of trial by a jury of peers.

Thor: The pagan Scandinavian God of thunder and fertile harvests, of strength, honor, and oaths, and the mightiest warrior among the Scandinavian gods.

thrall: A slave in Viking-age Scandinavian society.

wergild: The amount that must be paid to make recompense for killing a man.

White Christ: The Vikings' name for the Christian God, believed to be a derogatory term implying cowardice because he allowed himself to be captured and killed without fighting back against his captors.

ACKNOWLEDGMENTS

By the time it finally reaches the hands of its readers, every book is the result of a team effort. Although I cannot know the nature and extent of all the work put in behind the scenes by so many—most of whose names I do not even know—to help bring the Strongbow Saga and this book into being, I would like to take this opportunity to thank them all for their diligent efforts.

My special thanks go to Sarah Thomson, who edited *Dragons from the Sea*, and whose hard work and excellent ideas played a critical part in achieving the final version of this novel. Thanks also to Master Nathan, for his sharp eye.

HISTORICAL NOTES

The distortions caused by the passage of many centuries have left a popular misconception of the Vikings as unruly barbarians who were the scourge of the supposedly more civilized European countries. It is not so widely known that during the eighth and early ninth centuries, it was the Franks—now viewed as paragons of civilization and culture during a dark time—who terrorized their neighbors. In the latter decades of the eighth century, the Frankish King Charles the Great, or Charlemagne, waged a brutal, prolonged war against Saxon tribes living below the base of the Jutland peninsula. The Franks massacred thousands of Saxon captives, sold thousands more into slavery, and drove the remaining Saxons off their lands and into the wilderness regions along the eastern border of the Frankish empire.

Charlemagne also turned his eyes toward the

Danes, and in the early years of the ninth century, he launched an unsuccessful campaign against them. Godfred, the Danish king at the time, repaired and extended the Danevirke, a massive defensive earthen wall stretching all the way across the base of the Jutland peninsula, the Danish mainland, in response to the Frankish threat, and attacked Frisia with a fleet of swift-moving longships to draw off the Frankish armies. The Franks again attacked Denmark—unsuccessfully—during the reign of Louis the Pious, Charlemagne's son.

By the year A.D. 845, when *Dragons from the Sea* is set, Louis the Pious had been succeeded by his three sons, who split the Frankish empire into three kingdoms. Although relatively small-scale Viking attacks had plagued the Frankish coastline for years, during the year 845, two large-scale assaults were launched against the Franks by the Danes. One fleet, which may have been led by the Danish King Horik himself, struck up the Elbe River and attacked the Frankish fortress-town of Hamburg. The other, a fleet composed of 120 Viking longships, sailed up the Seine River, invading the Western Frankish Kingdom of Charles the Bald. According to Frankish sources, the leader of this army was named Ragnar.

Ragnar Logbrod, his sons Ivar the Boneless and Bjorn Ironsides, and the chieftain Hastein were all real Viking leaders who helped shape many of the major events of the latter half of the ninth century. In all probability, the Ragnar who led the attack up the Seine in 845 was Ragnar Logbrod. Readers who would like to learn more of what is known about these men, their exploits, and the world in which the Strongbow Saga is set are urged to visit www.strongbowsaga.com, an educational website dedicated to the Vikings and their age.